HEARTS ON FIRE

Part 2

MARINA SIMCOE

THE RIVER OF MISTS

Hearts on Fire, Part 2
World of the River of Mists

This book is a work of fiction. Names, characters, places, and incidents are a product
of the author's imagination. Locales and public names are used for atmospheric
purposes. Any resemblance to actual people, living or dead, or to businesses,
companies, events, institutions, or locales is completely coincidental.
Spelling: English (American)
Editing by Cissell Ink
Proofreading by Nic Page
Cover image source Depositphotos.com

Hearts on Fire is the final book in the Fire in Stone duet. It contains graphic
descriptions of intimacy, some violence, and discussions on adult themes.
Intended for mature readers.

Hearts on Fire

PART 2

MARINA SIMCOE

To my Captain

Thank you for making me fly.

One

AMBER

Nocking an arrow into the bow, I squinted at the painted center on a piece of wood attached to the farthest part of the wall. I carefully aimed the iron tip of the arrow at the red circle about the size of an apple—or the size of a dragon's eye.

I lingered, making sure everything was just perfect. I'd already broken one arrow by sending it too far to the right. It'd hit the rock wall instead of the wood and snapped in two. Now, I only had six arrows left in the quiver, and I had to be careful.

Holding my breath, I released the arrow. It flew across the courtyard. Its tip sank into the corner of the wood. The power of the impact made the arrow sing, the feathered tip of it swaying.

"Good," Zenada approved.

She crouched by the fire that was heating a round oven in the other corner of the yard. Iolena, another woman of the Sanctuary, brought a tray of flat, round bread made from a simple dough of salt, water, buckwheat flour, and a rising agent. Once Iolena left and the oven was hot enough, Zenada put the bread rounds inside it, slapping them on the thick, heated walls of the oven to bake.

Her cheeks glowing from the heat, she brushed a few long, black strands of her hair from her face.

"You're getting really good at shooting, Amber," she said, stretching her back.

"*Good* would've been getting it straight into the center of that 'eye.' Anything outside of it would get me killed out there." I sighed, heading to my target to retrieve the arrow.

I'd been practicing daily, sometimes twice a day if my chores permitted it. I was getting better at it. Just not good enough for my skill to be useful yet.

"You're getting there," Zenada encouraged.

Mother allowed me to train without arguing. Other women were encouraged to train with weapons as well. With Isar gone, the Sanctuary had lost its most capable guard and protector. Now, everyone had to step up.

Zenada removed the baked bread from the oven, piling the flat, dark rounds onto a wide, ceramic platter.

"Here." She shoved one round into my hand. "Have it now, before the meal."

Perpetually hungry, I had no willpower to refuse, biting off a huge chunk of the warm, fragrant bread right away.

"Thanks. Do you want some? I can share." I ripped the bread in half.

I knew the *salamandras* were hungry too. Just because their bodies were better equipped to deal with the lack of food, showing almost no signs of malnutrition, it didn't mean they didn't suffer from the gnawing pangs of hunger.

"No, thank you." Zenada averted her eyes from my offering. "I'm good."

A winged shadow fell on the stones of the courtyard. I ducked instinctively, my heart nearly stopping with a loud thud of panic. After more than two weeks in Dakath, I expected nothing but bad things to come from the sky.

"It's just a cloud owl," Zenada said, her voice lifting.

The shadow was smaller than that of a gargoyle man and

much smaller than that of a dragon. Still, it was bigger than any bird I'd ever seen.

I looked up, following the flight of the magnificent white bird. Gliding over the courtyard in a slow, graceful arc of descent, the owl flew past us and through the open doors into the Sanctuary.

"Why did it fly inside?" I stared after it.

Zenada's obsidian eyes lit up with excitement. "It's a messenger owl. From the king."

"But I didn't see it carrying any messages." There was no letter in its beak and no scrolls in its claws.

"It'll speak the message directly to whom it's intended. To Mother, of course."

"A talking owl?"

"Yes. Its kind comes from the Sky Kingdom that's high above the clouds where the sky fae live. King Edkhar got one as a gift long ago."

I remembered Mother saying she would write to the king. They clearly had some form of communication. I'd just never imagined it involved a magical talking owl.

Zenada shifted from foot to foot impatiently.

"I should take these to the kitchen." She placed the bread platter on her shoulder. "If Mother has any news from the king for us, she'd announce it inside. You probably should come with me if you want to hear it."

I didn't feel nearly as eager as Zenada to hear what the king had to say. After that tragic and turbulent first week at the Sanctuary, life here had finally settled into some routine. Despite the back-breaking labor it took to simply survive in these harsh conditions, the slow pace of life here appealed to me. My body had all but healed by now. And my soul had grown numb enough for me to go on in relative peace.

I wasn't looking forward to any potential disruptions of this quiet existence. But I followed Zenada to the main hall of the Sanctuary to find out the news.

We weren't the only ones there. Almost all of the *salamandras* of the Sanctuary had already gathered by the stone perches around the statue of their goddess. The Sanctuary was small enough for the news of the cloud owl's arrival to have spread almost instantly.

Mother exited from the semi-darkness of the inner rooms. The snow-white owl was perched on her shoulder. With its wings folded, the bird wasn't as big as it had seemed before.

"Get ready, sisters," Mother said, tilting her head in a dignified manner. "King Edkhar wishes to see us in the Bozyr Peak. We're leaving tomorrow, right after sunrise."

A wave of whispers rustled between the women. Some seemed excited, like Zenada, who clenched her hands to her chest, her eyes alight with anticipation. Others looked worried.

"How many of us will go this time?" someone asked.

"Everyone," Mother replied.

"Me too?" I blurted out, unsure how I felt about going.

Mother rested her stare on me. Long and unblinking, it sent a shiver of unease down my spine.

"You too, Amber," she said somberly, then moved her attention to the others. "We'll all go. The Sanctuary will be locked for the time being."

Zenada took a small step forward. "We can't leave right after sunrise. The dragons won't have enough time to come get us."

Mother pursed her lips before replying, "The king is not sending anyone to get us this time. He wishes for us to walk."

"All the way to the castle?" someone gasped.

"Yes. All the way to his castle on the Bozyr Peak." Mother's gaze hardened. She clenched her hand around the lizard pendant over her chest. "That is his punishment for harboring a venomous one."

The memory of the day when Isar was taken resonated painfully in my heart. Getting his hands on the woman clearly wasn't enough for the vengeful king. He also wished to punish all those who had shared the Sanctuary with her.

Someone said softly behind me, "This won't be the end of the punishment, I fear."

I whipped around to see who had said that. Everyone in the group of women behind me, however, stared straight ahead with the same expression on their faces. Their mouths shut. Their faces serene. Resigned to their fate.

"Amber," Mother said on her way to the exit to release the messenger owl. "You don't need to use the scarlet root paste for your hair anymore."

She went out into the courtyard, leaving me puzzled.

What did she mean? Did she want me to let my hair grow now? After making it clear how dangerous it was?

I knew I didn't trust Mother. Only now I wasn't sure which version of her I should trust less, the one that wanted me bald or the one who didn't.

A weight pressed on my chest. At least now I knew how I felt about going to the Bozyr Peak—I dreaded it.

Two

AMBER

We'd been walking for hours along the snow-covered passage between the mountains, hours that felt like years. By now, I could hardly remember when the world around me was not just endless black rocks, freezing snow, and bitter cold wind.

I fell behind our line of women in red. Zenada stopped, waiting for me to catch up.

"Not long now," she said, grabbing me under my arm.

Gusts of wind tore at my robe. I'd tied a piece of cloth over my head under the hood, to keep it warm, and a thick strip of wool around my neck to prevent the wind from blowing the hood from my head. The wide ribbon of lace that trimmed the hood hung low over my face, shielding it from the wind somewhat. Despite that, my cheeks felt numb, and I hadn't felt my nose for some time now.

"Just up this path, and we're there." Zenada gestured up the narrow passage between the snow-covered rocks jutting out on either side. The line of women climbing up the path stretched like a red-skinned snake ahead of us.

At the very summit, the mountain peak split into tall towers and spiky turrets. The dark cluster of them stood out sharply against the pale-blue sky of the winter afternoon.

The Bozyr Peak, the castle of the Dakath King, appeared dark and oppressive when I looked up at it from below. Maybe that was the point of whoever created it? The king's castle was meant to tower over the kingdom, instilling fear and reverence into the king's subjects. Despite the long trek being almost over, I wished I could just turn around and leave the way I came. The worn, stifling walls of the Sanctuary now seemed far more hospitable and inviting than the royal castle.

As if sensing my mood, Zenada patted my shoulder reassuringly.

"King Edkhar is famous for his feasts. We'll have plenty of delicious food to eat at the castle," she said cheerfully.

The excited anticipation in her voice wasn't just about food, I sensed. The way a warm smile teased in the corners of her mouth and how her eyes flicked to the castle every few seconds told me Zenada was looking forward to more than just a good meal.

"Zenada," I panted, trying hard to keep up with her and the others. "King Edkhar is responsible for us trudging through the snow and wind all day. He could've easily sent someone to get us, but he forced us to walk out of spite. Don't you think it's rather petty, especially when coming from a king?"

Her expression dimmed somewhat.

"The king wished to make a point, I guess..." she muttered uncertainly.

"Well, he sure has made it," I huffed, climbing over the slippery icy rocks in our path.

"The king has the entire kingdom to rule, Amber, and a war to fight. Who are we to judge him for the decisions he makes?"

"Including the decision to snatch Isar? He didn't mind sending dragons all the way to the Sanctuary *that* time, did he?"

Other than a few words the morning after that day, we hadn't spoken about what had happened to Ertee and Isar.

Maybe this wasn't the best time to bring it up. I was exceptionally bitter and cranky after the long, tiring hike through the mountains. Zenada wasn't responsible for the king's actions, and I shouldn't be taking it out on her.

But I missed them both, Isar and Ertee. In the little time I had spent with them, I grew to admire Isar's tenacity and strength. The way she was taken from us, unjustly and without a trace, made it even worse. Neither did the Sanctuary feel the same without Ertee's calming presence.

Zenada was quiet for a moment or two, climbing up the path alongside me.

"The king... He must have his reasons," she finally said.

Anger stirred inside me, making my hackles rise. It was directed at the king. But some of it spilled over, enough for Zenada too. I couldn't blame her for his actions, but it angered me that she didn't condemn them. Her defending him made it feel like she agreed with what he did.

"How can you say that?" I fumed. "What could possibly excuse what he did to Isar?"

"Well... The king is not alone in that castle, you know. He's surrounded by people, and not all of them are good. The High General, for example, is a despicable person."

I shook my head, not buying her excuses. "He is the king, Zenada. He chooses the people who surround him."

She bit her lip, turning away from my glower. It pained me more than anything she could've said or done. The king didn't just use Zenada's body, he had her heart.

"You love him, don't you?" I asked, dreading to hear her answer.

She dropped her head, not saying a word, but her silence was confession enough.

"God, don't let me fall in love with an undeserving man," I prayed. *"Never again."*

The closer we got to it, the bigger the castle appeared to grow. It took up the entire top of the mountain, accessible on foot only from this one side. But even here, the path we took didn't seem to be used that often. The majority of the castle's visitors appeared to prefer to fly.

By the time I reached the castle gate, the rest of the women had already entered. Beyond the gate, the space between the outer and inner walls of the castle looked more like a wide terrace than a bailey or a courtyard. It ran around the mountain, following every dip and curve of the landscape, edged by the walls with spiky towers.

We followed the path along the inner wall to a side entrance of the castle where a servant let us in.

"Dinner is in a half-hour," he informed Mother. "The king expects all of you to join him in the Dining Hall."

Unlike the women in the Sanctuary, it appeared the king took more than one meal a day since he had dinner.

Was a half-hour enough time to even catch my breath after hiking through the freezing mountains all day? It felt like I needed days just to melt the icy needles that seemed to have formed everywhere in my body. It felt as if my insides had turned into a solid icicle.

I also wished I could take a nap in a pile of warm blankets somewhere, so I could stand without swaying from exhaustion.

But we couldn't possibly make the king wait. Mother promptly ushered us to follow the servant to a long, narrow room with stone perches lined up along the walls. There was a wide window at one end, closed with wooden shutters. A dark fireplace at the opposite wall had no fire. The air in the room was barely warmer than that outside.

"Get ready," Mother ordered.

The women spread out through the room, taking apart the

bundles of clothes and other belongings they'd brought with them. Some brushed and re-braided their hair. Others straightened their clothes. One of the *salamandras* fetched water from the kitchen, so we could at least freshen up a bit after the long hike.

I rinsed my face and hands. Having no hair to brush or braid, I just re-tied the linen cloth I wore on my head and adjusted the robe over my dress.

"Put your hoods on," Mother said on her way out of the room. "And lower the lace over your faces, everyone."

The women did as she told them.

"Why do we have to cover our faces?" I asked Zenada.

She shrugged. "The king's orders."

Another woman muttered, "Maybe he's afraid of what he may find in our eyes, so he orders them hidden behind the lace."

Zenada's chest expanded with a sigh, but she said nothing in the king's defense this time, tightly pressing her lips together.

Mother led the women out of the room in a single line. I took my place at the end of the line and yanked the lace trim of my hood down and over my face, just like everyone else.

We went up a winding staircase inside a tower with tall windows on the same side at every level. The windows here had no glass and no shutters. I was glad I'd left all my clothes on. The cold mountain wind blew up and down the staircase unimpeded.

Following a wide hallway after that, we came to a set of double doors guarded by two men dressed in identical red and gold uniforms. They opened the doors for us, and we entered a long hall with a large table in the middle and a fireplace the size of a two-car garage to the side.

At least the fireplace was lit here. Thick logs burned inside. A metal rack was positioned over them, with several rods rotated by servants in uniforms. Large, juicy chunks of meat roasted on the rods. The men poured a fragrant sauce over the meat, ladling it from a black cauldron by the fire.

The appetizing aroma filled the king's Dining Hall, making

my mouth water. I didn't even mind not getting any rest after the long journey to the castle if this meat was our prize at the end.

The women moved faster, obviously looking forward to the meal as much as I was. Only instead of heading to the main table in the middle, Mother took us to the wooden benches by the wall. Plain wooden tables stood in front of the benches. They were much narrower than the main one and set with plain metal plates and simple goblets for us.

"I guess we aren't welcome at the table with the king," I commented, sitting down on the bench next to Zenada.

Mother shot me a stern look. "Only the king's men and lords of the court dine at the royal table."

Since I wasn't either, I had to be content with where I was placed. Not that I cared much, anyway. The royal court's hierarchy meant little to me, as long as I still got some of that roasted meat.

The double doors opened again, and a group of men entered. I assumed they were musicians, judging by the instruments they carried. They spread along the entire perimeter of the room, taking places along the walls. Some opened their wings and flew up to hover under the domed ceiling.

When they started to play, it was impossible to tell which direction the beautiful music was coming from. It simply filled the room wall to wall and floor to ceiling, permeating the air with beauty.

A procession of uniformed guards entered next, followed by a man who announced the arrival of the king.

King Edkhar was a tall, broad-shouldered man. His bright red hair lay in curls over his shoulders. A well-groomed beard of the same color reached down to his chest. I recognized him as the king by a crown on his head and by the way he entered the room ahead of the lords that came with him.

The royal clothes screamed status and opulence. The king's long scarlet coat was embroidered with gold and set with so many gemstones, it shone in the light of the fireplace. Gold and gemstones glistened in his beard and hair, too. A long crimson cape lined with white-and-black fur was draped over his shoulders, dragging on the stone floor behind him.

Zenada stared at the king in rapture. We all did. The man presented quite a sight, and he obviously expected attention.

The king strolled to the head of the table, where a massive stone-carved chair stood draped with red silk and furs—a seat fit for a king.

A group of courtiers followed their sovereign. They spread along both sides of the long table, taking their seats in tall-backed wooden chairs.

A man dressed in black, with an eye patch over his eye, took a seat to the king's right.

"That's the High General on the king's right," Iolena, who was sitting close to me, whispered. "But I don't know who's on his left."

I peered through the lace over my face at the dark-haired man taking a seat at the king's left, and my heart leaped with recognition.

Oh, I knew that man!

The last time I saw him, he wore a red t-shirt and a pair of cheap sweatpants. Now, he was dressed in a gorgeous black coat stitched with golden poppy flowers and pants of the same material, either a very fine suede or black velvet; I couldn't tell from a distance. A scarlet cape, trimmed with short black fur, was draped over his shoulders, and a long dagger with a bejeweled handle hung at his hip.

Elex.

I hardly recognized him in all that finery, but it was most definitely him. He survived the crossing of the River of Mists. He hadn't been carried off to another world by its milky-pink stream.

He was here.

For a few long moments, I just stared at him as the servants served the food, setting the tables with delicious-smelling dishes.

He'd shaved his beard, though his facial hair was so dark, the shadow of it permanently remained on his cheeks and jawline. His hair had been trimmed, too, but not by much. It was long enough to still curl over his ears and frame his handsome face in thick, glossy curls, one of them falling over the side of his forehead. Sitting at the king's table, he ran his eyes over the row of the *salamandras*.

My heart fluttered and raced. Excitement filled me, bursting through with a smile I couldn't contain. Elex needed to know I was here. Surely, he'd been wondering what happened to me. He must be worried about me, too.

I brought my hand to my hood and shoved it back to reveal my face. Lifting the lace, I waited until his gaze crossed with mine. Joy flooded me in a wave of warmth when his onyx-black eyes met mine. He was the only one in this entire world who knew me from before I came here.

For one tiny moment, the castle ceased to exist as memories took over. The memories of the open skies and his strong arms around me. Of the two of us flying far above the ground and away from any problems it brought.

A flash of recognition flickered in his eyes, then...his expression dulled. He turned to face the servant who was filling his goblet with wine.

My heart dropped. And with it, my spirit plummeted from the sky where it had soared.

"Amber," Mother hissed in warning.

I yanked my hood back down and lowered the lace over my eyes once again.

Did Elex not recognize me? Was I mistaken by that spark in his eyes?

I lifted my hand to my shoulder, displaying Elex's ruby ring on my finger for him to see. But he didn't look my way again.

My shoulders drooped, weighted down by bitter disappointment and...hurt. I didn't know what I'd expected his reaction at seeing me to be. Happiness? Excitement? Joy? I didn't know. But I certainly hadn't expected this complete and utter indifference.

Through the golden haze of the lace, I studied him furtively.

He lifted his goblet of wine to toast the king. The gems in the rings on his fingers twinkled, reflecting the light of the fireplace. In his fine clothes, at the king's side, Elex looked every bit the prince he was born to be.

I smoothed my hands down my robe, its material worn, the red color faded from the fabric due to it being scrubbed in the water of the cursed well at the Sanctuary way too many times.

I'd been blind, not seeing the distance between Elex and me before. It was far, far greater than the several yards separating our tables. The distance between us might not have been that apparent back in the human world. But here in Dakath, it became glaringly obvious.

Elex was a prince, born into royalty and raised in a castle. He looked so natural at the king's table, as if he'd always dined here. Despite his previous absence, he'd fit right back in upon his return.

He must have recognized me. He just didn't *want* to know me.

I didn't belong in any castle. I didn't even belong in this world. But I was stuck here now, and no one would be able to help me.

Elex might be a prince, but he wasn't my Prince Charming. He didn't show up here to rescue me. On the contrary, I was trapped in this world because of him. He was the one who brought me here. I should never forget that.

After filling every inch of the king's table with dishes, the servants finally brought some food for us, too.

Tantalizing smells wafted from the platters of grilled vegetables, creamy sauces, and roasted meat. My stomach might be twisting in knots from anguish and disappointment, but my mouth watered.

I'd be damned if I let the gorgeous, stuck-up fae prince deprive me of my appetite, now that I finally had more food in front of me than I could eat.

Grabbing a goblet of wine, I emptied it in three huge gulps. The effervescent warmth of intoxication rose from my empty stomach to my brain quickly. For the time being, it even muffled the pain of rejection.

No longer paying any attention to the men at the "cool table," I loaded my plate with all the yummy things served to us. The roasted beets with oil and garlic. The pheasants with meat so tender, it slid like butter off their delicate bones. The rice cooked with meat, carrots, and onions in a fragrant sauce that dripped down my fingers as I stuffed my face with it.

No one used utensils. People rolled the rice into chubby delicious balls before putting them into their mouths, using their hands. When the servants lifted one spear of meat out of the fire and placed it on the table in front of us, we were given knives to slice chunks of it straight from the spear.

I ate and drank until my stomach cramped and breathing got difficult.

"Oh, try this," Zenada moved a plate with dessert my way. "Red plums from the valley with cream custard and lily honey from the Lorsan Wetlands. It's my favorite."

I barely found some space in my stomach for the dessert, but it was totally worth it. The lily honey smelled like flowers and tasted like summer. I closed my eyes, savoring every bite.

Until the end of the dinner, I did not look back at the king's table. Not once. However, every now and then, a rush of hot tingles would scatter through my chest as I felt someone's stare on me.

Three

〜⤳

AMBER

The king rose from the table, signaling the end of the dinner. All at once, his men stopped eating or drinking, too.

"Sunset is close," Mother whispered to the *salamandras* as we all got up from our benches.

King Edkhar slid a glance along the row of women.

"Join us for the celebration at noon tomorrow." This was the king's only acknowledgement of our presence here tonight.

As soon as the king and his courtiers left, Mother hurried us out as well. "The sun is setting. We don't have much time. It wouldn't do for us to spend our first night here in the stairwell or in a hallway somewhere."

Not pressured by the approaching sunset, I let them all go ahead of me. With my limbs heavy from exhaustion and my stomach full of food, I fell behind. Thankfully, I remembered the way we came and headed along the hallway, then down the winding stairs inside the tower.

The sound of rushed footsteps came behind me. Someone

followed me into the tower. Only who could it be? Did I miss one of the *salamandras* somehow? I thought I was the last one.

I stopped on the narrow landing by the window and glanced behind me, then quickly turned away, recognizing the black clothes stitched with gold and the flash of the red cape.

"My little spark," Elex murmured, stopping right behind me.

The familiar deep voice enveloped me, trapping me in a web that was both sweet and painful. His nickname for me wasn't just empty words, it carried a meaning. He'd said I'd brought him back to life; I was the spark that had awakened him from the *womora* induced state. It'd made me feel like there was a time, a while back, when I mattered to him.

My heart beat faster, threatening my resolve. It took all I had to stay where I was instead of grabbing him into a hug.

"Do you not want to look at me?" His voice sounded light and playful, as if we were still flying over the Atlantic together. As if the past weeks never happened and there was no distance between us at all.

I closed my eyes, drawing in a long breath of the chilly air blowing through the open window. Bracing myself to face him, I dreaded to see what I might find in his eyes this time.

"Amber." Elex placed a hand on my shoulder.

My knees nearly buckled at his touch. Slowly, ever so slowly, I turned, then lifted the lace of my hood, meeting his eyes straight on. A warm glow flickered deep inside their darkness. A smile teased in the corners of his mouth.

God, I almost forgot how breathtakingly beautiful he was!

His chest rose and fell with a deep breath, as if seeing me brought him relief. "It's so nice to see you again, Amber."

Nice. Like we ran into each other at the movies, back in my world.

He moved to hug me, but I stepped back, so he just placed his hands on my shoulders again.

I had to reply to him. With something like, *"Nice to see you, too."*

17

But that sounded so shallow somehow. I swallowed hard, gathering my resolve before finally speaking.

"I'm glad...very glad to see you alive, Elex," I said sincerely. "I feared you were lost or...dead."

"I'm not that easy to kill." His smile grew brighter. My knees went weak, my legs shaking. It was a good thing he gripped my upper arms tightly, steadying me.

His thumbs rubbed lightly over the material of my robe. He was touching, feeling, always exploring after the years he had spent as a statue and was denied the sense of touch.

He quietly studied my face. The silence between us grew awkward, at least to me. Was I supposed to say something more?

"It's very nice to see you, too, Elex. Alive and well. And thriving." I pointedly stared at the rich embroidery on his chest.

He kept grinning, his gaze glued to my face. I wondered if he saw the dark circles under my eyes, my sunken cheeks, if he noticed that not a single hair was visible from under the cloth over my head.

"You took your silver ring out." He tapped the side of my nose with the tip of his finger.

The last of my piercings had long been removed by the *salamandras* on Mother's orders. I stiffened against the wave of darkness that flowed over me at the thought of everything that had happened from the moment Elex snatched me from my world and brought me to Dakath.

I lifted my hand to my nose, to the spot where only a tiny dimple of the hole now remained.

"I don't remember much of what happened right after we crossed the River of Mists," I said. "Somehow, I ended up on the riverbank. The women of the *Salamandra* Sanctuary found me. I've been with them ever since."

He nodded. "I know. I saw them take you."

His confession rushed over me with shock, chilling me like a cold shower.

"You did?" I muttered, stupefied.

All this time, I had wondered what happened to him. I'd missed and mourned him, fearing I'd lost him and would never see him again.

Yet there he was, spending his days in the king's castle. He'd known perfectly well where I was all this time. It'd be a short distance for him to fly, far shorter than it was for me to hike up here. Yet he hadn't even bothered to let me know he was alive.

He didn't care.

And why would he? I was no one to him. A "spark," who'd brought him back to life and had long served her purpose.

"I was there when the women found you," he said excitedly, rushing to get the words out as if catching up with a good friend. "I knew they'd take good care of you—"

"They sure did." Bitterness rose inside me, coating everything with the dark, sticky tar of resentment. "Do you want to see how well they did that, Elex? Do you want to know what else I've lost when I didn't even think I had anything left to lose in this life?" I ripped the hood off my head along with the linen cloth. "This is what they did with every hair on my body. Against my will."

His eyes flickered to my bald head for a moment, then down to my face again. His smile disappeared.

"Oh, Amber..." He slid his hands to my shoulders then up my neck. "I'm so, so sorry." He cupped my face, his thumbs skimming the skin above my ears.

My eyes burned with tears. A film of them obscured his handsome face from view. My throat tightened painfully.

"You should've left me back at the creek, Elex. You should've never taken me..."

He moved his hands to the back of my head, his fingers splayed on my skin. My skull tingled, heat rushing from his hands, warming my head. Something moved against my skin—a warm caress against the freezing wind from the window. A tickle brushed both sides of my face.

"What's happening?" I asked Elex, who stared at me intently.

The glow in his eyes grew, sparkling through the darkness of his irises. "Elex?"

I reached to touch his hand splayed on my head. My fingers sank into thick, silky hair... my hair. I tugged at the strands to feel the sting at the roots growing from *my* head.

"What is this?" I raked my fingers through the long tresses that stretched all the way down to my waist. "How..."

Letting go of my head, he staggered on his feet, then grabbed onto the wall by the window to steady himself.

"The magic of Dakath," he explained in a raspy voice. "It takes its toll when one uses it. But it is powerful." He shut his eyes tightly then opened them again. "It made me dizzy this time." He focused on me, the corners of his mouth lifting in a smile again. "Gods, you're so beautiful, Amber. Both with and without the hair."

His gaze darted to my mouth. The glow in his eyes heated dangerously. He leaned closer, parting his lips for a kiss. "I missed you."

But he wouldn't spare me even a smile of recognition in the company of the king and his fine lords. Instead, he met me here, in this cold deserted stairwell where there was no risk for the handsome prince to be spotted with someone like me.

My skin tingled either from the magic he'd used on me or from some new spell he was weaving. I trembled from head to toe. As if on its own, my body swayed his way, ready for him to catch me.

"I couldn't wait to see you again, little spark," he whispered against my lips.

Yet he *had* waited.

For over two weeks, he'd been here in the luxury of the castle, embraced by the king. While I'd been hiding in the Sanctuary, helplessly watching my friends suffer and die.

Elex and I finally met again, but not because he flew to me. I had trudged through sludge, snow, and ice, climbing this damn mountain to get to him.

I tugged at the hair on my head. Did he think this was all it took to "fix" everything?

If only it were that easy.

The setting sun tinged the sky with blood-red in the window behind Elex. If I stepped into his arms and met him in a kiss, the sun would set, and I would be trapped in Elex's embrace, his lips pressed to mine.

The prospect of spending the night in his arms didn't scare me nearly as much as the burning desire to let it happen. I wanted to have his hands on me, to feel his lips on my body. I wanted him, against all logic and despite all caution. And I had so little strength to fight it.

"I said no, but you didn't listen, Elex." This was a bitter reminder for me as much as for him. "You ripped me out of the only life I knew and brought me here, just to leave me for strangers to find."

Instead of stepping into his hug, I pressed my hands into his chest and shoved at him with all my might.

He staggered back, more from shock than from the impact, considering his strength. His arms flailing, he lost his balance, and I gave him no chance to regain it. I shoved against his wide chest once more. The back of his knees hit the windowsill, and he tipped backwards, falling out of the window and into the scarlet glow of the sunset.

His cape flew aside and his wings sprung open, as I knew they would. The wings took him down to the castle wall below. He landed in a crouch, the moment the last sliver of the sun melted into the horizon.

His wings surged up, ready to take him off into flight again. But they froze, like two sails in the bitter wind. The sun had set, making his black stone blend with the night.

He was looking up, facing the window with me standing in it. I couldn't see his expression from here, but I sensed his shock and disappointment. And I cruelly hoped he felt at least a fraction of the pain he'd caused me.

"Good night, Elex," I said, even though he probably couldn't hear me over the howling wind. "If you couldn't leave me alone back in my old world, you most definitely should let me be now."

Grabbing my head cloth from the floor, I headed down the stairs to the women with whom I belonged.

Four

AMBER

Instead of going to bed, I visited the castle's kitchen. It wasn't hard to find. Mother had warned us on the way to the king's castle that we were expected to do chores as well as help the servants with cooking. We weren't merely guests here. The room in which they put the *salamandras* was on one of the lowest levels, so I figured the kitchen must be somewhere close.

I padded by the closed door to the *salamandras'* bedroom. Making sure there were no sleeping gargoyles in the narrow corridor behind it, I followed it to a short, wide hall that led to an arched entrance into an open space with several fireplaces, stoves, and long, wooden tables in the middle.

There was no one here, either. The fire in the hearths and stoves had been put out, though the scents of cooking lingered in the air.

Huge barrels of water stood next to the tables. The barrels were filled with dirty dishes. Since the king had dinner served so close to sunset, the servants had not had time to clean the dishes, leaving them to soak in the water overnight to deal with them in the morning.

That was the nature of this world. The sun was the great equalizer. Everyone got the same amount of rest, from the king down to the lowest servant. That didn't mean, of course, that the servants didn't work twice as hard during the day to keep up with the demands of the king and his courtiers.

Like most windows in the castle, the ones in here were closed with wooden shutters, letting only tiny slivers of moonlight in.

There were more doors in the walls between the fireplaces. But I didn't go see what was behind them, afraid I may stumble upon the bedrooms of the kitchen staff. Instead, I made my way around the tables and the barrels with dishes and found a knife block then took a long, serrated blade out from it.

Winding the thick mass of my new hair around my wrist, I brought the knife under it, as close to the roots as I dared.

Long hair was a nuisance. In my case, it was more than that. Mother had called red the royal color. She clearly feared for it to be discovered, and I had no desire to bring the king's attention to me for any reason.

Elex thought he was "fixing" a problem. Or maybe he believed he did me a favor by giving me my hair back and then some. But he'd only made it worse.

I gripped the hair tighter. With this blade that was probably used to saw through the bones of mountain goats, it wouldn't take me long to cut off a bunch of hair, no matter how thick it was. Or how silky it felt... I slid my hand down, enjoying the softness of my new locks.

Lifting my eyes, I met my reflection in the dark glass of the dish cabinet by the wall. I'd never had hair this long. I never had the patience to let it grow. I also used to like cutting it in fun, edgy styles, either by myself or with the help of a friend.

This was new to me. I never thought I could have something this beautiful. I released my grip, letting the rope of hair unwind from around my wrist. It sprang free, unraveled, and draped over my shoulders, cascading down my chest in rich, copper waves. The shine of my new locks in the moonlight would rival that of the fae. Or maybe Elex's magic was still glowing through it?

My hand trembled, and I put the knife down. Hair this long meant trouble. It'd be hard to conceal. But I had never possessed anything so pretty in my life, and now I wished to keep it for as long as I could.

Parting it in three sections, I braided the hair into a long plait, then tied it into a knot on the back of my head. Using the cloth, I covered my head, hiding every single strand, then tied the ends around the braid in the back, making it look like the knot was made entirely from the fabric.

Satisfied with the result, I carefully put the knife back into the knife block, then returned to the bedroom of the *salamandras*.

The women sat on their perches, motionless in their stone forms. The sight of the statues, not dead but not fully alive either, used to unsettle me. By now, however, I'd gotten used to sleeping among them. It even brought me comfort to know I wasn't alone.

I hoped they were all asleep. There was no way of telling for sure, though.

After kicking off my worn leather boots, I climbed under the covers on my perch. Despite the exhausting day, sleep wouldn't come to me. I remembered wishing for Elex to be in this world, thinking his presence would make life here more bearable.

Now that he actually was here, I wasn't so sure anymore. None of the emotions he caused in me were simple. And what lay ahead was troubling in its uncertainty.

The blanket was ripped off me with a swoosh.

"Where were you?" Mother's stern voice demanded. "Where were you last night at sunset?"

I blinked, the events of yesterday rushing into my memories. Snow-covered mountains. Wind howling between the rocks of the passage. Mind-numbing exhaustion. Dinner with the king. Elex...

I quickly patted my head to make sure the cloth was still on and my hair remained hidden.

"I asked you..." Mother stood over my perch, holding my blanket in her hand. Other women pretended to be going about their morning, washing their faces and brushing their hair and teeth while throwing furtive glances our way. "Where were you last night at sunset?"

"Here," I mumbled, rubbing the sleep out of my eyes. "I'm here now."

Despite the longer winter nights, I had a hard time falling asleep yesterday and would have loved to stay in bed just a little bit longer. There was no chance for that, of course. Judging by the furious face of Mother, I had an explanation to give. And it'd better be a good one.

"You didn't come with everyone else last night. It took you a while to show up," Mother seethed with anger.

Apparently, she had a hard time falling asleep too. Solid and unmoving in her stone form, Mother had been sitting on her perch, watching and listening. She had been awake when I went to bed.

"I..." I winced, trying to kick my brain into gear. "I went to the kitchen to get some water. I got thirsty after all that food." I looked up, straight into Mother's blue eyes lined with the fine web of fissures. Her face was distorted with anger, but there was desperate fear in her eyes too.

There was no harm in telling her about Elex. Or was there? If I told her the truth, I'd gain nothing. But there might be something either Elex or I would lose. It was best to stick with the lie.

"It took me a while to find the kitchen. But I had some water and came right back," I said.

"Did anyone see you?"

Elex was the one who did. But he wouldn't tell on me, would he?

"No. There wasn't anyone there."

She dropped my bed cover back onto my perch.

"Well, let's hope nothing bad comes from it. From now on, you're to be here at sunset, like everyone else. No wandering through the castle at night," she ordered, then added, muttering under her breath, "The last thing we need is to be accused of bringing a spy to the castle."

It couldn't have been easy for Mother to look after the safety and wellbeing of the women in her charge while also trying to appease the king at the same time. The king's wishes weren't always in line with the *salamandras'* interests, I imagined.

"I'll be here at sunset," I promised. "Every night."

She nodded, looking somewhat relieved.

"Get ready, everyone," she announced in a calmer voice. "Time to go to the water caves."

Her words stirred a wave of excitement among the women. They put their robes on hurriedly, then lined up by the door.

"What are the water caves?" I asked Zenada, who lowered the lace of her hood without a prompt.

"They are exactly that, silly," she laughed. "Caves with hot water springs running through them. We'll get to bathe, Amber. You'll love it."

"Here." Zenada grabbed a couple of plums from a small table by the entrance to the caves and shoved one into my hand. "I told you, food is everywhere at the king's castle." She smiled, biting into her plum.

The tables with fruit, candied nuts, and small pastries lined the walls of the wide arched entrance. Long loungers were carved from the stone between them and everywhere inside the caves. This place was clearly meant for enjoyment and relaxation.

The air inside was warm and rich with moisture.

"Come on, Amber, take off your clothes," Zenada urged at the nearest pool. She'd already finished eating her plum and was disrobing quickly.

I gaped at the beauty of this place. The caves of different sizes cascaded inside the mountain with water rolling down in a series of wide waterfalls. The dark burgundy walls with veins of pink quartz spread out wide. The ceiling of the main cave where we stood rose so high above us, I could barely see the glistening stalactites up above.

Steam rose from the water, giving the entire underground space a mystical appearance. It looked like a dream. And it was so warm here, it must be the warmest place in all of Dakath.

Completely naked now, Zenada approached the dark, steaming water.

"Oh, it's so nice," she moaned, dipping her toes into the pool. "Come Amber. You'll love it."

I shoved the rest of my plum into my mouth, then spat the pit into a small plate left for that purpose on one of the tables nearby. Untying the laces of my robe, I took it off and folded it on one of the stone loungers nearby. Next, I lifted the skirt of my dress. While taking it off over my head, I glanced up.

Carved paths ran between the pools and waterfalls of the caves. Some had narrow balconies with curled metal railings or stone parapets. There were people on the paths—men. Dressed in loose robes of light, flowy material, they strolled between the caves or casually leaned against the railings, watching the naked women bathe in the streams and pools below.

I pressed my dress to my chest, keeping my long shirt on. "Zenada, there're men up there."

She looked up for a moment, not at all concerned.

"They can watch all they want." She shrugged. "But no one can touch us without the king's permission."

That didn't make me feel any better. Crossing my hands over my chest, I stood at the pool. I would give anything to have a bath.

But the idea of being watched by strangers while doing it made me tense with unease. This would not be as relaxing as I'd hoped.

Wading out of the water, Zenada came to me.

"You're right. It's best for them not to see you." She took my hand, then led me away along a side path. "If they see you naked, they'll know you're not a fae."

Zenada's brown skin shimmered in the glow of the caves. Her coal-black hair glimmered with burgundy highlights from the reflected light cast by the quartz walls. Her body was flawless, perfectly proportioned, with a narrow waist, a delicate flare of hips, and breasts of just the right size.

With my bony shoulders, lanky limbs, and the breasts barely big enough to fill an A-cup, I didn't need to stand naked next to her to know that the physical differences between us would be striking. Most importantly, however, my human skin looked dull compared to hers that glowed with fae magic. Anyone seeing us naked together would know we're not of the same species.

"Come here." Zenada pulled me into a small cave off the path. A side stream filled the bottom of it, pooling in the middle into a small, round pond.

The ceiling in this cave was low, barely high enough for us to stand at full height.

"No one will see us here." Zenada took my dress from me, then lifted my shirt, taking it off.

She reached for the cloth on my head, but I stopped her, not trusting even her to see my new hair.

"I'll keep this on." I pressed my hand to my head.

She stepped back, not insisting I remove it.

"You have nothing to be shy or embarrassed about, Amber. Every man in this castle will want you. And if they knew you were a human, they'd fight each other for you."

She clearly meant to make me feel better, but her words had the opposite effect. Worry zapped through me.

"Why would they want me?"

I far preferred to remain in obscurity, out of the men's sight and away from their attention.

She shrugged. "You're a human. The only one in Dakath. Rare, exotic, and different."

Everything *different* attracted interest in Dakath. Only not the kind of interest I wished for. Being different could kill one as I'd learned.

"More reasons for me to stay away from the king's men," I muttered under my breath, walking to the water.

Zenada followed me to the pool. "Not necessarily. Having a lord for a lover has its advantages."

I failed to see any. Zenada had the king for a lover, and he kept her in the Sanctuary. Even now, with all of us in the castle, he hadn't brought her to his chambers to stay or given her a room of her own. She still slept and ate with us, stealing plums for a treat.

But she'd been so full of smiles and giddy with happiness ever since we'd arrived in the castle, I had no heart to argue with her.

Warm water caressed my feet when I stepped into the pond, and everything else shifted into the background.

"Mmmm," I moaned, walking deeper.

The water sloshed around my legs. The needles of frost that seemed to have permanently lodged in my body ever since I came to Dakath finally melted as I walked into the pool up to my shoulders.

"Oh, this is heaven." I lay on my back, letting the water hold me.

The stalactites in this cave were short and chunky. Their glow reflected in the ripples of the water below, bouncing back to the ceiling. The result was mesmerizing as the shimmer filled the entire cave, making it look as if it had a glowing pink disco ball suspended in the middle.

"This is now my favorite place in the castle," I declared. "In whole of Dakath, actually. The rest is mostly cold, harsh, and unwelcoming, anyway."

Zenada laughed softly, floating next to me.

"Dakath is very beautiful once you get to know it better. The valley and the foothills will become green soon. The spring is gorgeous in the mountains too. When the snow poppies bloom, it's the most beautiful sight you'll ever see."

"How long is it until spring?" I asked.

"Not long now. We've already had a few sunny days. That's how it starts. First, the light banishes the clouds. Then the air gets warmer. The snow melts and the poppies bloom."

I tried to imagine the lovely picture she described.

"Warm is nice. It's always too cold here. Even in the castle."

"You need a dragon with fire in his blood," she giggled. "He'd take you flying and warm you up."

Zenada didn't know it, but I'd been there. I'd flown with a dragon. It was magical. But it hurt when it ended. I closed my eyes, waiting for the ache of the memories to pass.

"I saw one of the king's men staring at you at dinner last night," Zenada lowered her voice.

"Did you?" I guessed whom she was talking about. Elex's glances had been so short and uninterested, however, I was surprised anyone noticed them at all beside me.

"The new lord at the court seemed to notice you. I caught him staring. And if so, it may be good. The king appears to favor him. You'll be smart to accept his advances. Some say he's of royal blood."

"Who says that?" Elex must have revealed who he was, at least to the king. That would explain him gaining royal favor so quickly. The two were family, after all.

"It may be just rumors. But there is often some truth to the court gossip. The new lord may be the king's long-lost brother, or his nephew. Or maybe even his bastard son. In any case..." She splashed, standing up. "It's good you caught his eye. His magic is strong. If he claims you, he'd be able to protect you from all the others." She swam back to shore. "I'll get us some soaps and oils. They'll add some shine to your skin."

"Zenada." I stood up, too, facing her. "Why are you so good

to me? Why do you care about me at all?"

From day one, she'd been feeding me, healing me, and keeping me warm. And lately, she seemed to search out my company even more, spending whatever spare time we got with me.

She blinked, staring at me, as if thinking about that for the first time herself.

"Well..." She twisted the end of her wet hair around her finger. "You were hurt and looked so weak when we found you."

"You felt sorry for me?" I wasn't offended if she did. I was in a sorry state when they found me.

She shrugged, not denying it. "I'm rooting for you, Amber. I want you to find your place in this world and be happy. Besides," she flashed me a grin. "Everyone needs a friend, right?" Her smile faded quickly. "I don't have many of those left."

Zenada had been close with Ertee and Isar. I understood the loss she was feeling. But I didn't trust friendships, just as I'd lost faith in love long ago.

Was it possible, though, to go through life completely on my own? This world was so cold already, wouldn't staying away from people make it even more miserable and harsh?

I smiled at Zenada. She nodded briefly before leaving the cave to get the soaps. I followed her with my gaze to the main cave visible through the entrance. Women splashed and swam in the water under the stares of the men on the paths above.

Some of the *salamandras* washed quickly and left. Others floated on their backs, displaying their bodies to the men. They washed leisurely, stroking their hips and rubbing fragrant oils over their breasts.

Maybe like Zenada, they appreciated the importance of having a lord for a lover and wished to attract one. Maybe they just enjoyed the men's attention after being deprived of male company in the Sanctuary.

I wasn't going to judge the women for trying to bring a little fun into their lives of hard work and solitude. But I feared that in the king's castle, male attention came with a price.

Five

AMBER

New clothes waited for us when we returned to our room. There were feather-light, long shirts with wide sleeves held at the wrist with embroidered cuffs. The dresses to wear over them had no sleeves, similar to the garments we wore before. Only unlike our old baggy dresses of scratchy wool with a rope around the waist, these gowns were made of shiny jacquard and tailored with darts on the sides. Open in the front, they were held together with two metal clasps under the breasts.

The women gushed and gasped, changing into the fine clothes. Zenada grabbed a bright orange dress and thrust a blush-pink one into my hands.

"Try this one," she said excitedly. "It'll give some nice color to your cheeks."

No one seemed to care about modesty, changing in the open. I shed my old, worn clothes, too, then pulled the shirt over my head, careful not to dislodge the wet cloth hiding my hair.

The light fabric of the shirt whispered down my naked body, and the voluminous sleeves caressed my arms like silky clouds.

The embroidered hem reached down to my ankles, but the material was rather transparent. The pink of my areolas was clearly visible through the milky-white of the shirt.

Thankfully, the dress covered my nipples completely. But the last clasp in the front was just above my belly button, allowing the skirt of the dress to fly open with every step I took. The nearly transparent shirt was the only thing that kept me from exposing myself completely while I walked.

I was glad to see the women putting their robes on over their rather revealing clothes and grabbed mine too.

Before long, all of us were dressed in the new clothes with the old robes over them. Instead of the worn boots, we now had light slippers on our feet.

"Lower your hoods, sisters," Mother ordered.

I draped the golden lace over my face. As annoying as it was to look at the world through the yellow mesh, I was glad for the protection it provided against the uninvited stares as we walked out of our room and into the rush of the servants and courtiers in the corridors.

As we ascended the winding staircase, I stole a glance at the wall outside the tower window—the spot where I saw Elex last.

Of course, he wasn't sitting on the wall anymore, but the thought of him made my stomach feel warm and jittery, as if a sparkle of fireflies swarmed inside it. I wondered if he'd be at the celebration today. He probably would since it was the king's event, and Elex was the king's favorite, according to Zenada.

We exited the tower a floor higher than last night, then stepped into a much larger room than the one we'd had dinner in before.

This one was perfectly round, with a high dome above. Windows and fireplaces were spaced equally along the circular walls. Fire burned brightly in the fireplaces. But the shutters on some of the tall windows were open, letting in daylight and winter wind.

Music filled the air. The musicians sat on a narrow platform by the entrance. High under the dome, a myriad of colorful crystals were suspended from thin golden chains. Prisms, diamonds, and pyramids swayed and turned in the wind, painting the walls and floor with a kaleidoscope of sparks.

Despite the mesmerizing light show, the place appeared rough and neglected. Scorch marks and ash smeared the interior. Deep grooves marred the floor and the walls. Parallel in sets of four or five, they looked like the scratches left by dragons' claws.

The king sat in the wide throne in the middle, leaning against one of the fur-covered armrests. Stone perches were arranged on either side of the throne, forming a wide semi-circle. Each platform looked like a double-wide lounger carved from stone, then covered with feather beds and animal hides. Placed between the perches, low wooden tables had been set with all possible kinds of food.

The king's men occupied the loungers. Some were sitting. Others were reclining in the pillows or leaning against the thick armrests carved on each side of the perches.

As if on its own, my gaze went to the place on the king's left.

Elex sat in the position that reminded me of the night I first saw him as a statue. With his one foot propped on the perch, he rested his forearm on his bent knee.

Without the long coat this time, he wore only a wide-sleeved red shirt with its ties open at his throat. A matching red sash was tied around his trim waist, the tasseled ends of it draping down one hip. The short, suede boots matched his black pants, stitched with dragon scales along the side seams.

His pose was relaxed and casual, but his gaze was scanning the row of *salamandras* intently. I drew my head deeper into my shoulders, glad for the robes and hoods that made us all look the same.

The women kept close to the door. Only Mother took a step forward.

"It's an honor to be here, Your Majesty." She bowed her head in greeting and supplication.

35

The women did the same, bending their knees to make themselves smaller. Not wishing to stand out in any way, I did like the others, dropping my head low and sinking into a curtsy.

The king grabbed a huge bone with meat that dripped with sauce and raised a goblet in his hand for the servant at his throne to refill it.

"One of the rebels, Lord Orirel, was poisoned yesterday." By the glee in the king's voice I gathered he must be talking about one of his worst enemies. A boasting note in his tone also hinted that the king had something to do with Lord Orirel's misfortune. "Today, we celebrate."

Taking a huge sloppy bite of the meat, he snapped his fingers at Zenada, who had slid her hood back to show her face. She sucked in a breath of excitement before rushing to him. The king slapped his thigh in invitation, and she lowered her bottom into his lap.

Mother quietly exited the room, leaving the rest of us at the mercy of the king and his men.

Some of the women lifted the lace from their faces. One by one, the men raised their hands, clicking their fingers at the *salamandra* of their choice. With a varied degree of eagerness, the women then joined them on their loungers.

Elex squinted at the few of us remaining by the wall unclaimed. I jerked my head down, keeping my hood low. But his features relaxed with recognition. Lifting his hand, he clicked his fingers, making the light blink in the stones of his rings. He had one on each finger now, having replaced many times over the ruby ring he'd given me.

The woman next to me shoved her elbow into my side.

"That one wants you," she hissed from under her hood.

Somehow, he had recognized me, even with my hood on and the lace down. Since I didn't move, he clicked his fingers again, flicking his wrist impatiently.

Clearly, I was expected to run to him, literally, at the snap of his fingers.

"Well," he scoffed, with a glance at the king. "That one is either blind or stubborn."

The king guffawed loudly. "Either way, she needs help to obey."

Zenada glanced my way, her eyebrows pinched into a frown of concern. I was attracting too much attention for my liking, but I simply couldn't move a muscle. I couldn't go to him. I couldn't sit next to him. I couldn't...

"This is going to be fun." Elex got off his perch and sauntered my way.

I hiked up my shoulders to my ears, planting my feet into the floor, and held my breath as he approached.

It didn't help. His warm scent reached me. It was both new and familiar. He smelled like spiced hot chocolate and a warm night by the fire. Magical and so disarmingly cozy.

He threw one arm around me, pressing me to his side.

"If not me, it'll be someone else," he whispered in my ear. "Is that what you want?"

I flicked my gaze between the available men. The High General's silver-blue eye peered at me with cold curiosity. The rest of the men focused on the remaining *salamandras* by the wall.

No, I didn't want any of these men. I wished to be back in the *salamandras'* room, alone on my hard, cold perch. But that clearly wasn't an option, so I kept quiet.

Taking my silence for compliance, Elex headed back to his lounger, half-leading, half-carrying me along.

He reclined into the furs, dragging me down with him. I propped my hands on his chest to keep at least some distance between us. It wasn't easy, and I ended up sitting on his lap.

"The window is right there." He tipped his chin at the open window behind us.

"Why would I care about the window?" I mumbled, confused. With him being this close, his scent invaded my senses, making me feel lightheaded.

He casually draped an arm around my waist. "Just in case you want to toss me out of it again."

A teasing smile broke on his face, and I had to glance away before I lost my mind and did something stupid, like kiss him.

I wished I could just toss him out of the window again. Last night, it proved to be a great way to deal with the turmoil he caused inside me.

I knew I should at least shove him away right now. But the freezing air from the window curled through the room like long, icy fingers, reaching under my robe and through the thin material of my clothes.

And Elex was so freaking warm.

Heat radiated from his body like from a furnace stocked with coal. Instead of shoving him away, I leaned closer into the warmth. I tried not to make it too obvious, pressing my side to his front but angling my head away from him. The position was rather awkward, but it kept me from outright lying on top of him.

"So..." I furtively tucked my numb, cold fingers under my side, pressing them against his warm stomach. "Now that I'm planted here on your lap, does it mean you've claimed me? I mean, will that keep the other men away from me?"

"I sure hope so." He shrugged casually, though the focus in his eyes sharpened with warning as he moved his stare along the perches with the king's men on them. "I'm new to all of this."

"New? But weren't you born and raised in this world? In this very castle?"

He lifted the wide strip of lace over my face and folded it back. Nothing stood between my eyes and his now.

"I was born and raised in this world, true. But it was during a very different time. This place is nothing like my father's castle used to be. I hardly recognized the Bozyr Peak when I first got here."

Somehow, I had assumed that since this world was his, Elex would fit right back into it. And it seemed like he did. Wasn't he sitting here in the royal hall, wearing fine clothes, celebrating the murder of one of the king's enemies?

But there had been some adjustments for Elex to make, too.

"How far from your time are we?" I asked. "Who is the king to you?"

He brought his lips to my ear, lowering his voice and making it look like he was whispering sweet nothings to me. "King Edkhar is my great-great-grandfather."

"Wow..." I released a breath with a little whistling sound. "How far back into the past are we, then?"

"About a thousand years."

"That's a long time." A thousand years would mean a big change in life back on Earth. It'd be like going from flying on airplanes to the end of the dark ages. "But you knew that might happen, right?"

He nodded. "I did. I had plenty of time to think it through while sitting as a statue in Ghata's menagerie. I had the time to mourn the life I left behind when the *bracks* took me and to accept that I may never see anyone I knew ever again. And I decided to return to Dakath, no matter the cost."

That was the difference between Elex and me. I'd never had a chance to even absorb what was happening when he'd snatched me from my world, no time to think it through or to make any decision at all.

"Well..." I searched for something positive to say to him—a silver lining in all this mess. "At least you're back in the castle. The king likes you. Maybe he'll grow fond of you enough to pass the crown on to you one day. You'll be the king, like you were born to be. Apparently, there are rumors that you're King Edkhar's illegitimate son. It wouldn't be too much of a stretch for him to officially adopt you."

He looked at me with amusement as I babbled away.

"Is that what you think I want, Amber?"

"Why not?" I shrugged a shoulder.

"King Edkhar doesn't like anyone. He uses some people and

tolerates others. He knows I belong to the royal bloodline because I have access to the magic of the Dakath Mountains." He slid a hand inside my hood and pulled out a tendril of hair from under the cloth on my head. "The same magic that let me do this." His expression turned dreamy as he curled the lock around his finger.

I slapped my hand over the hood, trapping his finger inside.

"No one can know about this."

He moved his eyes to mine. "Why?"

"They got rid of my hair before. They'll do it again, Elex. That's why."

A deep groove formed between his eyebrows.

"Why did the *salamandras* do it to you? Did Mother make them? Was it the king's order?" His voice lowered to a growl. He looked ready to rip apart whoever I pointed my finger at.

But I'd never held a grudge against the three women who waxed my hair off. It wasn't their fault that the circumstances were against us all. Out of the three, Zenada was the only one left alive now. And I certainly wasn't going to sic Elex on her.

Dropping my gaze down, I removed his hand from my hood, then tucked the loose strand back under the cloth.

"It doesn't matter who did it. It was done for my safety and theirs." He kept staring at me with that dangerous frown on his face and murder in his eyes, so I tried to explain. "Here is what I've been told, Elex. In this world, nothing good comes to those who are different. I'm the only human in Dakath, which makes me *very* different. In addition to that, apparently, the color of my hair is also somehow important."

"King Edkhar likes red," he muttered under his breath.

"Why? I don't feel all that special being a redhead. It often feels like a nuisance as it comes with all these freckles and the risk of sunburn at the slightest exposure to the sun."

He slid my sleeve up, then traced the freckles on my forearm with the tip of his finger, as if connecting the stars into a constellation.

"Red is the color of fire," he said. "And fire is the symbol of power. Long ago, it was also believed that in gargoyles with red hair, magic also manifested the strongest—" he cut himself short, as if thinking of something. "Well, since 'long ago' is now, it's not *was* but *is*. It *is* believed that red hair means more magic and more power."

"But I have no magic. None. I'm a human, remember?"

He stroked the side of my face with his finger, his expression softening.

"How could I ever forget that? My dearest, most beloved human."

Slowly, deliberately, the warm pad of his finger traced the shape of my face, from my cheekbone down to my jawline. His eyes stayed on mine. The red spark deep inside them flickered and churned.

I was no longer cold. My body heated, making me wish I could take the woolen robe off. I shrank away, turning my head to evade his touch.

He wouldn't let me get away, though. Cupping my chin in his hand, he turned my face back to his.

His eyelids dropped a little, as did his voice. "Am I so hideous to look at that you keep avoiding it, my spark?"

Yanking my chin from his hand, I turned to his left. The man in the lounger a few feet away from us had a *salamandra* in his lap. Her hood was off, and I recognized the woman. Her name was Delsandra. She was a quiet one who spent a lot of time indoors. I'd hardly ever seen her in the courtyard back in the Sanctuary.

One of the man's hands was buried in the hair on the back of her head as he kissed her. The ties of her robe were undone, the man's other hand was in the neckline of her shirt, fondling her breast.

Delsandra gyrated her hips. Her moans mingled with his in the kiss. With her skirts pooling in his lap, it wasn't clear whether he was inside her or if she simply rubbed herself against him through their clothes. Either way, this was a private scene, not for me to watch.

I turned away, meeting Elex's heated gaze again.

"This 'celebration' is turning into a real orgy," I muttered, my cheeks burning hot from what I'd witnessed.

Even without looking at them, I couldn't escape the sounds of the people kissing and moaning next to us. On the right, similar sounds came from the king's throne.

Elex didn't seem bothered by what was happening around us. His attention was fully on me.

"Is this something all gargoyles do?" I blurted, just to say something as his stare started to burn a hole in my self-control. "The orgies? Did you have them in your time, too?"

"Orgies?" He swept the room with his gaze as if noticing his surroundings for the first time just now. "We had celebrations often, but not like these."

"Were yours without sex?"

"Why without?" He grinned. "Not our family celebrations, of course, but I've held parties with my friends, other lords and ladies, where everything was allowed."

"Everything?"

He nodded. "As long as everyone enjoyed themselves."

That was the most upsetting thing about the current situation—I didn't believe that everyone was enjoying themselves in equal measure. The balance of power here was severely skewed in favor of the men. I wondered how many women wouldn't be here at all if given a choice.

Just a little while ago, I would have rather left this room, too. Now... Now, I no longer felt in a hurry to trade Elex's warm lap for my cold perch in the room I shared with three dozen other women.

Other than his arm around my waist, he wasn't touching me. After lifting the lace from my face, he hadn't removed any of my clothing. I didn't feel pressured to do anything the other couples were doing. He seemed to be content with simply talking to me. And I... I'd always loved talking to Elex.

I touched the soft silk of his shirt. The material was so thin, I could easily trace the landscape of his muscles underneath.

"So, what did you do with all those lords and ladies at your parties?"

He grinned. "Well, personally, I've always preferred ladies."

"Ladies who liked doing *everything* at the parties with you?"

He paused, studying my face with unnerving intensity.

I was fine with our light conversation. I was even okay with flirting. I could possibly handle even more, as long as it remained light and easy.

But I had no idea what to do with this serious stare of his. I was losing control of the situation.

"That's not what I'm after, Amber," he said softly as his gaze caressed my face. "I have no interest in King Edkhar's parties or the ladies of his court. For some time now, my mind and my heart have been solidly occupied by just one woman."

Breath caught in my throat. I wasn't ready for that turn of the conversation. I didn't want to know which woman he was talking about. And I certainly didn't wish to discuss any of that over the noise of sex happening in this room.

He slid his hand inside my hood, cupping the back of my neck.

"Amber..." He brought me closer, so close, my chest pressed against his.

I hooked one arm around his neck, splaying the other hand flat on his chest. The crimson silk of his shirt cast a red glow on my skin, like a hint of blood. Or the light of sunrise.

"I dream about you." He stroked my cheek with his thumb. "Even during the day. When I'm hurt or alone, I close my eyes and think about you. I remember your kisses, and how you made me laugh. The memories of you fill me with light even when it's dark."

His voice was earnest, his expression open and warm.

Stunned, I had no idea how to react to his confession. My inner barriers cracked, and I just stared into his eyes, my head spinning while I was losing myself in their depth.

"You're the spark that brought me back to life, Amber. And you're still lighting my way during the darkest times."

My heart raced. So many emotions filled me, I feared they would overflow. Then, I might say or do something irrevocable. Something that would get me hurt. Again.

Elex was not my Prince Charming. He wasn't my anything.

I had to stop this. To change it. But I didn't know how.

I slid my hand up his shirt and slipped my fingers into the opening on his chest. He sucked in a sharp breath the moment I touched his skin. Heat flashed in his dark eyes.

Distraction. That was what I needed. And it worked—he stopped talking.

Encouraged, I reached down with my other hand and pressed my palm to his hard length through his pants. With a soft moan, he tossed his head back, thrusting his hips into my touch. His response proved invigorating.

"You like this, don't you?" I whispered, pressing the side of my face to his, my mouth next to his ear. "You like my hands on you."

He just groaned in reply as I squeezed my hand tighter. He'd spent so much time as an unfeeling piece of rock, every sensation must feel so much more intense to him now.

I wished to give him more.

Leaning back a little, I tugged at the silk sash around his waist, loosening it. He didn't stop me, and I untied the lacing on his pants next, finally slipping my hand inside.

He was even hotter here, his length hard and pulsing.

"Amber... Amber," he kept repeating my name like a mantra as I wrapped my fingers around him. "Gods...yes."

He flexed his hand on my nape, bringing my face to his, but I turned my head, evading his lips.

"Kiss me," he begged. "Please."

I didn't. I buried my face in his shoulder instead, rubbing him harder with my hand. He writhed under my touch, completely in my power. I had control, but only as long as *I* touched *him*. If I kissed him, if I let him touch me back, I would lose myself to him, and I'd fall for him fully and completely.

I couldn't let that happen.

"Come for me, Elex," I whispered, instead.

A growl vibrated deep inside his chest. His hand found its way under my robe. He deftly opened both clasps of my dress. Then both his hands were on my body, touching me through the barely there fabric of my shirt.

The heat of his palms seeped through the material to my skin. He slid his hands up my sides to my breasts. A pleased rumble sounded in the back of his throat as he cupped them. My nipples hardened, pushing against the fabric, and he found them by touch with his thumbs.

"I want to hear those little moans you make when I play with these, my spark." He pinched the tips through my shirt, sending a shudder of pleasure through my body.

Breath rushed out of me as I arched my back, pressing my pelvis to his.

"Just like that," he murmured approvingly at my needy whimpers. "Oh, how I missed these sounds."

I felt my control slipping after all. My body ignited with need. The desire for him rushed through me with hot sparks. I no longer cared where we were or what was happening around us. It was just Elex and I. Soaring, as if we were high in the sky again, where nothing else mattered.

"Kiss me," he pleaded, searching for my mouth with his.

I jerked my head away, snapping back to my senses. Squeezing my fingers tighter, I moved my hand faster along his length.

"Come, Elex," I begged. "Come, now."

I feared that if he took just a little longer, I'd give up. I'd give him my body and soul. And I'd lose every bit of myself to him, without him ever asking for any of that.

He gripped my sides, his body tensing under me. His lips parted. Air left him in sharp breaths as he came in my hand. I trembled, as if I came with him, which of course I didn't. My hand shook when I removed it from him, taking it out of his pants.

His body relaxed. But the look in his eyes remained as intense as ever. He searched my eyes with his, and I looked for distraction once again.

"Well..." I held my hand between us. His release glistened on my fingers. "I guess I'll have to go wash my hand now." It was as good an excuse to leave the room as any.

I made a move to get off his lap, but he grabbed my wrist.

"Wait." He yanked the sash from around his waist. "Let me clean it." With the red silk of his sash, he wiped my fingers thoroughly, one by one. "Here you go." He placed a kiss in the middle of my palm. "All done."

"But it still smells like you," I mumbled.

The faint spicy scent was pleasant.

Why? Why did he need to smell so nice?

He arched an eyebrow. "And is that a bad thing?"

I stared at him firmly. "I don't want to smell like you."

Silently, he reached for his goblet on the table next to us and dipped the end of his sash into the wine.

"Here," he said, wiping my hand with the wet silk. "Now, you smell like pomegranate wine. Better?"

The scent of wine was nice, but not nearly as pleasant as his. Not that I was going to tell him that.

He lifted my hand to his mouth and kissed my fingers, catching an errant drop of wine on his tongue. The caress of his lips teased my unfulfilled desire. I had to leave. I needed to climb off his lap and leave this room, whether it was allowed or not. But Elex had robbed me of my excuse to leave, and I was too distracted by the caress of his lips on my fingers to come up with another one.

He slid his hand up and down my back. The gesture was

soothing, simple but intimate. And I gave in. I curled against his chest, resting my head on his shoulder.

"Amber," he started.

There was urgency in his voice, and I pressed my finger to his lips.

"Shhh," I whispered, relaxing in his arms. "Not right now. Please."

This very moment, I found myself in a happy place, even if against my will. Now, I just wanted to stay like this for a little while longer, basking in the warmth of his body and enjoying the few stolen moments of peace it brought me.

Six

AMBER

"**D**ance for us," the king's voice boomed from the royal throne.

The cozy bubble around Elex and me burst at the sound. Reality rushed back in.

The music still played. The musicians clearly possessed inhuman endurance. Zenada climbed off the king's lap with some reluctance. She must be wishing to stay in her own bubble, too.

"Good girl." The king slapped her butt, making her giggle. With a bow to him, Zenada left the room to get ready for her dance.

The king sat up on his throne, then ripped another meaty bone from the dish on the table nearby.

Elex ducked his head to see my face under the hood. "Are you hungry, Amber?"

When was I not hungry? The few pieces of fruit I'd eaten in the caves that morning didn't last long.

I said nothing, but he knew the answer anyway.

"Here." Leaning to the left, he dragged an entire table to me. "Try these. They were my favorite growing up."

From a large brass platter, he picked a twig with what looked like a handful of ground meat stuck around it like an elongated meatball. He dipped the meat into a dish of cherry-red sauce, then offered it to me. Circling his wrist, I took a bite as he kept holding the end of the twig.

I wished I could pause to savor the full complexity of flavors of the sauce or to appreciate the mix of spices in the meat, but I swallowed the first bite with hardly any chewing, then stuffed the rest of the meatball in my mouth, sliding it off the twig with my teeth.

"It's good." I nodded, quickly reaching for another one.

Elex rinsed and refilled his goblet for me, and I washed the meat down with some wine, then kept eating. There were vegetable disks that looked like grilled eggplant and purple potatoes drizzled with oil and roasted with garlic. The greenish pancakes tasted like the most tender zucchini latkes I'd ever tried. They were served with a creamy dill sauce that was just to die for.

I tried every savory dish before moving on to the dessert of syrup-soaked cherries and roasted nuts.

Snacking on a handful of candied cranberries, Elex watched me silently. Every now and then, he would refill my goblet or move a dish closer to me, but his expression grew darker the more I ate.

"Does Mother of the Sanctuary know humans need to eat more often than fae?" His voice sounded grave.

I nodded. My mouth was too full and sticky with dessert to reply with words. He drew in some air, possibly to ask more questions, but the doors to the room opened again, and Zenada entered.

She wore her robe with the hood up and the lace drawn low over her face. In one hand, she carried a large leather sack with metal rods sticking out of it.

Dropping the sack at her feet, she stopped in the middle of the room and faced the king.

"Isn't she lovely?" The king rubbed his hands, his face lighting up with excited anticipation.

I wasn't sure how he felt about the woman, but he certainly was looking forward to the entertainment she was about to provide.

Bringing her hands to her hood, Zenada lifted the lace, giving the king a heated look. She then slid the hood down, revealing her hair braided into two long plaits with golden ribbons woven through.

Slowly, she tugged at the ties of her robe at her neck, then shrugged out of it, letting the robe fall to the floor. The deliberate, artistic way she was undressing told me it was also a part of the act.

The king clearly appreciated it, shifting to the end of his throne. His eyes sparked with excitement as he watched her every move.

Zenada opened the clasps of her dress, then dropped it to the floor on top of her discarded robe. There was no shirt underneath. Instead, she had a short leather bustier on, with a pair of matching pants. The pants sat low on her hips, emphasizing the dip of her narrow waist. Each pant leg was split open from the knee down, giving them a flared shape. The dark-brown leather of her outfit was embroidered with golden thread and ruby beads that twinkled in the light as she moved.

She took two metal torches out of her bag, then shoved the bag and her discarded clothes away with her foot, giving herself some space.

The king suddenly stood up from his throne, then walked behind it, disappearing from view. The next moment, he grew, his head rose above the high back of his throne, his shoulders spreading wider. His neck elongated, his skin turning to bright red scales that shimmered with gold.

Zenada's chest rose with a deep breath. She braced herself before raising her torches up over her head. They were unlit. And I saw no buckets of flammable tar anywhere.

The king fully transformed into a dragon now. He lay behind the throne, his long neck curled around its back with his head leaning on the armrest.

"Are you ready, my fire dancer?" the dragon's voice thundered, making the crystals under the dome tremble and clink.

Zenada nodded, her pose tense. The dragon opened his mouth. A cloud of smoke churned over his long tongue with sparks of fire. He formed a circle with his lips and blew. A long ribbon of bright sparkling fire shot out of his mouth, snapping over Zenada's head like a whip. She caught the fire with her torches, setting their ends aflame.

The music leaped higher as Zenada took off in a dance. Moving smoothly, she tossed and twirled the torches. Their fire licked the leather of her outfit and skimmed the bare skin of her arms and midriff.

"Oh, she is so beautiful..." I whispered, mesmerized.

With another surge of music, Zenada flicked her wrists. The torches opened like two large fans—or dragon wings—each spike burning with fire at its end.

The musicians played faster as Zenada sped up her tempo. Instead of two torches, she now had twelve sparkling balls of fire on each end of a spike. They blurred into two continuous ribbons of light as she danced, twirling faster and faster.

I gripped Elex's thigh, my eyes glued to the limber woman dancing inside what now looked like a hurricane of fire. It sparked and twisted around her, continuously changing shape with her every move.

The dragon-king's eyes glistened wildly, his head moving slightly as he followed her movement along the floor.

Without warning, he blew another flame from his mouth. But Zenada must have expected it. She brushed through the flame with one of her metal fans, gracefully moving her body out of harm's way.

The dragon blew another stream of fire and sparks out of his mouth. Zenada evaded it again. Raking the ends of her fans through the flame, she cut it into smaller ribbons, each curling and twisting in its own way. They created unforgettable designs in the air before disappearing into tendrils of smoke.

The dragon wouldn't let her rest, blowing more fire, faster and faster. This didn't look like teamwork anymore, but competition. The king no longer worked with her but against her. He clearly tried to trap her, to force her to make a mistake, and to hurt her. The cold glint in his eyes said he *wished* to hurt her.

He blew the fire to her right, then almost immediately to her left. Zenada wasn't fast enough. The second blast lashed against her midriff, searing her exposed skin and scorching the leather of her bustier.

She cried out in pain, stumbling on her feet and messing up the next step of the dance. I jerked instinctively, trying to get to her. But Elex flexed his arm around my waist, holding me in place.

The dragon-king chuckled. "Still not fast enough, my little *salamandra*."

It occurred to me that the king never called Zenada by name. I wondered if he even knew or cared to know it.

Zenada pressed her arm to her side, then jerked it away with a hiss. Her skin blistered and puckered, turning red where the king's fire had touched her. It would add another scar to the many she already had.

"Zenada!" I fought against Elex's grip, needing to get to her.

She threw me a warning look. Her dark eyes filled with tears, but she bit her bottom lip, not letting another cry of pain out. Hunching over, she picked up the bag with her equipment and her clothes, then limped out of the room.

The dragon leveled me with a stare.

"Still not tamed?" he growled, displeased. "Will you teach her how to keep her mouth shut, Lord Elex? Or should I do it for you?"

I stiffened, afraid to breathe. What was I in trouble for? For saying my friend's name out loud? It made no sense. Yet the impending punishment seemed as real as ever.

Elex rose to his feet, hauling me up with him.

"My apologies, Your Majesty. I'll take care of it outside, so as not to disrupt your celebration." With his arm around my middle, he tossed me over his shoulder.

I clenched my hands into fists. Indignation burned through me like acid. Yet I knew protesting would only make it worse.

The dragon-king grimaced, obviously annoyed by my behavior, but he didn't stop Elex from carrying me out of the room.

After the heavy doors closed behind us, Elex carried me down the hallway, then around a corner and out of sight of the guards by the entrance to the hall. The moment we were alone, I slammed my fists into Elex's hard bottom.

"Put me down! Now."

He set me down with my feet on the floor.

"It had to be done," he explained, running his hands through his hair. "I couldn't let the king near you."

"I know." I breathed deeply, trying to calm my nerves, my fear, and indignation. "I have to find Zenada."

"Wait." He took my hand. "Tell me what life is like in the *Salamandra* Sanctuary?"

I scoffed. "What do you think?"

He spread his arms aside in a disarming gesture. "I honestly don't know what to think, Amber. In my old time, my mother looked after the Sanctuary. She ran it along with two *salamandras* who lived there. As far as I remember, it was always a safe place for both men and women. Those who were going through hard times, who had nowhere to go and no one to take care of them, found a true sanctuary there. According to the legends, Mother *Salamandra* created our people by teaching her sons love and compassion. She united dragons and saurians, creating the gargoyle race. The Sanctuary bears her name as the symbol of unity, love, and compassion."

I hugged my arms. "Beautiful words, Elex. And maybe that's what the Sanctuary was during your times. But that's certainly not what it is now."

"Tell me," he demanded.

I used to think Elex grew up sheltered and ignorant. But that clearly wasn't the case. Elex was smart and inquisitive. He didn't shy from the truth and didn't fear it. He wouldn't have spent a hundred years of his life willingly blinded to the life outside of the castle. The Kingdom of Dakath just used to be very different during his time—much better, by the sound of it.

Now, I had to tell him the truth about his own world. I heaved a breath, wondering where to even begin.

"Dakath women are not allowed to exist independently. Their value is only as good as what they mean to a man. The *Salamandra* Sanctuary is filled with widowed and unmarried women who have no man to belong to. Men aren't allowed inside, unless they're sent by the king. In which case, he can order them to do whatever he wants. Oh, and as I recently learned..." I tipped my head in the direction of the king's party room. Bitterness filled me, and I made no effort to keep it from my voice. "The women are expected to run to the castle at the snap of the royal fingers, to entertain the king and his men, and to provide sexual favors along with whatever else tickles his fancy. They get nothing in return, just the scorn of the 'respectable' villagers and burn scars."

Elex gritted his teeth, working his jaw. He looked like he could barely contain his rage, which gave me hope.

"You can change this, Elex. You are the Prince of Dakath. You have what it takes to make a difference."

His features tensed in a pained expression. "Only by changing the present, Amber, I would risk changing the future. No matter how hideous life is now, in just a few hundred years, this world will be so much better."

"A few hundred years?" I felt deflated, hope deserting me.

He kept talking passionately. "Before the spring is over, King Edkhar will win the war. He'll defeat the Rebel Lords in the final battle at the foothills of the Bozyr Peak."

"He will?"

That was disappointing. I took no sides in this war, but from what I knew, the cause of the Rebel Lords appeared as a more sympathetic one to me—they stood up to avenge the kidnapping of a woman. King Edkhar had been fighting solely to assert and keep his power.

"This summer," Elex continued, "the king will marry his future queen, Lady Amree. And less than two years from now, his son Elex will be born."

"Elex?"

"Yes. I was named after the Great King Elex. He will be nothing like his father. Under his rule, the Dakath Mountains will thrive. The justice and liberties the people enjoyed in my time will begin during the reign of King Elex and his wife, the Fire Queen."

"The Fire Queen? Is that her name?"

"That's the name kept in chronicles of her. My great-grand-mother was the one and only fire bending *salamandra* in gargoyle history. Her magic rivaled even her husband's."

"Quite a power couple they made," I muttered, rather impressed.

"They were bonded mates, inseparable and practically invincible." He took my left hand in both of his and stroked the ruby salamander wrapped around my ring finger. "This ring belonged to her."

I wondered briefly if it was my responsibility to ensure the ring went on to the future queen for its history to continue. Or was I supposed to lose it at some point, for it to be created later for her in the future? Did time move in a line or a loop? I had no idea, and sadly time travel didn't come with a handbook explaining all the rules.

Maybe, one just had to go with the flow and let things happen as they did?

Elex kept my hand in his, warming my cold fingers with his gentle caress.

"The son of the Fire Queen, King Ahrit, will be my grandfa-ther. He will continue to build on his father's legacy. You see,

Amber, the present has to continue for the future to happen just the way it will."

Logically, his words made sense. But my heart refused to accept the current injustices, even if they were for the sake of some greater good in the future.

I gave him a hard stare.

"Well, now I know exactly where you stand."

I turned on my heel, ready to leave, but he grabbed my shoulders, spinning me back to face him.

"I want you to understand, Amber, my life is tied with the king's. I have to protect him and his crown."

"Then, what are you waiting for? Go protect your king, Elex." I gestured in the direction of the hall. "And I will go where I belong, to the women."

"No." The force and passion he put into that one word made me pause. "Stay with me. Please. My room is on one of the upper levels of the castle. You'll be warm and safe there."

Warm. He knew exactly how to entice me. But the other part of what he said made me scoff.

"*Safe?* Is there such a thing, Elex? Nowhere in Dakath is safe for a human. And how can you keep me safe from the king you serve?" I shook my head with regret. "Sorry, but I trust the *salamandras* to keep me safe more than I trust you."

"Amber." He flinched as if I'd slapped him.

I felt his pain. I really did. Deep inside I believed, Elex was a good person who wanted to do the right thing. Only what good did it do?

I swallowed around a tightness in my throat. "I shouldn't have come to Dakath, Elex. It would've been easier for both of us if you had just left me in my own world." I lifted my eyes to his. "You've never even apologized for that, for taking me."

I glimpsed sympathy in his dark eyes, but there was not a hint of regret.

"If I didn't take you, you would've been dead."

"You don't know that for sure. Maybe I could've made it. I've been in tight situations before."

He shook his head resolutely. "'*Maybe*' wasn't good enough for me. It looked like a life-or-death situation to me. *Your* life or death, Amber. I couldn't leave it up to chance."

"So you brought me here and left me right after. How was that any better?"

His cheeks flushed. His eyes sparked. He opened his mouth to argue, but I spoke first.

"You felt so sorry for me losing my hair, Elex. As if that was the biggest problem. You never apologized for what really mattered."

He stalked to me, grabbing my shoulders. His eyes roamed over my face. His expression was wild. But I was not afraid of him, not for a second.

Elex was clearly deeply affected by this conversation. He probably felt frustrated, maybe even angry at the situation. He might even be mad at me. Obviously, we saw some things differently. But I knew beyond a shadow of a doubt, Elex would never raise a hand to me. He was nothing like his great-great-grandfather who delighted in violence.

"Amber, please believe me—"

The doors slammed open at the end of the hallway. Then heavy footsteps rushed our way. I yanked my hood low and stepped away from Elex a moment before one of the king's guards turned around the corner to find us.

"King Edkhar wishes to know if Lord Elex and his *salamandra* are ready to return to the party?" the guard announced.

Elex reached for my hand, but I jerked it away from him.

"Tell the king I ate too much and have stomach cramps," I whispered to him quickly. "No. Wait." It occurred to me that King Edkhar wouldn't care how I felt. I'd be required to attend even with stomach cramps if that was his royal wish. "Tell him the zucchini didn't agree with me."

"What do you mean?" Elex looked puzzled.

"Oh, for Pete's sake," I muttered under my breath. "Tell him I have diarrhea. A really bad case. And I don't want to... um, *soil* his fine gathering in any way."

Not waiting for his reaction, I ran to the tower with the staircase at the other end of the hallway.

"What's *diarrhea?*" the guard asked Elex, sounding confused.

I guessed the fae didn't have that particular ailment—lucky for them. I didn't go back to explain, however, letting them figure it out on their own, or not. Either way, I trusted Elex to come up with a suitable excuse for the king if needed. He was so much better at court life than I could ever hope to be. And I had a different priority right now.

Running down the stairs, I made it to the floor with the kitchen, then to the corridor that led to the *salamandras'* bedroom.

Zenada lay on her uninjured side on her perch. Her leather top was off. Her pants had been shoved down. Mother sat next to her, applying a brown poultice to Zenada's freshest burn.

"How are you?" I padded closer, instantly subdued at the sight of my friend suffering in pain.

She gritted her teeth as Mother smeared another dollop of paste on her red and blistered skin.

"She'll be fine," Mother bit out. "It'll take a few days for the new skin to grow."

"For the *scar* to form, you mean?" I fisted my hands, wishing I could punch something... No, someone... I wished I could punch the king for burning Zenada for no other purpose but for some perverted kind of fun.

Damn you, King Edkhar.

Mother shrugged. "Is there a difference?"

Anger rose in me, burning my insides like fire.

"You know there is. The king could've had his entertainment by letting Zenada dance with the regular fire. If she burned herself with it, at least she could heal without a scar. But no, he wanted to burn her himself, with his dragon's fire. Because he knew it would really hurt her, leaving a mark on her—"

"Silence!" Mother jumped to her feet. The clay lid of the poultice jar rolled from her lap and shattered to pieces against the stone floor. "Don't you dare criticize the king." She slammed the jar on the perch nearby.

Fuming, I plopped onto my bed next to Zenada's. Mother kneeled at my feet unexpectedly, leaving me speechless for a moment. Then I realized what she was doing as she snapped a metal manacle around my right ankle.

"Why?" I yanked at my foot, making the chain attached to the manacle rattle. It stretched all the way to a ring mounted into the wall.

"This is to make sure you stay put at night," Mother hissed, locking my restraints then slipping the key into her pocket.

Hurt and indignity stirred in me. I'd promised her I wouldn't leave the room at night anymore. Did she not trust me?

Her haunted expression held so much fear, however, that I didn't even argue. Mother's actions had little to do with her trust or with any of her own feelings. She simply tried to please the men in power because that was the only way she knew how to survive.

Well, let her sleep better, thinking she had restrained me. There was no need for me to wander at night, anyway. But if that need arose, I'd just have to get my hands on something long, sharp, and flexible—like Zenada's hairpin, for example—to set myself free.

I was a thief, after all. And picking locks had been the skill I'd honed for years.

Seven

⤫⤬

ELEX

He spread his wings and pushed off a window in his bedroom. Silently, he glided around the mountain, heavily leaning into his newly healed right wing to test its strength. The royal hag knew her trade well. The wing healed so well, it didn't even feel like it'd been broken.

A warmer spiral of air brought him around the Bozyr Peak and onto the north wall of the castle.

The midday sun was high. It burned brighter as spring began. The ice on the black, spiky roofs of the turrets was melting, dripping down in icicles all along the wall. On the south side, it evaporated, rising into the air as steam. Here in the shade, it was a little cooler, but shadows helped him hide.

Folding his wings through the slits on the back of his shirt, he landed on the inner wall of the castle, not far from the spot where he'd spent a night two weeks ago, when Amber had pushed him out of the window.

Crouching behind a turret, he waited.

There weren't any guards on this part of the wall. The sky above the castle was guarded from much higher lookout points.

The outer wall on this side was built directly over a steep drop off of the cliff, inaccessible by land, which made guarding it a waste of time and resources.

Amber had figured it out, too, as she had been coming here daily while the king and his courtiers had their midday meal.

She'd refused to move to his room. And after everything she'd told him about life in the Sanctuary, he was sick with worry that something terrible might happen to her while she was with the *salamandras*, fragile and defenseless.

Having Amber close would make watching over her easier. But since she refused even to look at him lately, he did his best to guard her from a distance. He'd spent his nights on the castle wall, with a view of the window of the room where she slept. Over a week ago, he'd spotted her while exercising his healed wing in flight. Ever since, he made sure to be here every day just before noon, waiting for her to appear.

The sound of light footfalls reached his hearing, sending a shiver of anticipation through him.

Amber padded between the inner and outer walls of the castle. Like every day before, she carried a bow and a quiver with arrows. She only had six, but these were real arrows, tipped with iron and meant to kill.

With a quick glance around, she pulled out a square piece of wood she kept tucked by the inner wall, then propped it on the base of a turret. In the middle of the square she had a circle painted in red, just one circle, about the size of a large apple.

Turning with her back to her target, she walked away from it. Her lips moved as she counted the steps. After counting to thirty, she turned around and squinted at the wood with the circle. Taking a red plum out of the pocket of her robe, she bit into it, staring at her target as she ate.

Elex loved seeing the shadows under her eyes disappear during the past week. Her cheeks had filled out, too, a little. By twisting the rules and using the king's name, he'd arranged for trays of food to be sent to the *salamandras'* room every morning.

Humans needed breakfast, and he made sure Amber got one daily.

He'd found out she liked the red plums from the valley, so he'd requested them to be added to the trays, as well as the flaky pastries that looked similar to those she'd fed him back in the human realm. And coffee of course, the best coffee Dakath had to offer.

After finishing the plum, she chucked the pit over the wall then nocked an arrow into her bow. The first shot ended up landing a bit off, but the next five hit within the red circle.

She'd been getting better. Even in the days that he'd been watching her, her aim had improved as did her confidence and strength.

She pulled the arrows out of the board, then untied her robe. Glancing around to make sure no one was watching her, she shrugged out of her robe and adjusted the cloth on her head.

Elex nearly groaned with disapproval. She still hadn't learned that in Dakath one had to watch the sky just as much as the ground. Though, he was glad her negligence allowed him to remain undetected.

Her simple dress and the stiff linen shirt hid most of her figure. But seeing her without her robe sent a warm shiver of excitement through his body. His blood heated. His fire surged whenever Amber was near.

She caught his interest the first time he'd seen her. But from the very beginning, he'd tried to keep their interactions fair, dealing with her in an almost business-like manner. She'd agreed to take him to the portal, he'd paid her with his great-grandmother's ruby ring. She'd let him touch her, and he'd made sure she enjoyed it.

Despite his best efforts, however, things had gotten rather messy after that. They had no straightforward agreements anymore, and she'd been taking from him, without him even realizing when and how she did it.

First, she took his sleep. Before she even came to the Bozyr

Peak, he would sit on the perch outside his bedroom, stare at the dark night sky, often until sunrise, thoughts about her keeping him awake.

He'd only spent two nights with Amber in the human world, but he had somehow gotten addicted to having her close. He had a difficult time falling asleep now without the sound of her breathing mixed with her cute, soft snoring. Gargoyles didn't breathe at night, staying completely still in their stone form. And he missed the sounds she made in her sleep, resenting the complete stillness of his lonely nights.

On those rare occasions when he managed to fall asleep, he'd wake up panicking in dead silence. Not hearing her soft, measured breaths felt like she was gone, like he'd lost her.

Next, she took his sanity along with his sleep. Worry about her wouldn't let him rest even during the day.

Was she safe? Had she eaten? Was she warm enough in this place with no glass on the windows to trap in the heat? Gargoyles could keep themselves warm even in the constant drafts of King Edkhar's castle. But Amber was a human. She had no fire in her veins and needed to be kept warm by external sources.

Watching her rub her hands now and blowing on them to warm up her fingers before nocking another arrow, he wished he could just grab her and bring her to his room despite her stubborn protests. He could keep her warm in his arms.

The only reason he hadn't done that yet was because he sensed she would be forever lost to him if he did. She'd built thick walls around her heart for protection, and he couldn't break through them without damaging the fragile being inside.

He wanted her to trust him, fully and completely. And for that, he had to be patient.

Trust couldn't be stolen, it had to be earned.

So there he was, hiding and watching, learning what he could about this woman, hoping to figure out how to earn her trust, her heart, and ultimately, her love. Right now, however, he would give everything just to have her look at him without a scowl.

She bit her lip, her eyes trained on her target, the string of her bow pulled back. Halting her breath, she released the arrow. It sang through the air and embedded into the wood, in the very center of the red circle.

"Yes!" she hissed triumphantly, her cheeks glowing with pleasure.

He wished he could kiss her. He wished he could do many other things to her. The memory of her slender fingers around his cock had kept him semi-hard ever since the king's celebration. It sent a rush of heat to his groin right now, making him shift his position to allow for more space in his pants.

Gods, he would do anything just for another chance to have a conversation with her.

One by one, she sent her remaining arrows into the piece of wood with the circle, each shot executed smoothly and methodically. This time, all six landed inside the painted target.

"Yes!" She pumped both fists into the air, jumping with joy. "Has anyone seen this? Anyone?" She giggled, obviously not expecting an answer to her question.

But he couldn't stay away any longer, wishing to share her joy. Snapping his wings open, he leaped off the wall and landed right in front of her.

"I did. I saw everything. Great job, Amber!"

With a strangled gasp of shock, she slammed both fists into his chest. "Dammit! You nearly gave me a heart attack."

He laughed, grabbing her by the waist and twirling her around, just once.

"Bullseye, Amber!" He set her down, then glanced at her target over his shoulder. "Or should I say *dragon's* eye?" The red circle, the single target she had painted on her board, was exactly the size of a dragon's iris. "Is that what you've been up to? Training to kill a dragon?"

She moved past him to yank the arrows from the wood and put them back into her worn leather quiver.

"That's none of your business. How did you know where I was, anyway? Aren't you supposed to be with the king?"

For the past two weeks, the king had been focused on strategizing for the final battle of the war. Every morning, Elex met with him in private. During these meetings, he recounted to King Edkhar the battle at the Bozyr Peak in every detail he could recall. The king knew he would win, but he wished to leave nothing to chance.

"I see the king in the mornings, before his meetings with the others," he said.

"Right. You're his favorite, aren't you?" The disdain in her voice made him wince.

"I have the information he finds extremely useful right now. The final battle is in less than two weeks."

She propped her hands on her hips. "But *would* it happen if you didn't tell him that?"

Amber was getting into the cause and effect of the events. There was no answer to that question as no one could live two different timelines to compare them. But he had seen the result of *this* timeline. He'd lived in the future. He knew what was the best outcome for his family and his kingdom, and he had no desire to jeopardize that.

"It has to happen, Amber. The king must win. But isn't the end of the long, bloody war a good thing?"

She shrugged. "I guess."

"You don't look convinced."

Amber had long become more than just the girl who saved him from Ghata and made his cock stand to attention by just looking his way. He'd been trying to glimpse deeper inside her soul and her heart, but she had walls built around her heart, higher than the Bozyr Peak. She wrapped her soul in so many layers of self-preservation, the more he peeled them off, the more he found behind them. And...the more he wished to know about the beautiful creature hidden inside.

What exactly made her happy? Why had he not seen her smile

for what felt like forever? Why instead of the intoxicating fragrance of arousal when she was near him before, could he only sense the darkness of despair rolling from her now?

"Doesn't the end of the war excite you?" he asked.

"It's not my war." She set the quiver down and reached for her robe.

He took the robe from her and helped her put it on. It shrouded her slender frame, turning her body into a shapeless blob, but it must at least keep her warmer.

"Doesn't the end of violence and murder need to be celebrated?" he insisted. "Even if those aren't your people who are being murdered?"

She glared at him.

"I'm not heartless, Elex. I would rejoice at the end of the bloodbath. Only I don't believe the violence and oppression would stop even after the war has ended. The people... *My* people will still cower behind the walls of the Sanctuary. They'll still be persecuted and murdered for being born the way they are. They'll be burned for the king's entertainment..." Her voice trailed off, and she glanced away, blinking a tear from her eye.

The heavy feeling he'd been carrying inside pressed on his chest even heavier. He knew which side to pick the moment he'd learned the exact year he'd returned to Nerifir. That didn't mean it didn't feel like the wrong side to be on.

"It will get better, Amber. In just over a century, King Edkhar will be dead. King Elex will take his place—"

She exhaled a humorless laugh. "A century is longer than a lifetime for someone like me. And how can you be so sure that life is just moving along this one predetermined path, like on a train track, with no turns, detours, or side quests?"

"Because I lived it—"

She jerked her head impatiently, not letting him finish. "You lived a thousand years from now. But you feel the sufferings of others are justified for the next hundred years as the sacrifice to your bright, shiny tomorrow. We all only have one life to live,

66

Elex, and the lives of everyone who is here today will be over before that shiny future of yours will arrive. So forgive me if I can't fully *rejoice* at what's about to happen."

She leaned to pick up her bow, but he stopped her by gripping her shoulder. He couldn't let her storm away again filled with anger and resentment.

"Don't go. Not yet. Not when you're mad at me."

"I'm not... I..." She blew out a breath, rubbing her forehead. "I shouldn't be blaming you for all of this. There is only so much one man could do anyway, prince or not." She looked at him with a little less fire in her gaze. "Just think about it, Elex, please. What if the history you learned was wrong? How can a son of a tyrant grow up to be the kind, just, benevolent king your namesake would grow up to be? It doesn't make sense. Apples don't fall far from the trees, as they say. It took three generations of ever-increasing depravity to result in the current state of affairs in Dakath. Why do you think it will all just fix itself with the arrival of King Elex?"

"I have trust in the future." It was the only answer he could give her.

She turned away with a sigh.

"Well, I don't. I don't trust anything or anyone. Yes, I'm training to kill a dragon, but I want no part in your war. I'll kill to defend myself, but not for anything else." She grabbed her quiver, ready to leave.

Every word of hers felt like an arrow shot straight into his heart. Her resentment burned, festering between them and keeping them apart. He couldn't stand it. He couldn't let her keep walking away from him.

He crossed his arms over his chest, leaning against the castle wall. "Then you need more than an arrow."

"What do you mean?" She paused.

He peeled his back from the wall and stepped closer. "Dragons can be more dangerous when they look like men."

She could've moved back, but she didn't, standing her ground.

He yanked the dagger out from the sheath on his hip. "What would you do if you let a dragon come way too close to use a bow and arrow?"

Her delicate throat moved with a swallow. "I won't let that happen..."

"But you already have. I'm here. Am I not?" He leaned closer. His forehead touched the edge of her hood. His chest was a breath away from hers. Yet it still didn't feel close enough for him.

The bow slipped from her hand, hitting the ground with a thud. He replaced it with the dagger, wrapping her fingers around the bejeweled handle.

"Aim it here." He lifted her hand, then pressed the blade to the side of his neck. "Where the blood pulses, carrying the fire of life through the dragon's body. Stab through the vein." He squeezed her hand tighter around the handle. "Twist the blade to let the blood out. But do not remove it after. Choose a weapon with Nerifir iron in it, the one that can kill a fae. Leave it in the wound for the iron to poison his blood and carry it through the rest of his body." He felt his pulse beating against the cold blade. "He'll be dead within seconds."

She stared at him, her summer-green eyes open wide.

"Y-you want me to kill you?" she stammered.

Confused and uncertain, she looked more vulnerable than ever. But she had killed him many times over already. Every time she glared at him with resentment, every time she stormed away and avoided him felt like a stab through his heart.

"No, my dearest." His lips twitched with a smile. "I want you to *kiss* me. In fact, I think I'd die for a kiss at this point."

She released a breath, her eyes flicking between his. When her gaze darted to his lips, his heart flipped. Was she actually going to do it?

The next moment, however, the look in her eyes hardened.

"There weren't supposed to be any more kisses, remember? The one by the creek in my world was our goodbye kiss."

She never forgave him for taking her that day. But she had touched him since. The memory of her hand wrapped around his shaft made him hard in seconds.

"If it's my only choice," he murmured. "I'd take you stroking my cock instead."

She rolled her eyes in that so-very-human expression of hers.

"Since we have no spectators and no pressure for me to do that," she snapped, "I'll pass."

She lied. No one had pressured her into touching him the way she did at the king's celebration. He had been content simply holding her in his lap and talking. She'd been the one who went for his pants, to his utter delight, of course. He just wished she'd let him do the same to her, too.

She shifted back, and he couldn't stand the distance returning between them. It felt like the closer he tried to get to her, the further she drifted away. Soon, he feared, the distance would be so great, neither of them would be able to bridge it. They'd be in the same world, but worlds apart.

"Don't leave. Please..." With her hand holding the blade at his throat, he hooked his arm around her middle, yanking her to him.

The blade slid along his skin. He felt a warm trickle of blood down his throat.

"Oh no!" She dropped the dagger with a gasp. "I'm so sorry. I didn't mean it..."

He grinned. "It's nice to know you didn't mean to hurt me, little spark." His smile disappeared, extinguished by the heavy feeling pressing on his heart. "I never meant to hurt you either. But I fear I inadvertently have." He cupped her face, directing her gaze to him. "I'm sorry, my spark, so sorry for the wrong I've done to you. I can't regret taking you with me, but I'm sorry for all the pain it has caused you. I'm sorry I ripped you out of your life, the only life you knew. I'm sorry I forced this change on you. I wish I knew how to make you happy again. Tell me what to do, and I'll do it."

He meant it with all his heart. All he'd ever wanted was to give her the life of a princess. For that, he hoped to secure his high standing at the king's court. But even that paled in comparison to what really mattered—just being with her. As long as they were together, he'd *treat* her as his princess, no matter where they were or what they did.

Something shifted in her eyes, as if a shield got lowered for just a moment.

"You still don't get it, do you?" she said softly. He had to admit, he had no clue. "I'm not angry with you for taking me to Dakath. It was sudden and painful, but I understand why you did it. And I agree, you probably did save my life that day. Things hadn't been good between Chris and me for a while. And the more I think about it, the more I believe he wouldn't have let me get away that morning."

"So you're not mad at me?" His heart lifted.

"Oh, I am, Elex. Not for taking me to Dakath, but for abandoning me right after. For leaving me alone on that riverbank. Everything you and I have gone through since would've been so much easier to bear if we stayed together, don't you think? You said you saw me. You knew where I was. Why did you leave? You didn't even let me know you were alive. That's something I can't understand or excuse. And it hurts..."

She rubbed her chest where it must have ached, and he felt her pain. His own heart squeezed so tightly, he could hardly breathe.

"Amber, I didn't abandon you. I would never..." He sucked in a desperate breath. She had to believe him. He had to make her see. "The king's men were there, looking for *salamandras*. At that moment, it felt safer to lead them away from you. I didn't know about the current state of the Sanctuary. I believed you were better off with the women. And I would've flown back to you, no matter how far, but I couldn't. Our crossing to Dakath was rough. The river rapids broke my wing—"

Her brow furrowed in a worried expression. "It was broken? How bad were you hurt?"

She didn't need to know all the gory details. He wasn't looking for her pity, just for her forgiveness.

"I couldn't fly. The royal hag had to heal me. I had to see you. But since I couldn't get to you myself, I manipulated the king into inviting the *salamandras* to the Bozyr Peak instead. "

Her eyebrows shot up almost to the edge of the cloth on her head. "It was you? How did you do it?"

"That was the easy part. The king likes to brag. He brags about everything, including his parties and celebrations. He claimed they were the best in all of Nerifir, with even the poor from the Sanctuary invited to join. I said I wished to see that. And he grabbed onto the chance to impress. Little did I know about all his cruel ways to entertain." He heaved a sigh of regret. "I'm sorry—"

"That's all you have to say." She rose to her toes and slipped her hands to the back of his neck, bringing him closer. "Now I understand. And I forgive you."

Then, she kissed him. She finally kissed him.

His heart plummeted into the hollow of his stomach, then soared to heights it'd never reached before.

Grabbing her under her arms, he lifted her up, then walked to the wall, all the while keeping his mouth on hers. Now that he got to kiss her again, he wasn't going to stop. Ever.

Her back to the wall, he wrapped her legs around his middle. She moaned, raking her fingers through his hair. Her clothes were in the way. He tore at the ties of her robe then her shirt, needing to touch her skin.

Tearing her mouth from his for a moment, she panted. "Wasn't it supposed to be just a kiss?"

He growled, re-capturing her mouth. A kiss was never going to be enough. A million kisses wouldn't, either. He needed her, all of her, now and always.

Always.

The realization struck him like lightning. There was no other future for him but with her. It didn't matter where or when, as long as she was with him. Together.

"Amber..." He searched her eyes. "If returning to the human world is what you want, then I'll take you there."

"What?" She stared at him in shock.

He was shocked, too, hardly believing the words that were coming from his mouth, but he stood by them, nevertheless. "I'll carry you back to the portal right now. I'll take you to the human world."

"Elex...What are you talking about?"

He felt drunk. His head was spinning. Maybe he wasn't well. Maybe he'd lost his mind. But he would do anything to see her happy again. Anything for just one smile of hers. Even if that meant to leave Dakath for good.

"I'll come with you. No matter what time in your world we will land. I'll take care of you. We'll be together."

"Oh, my God, Elex..." Wrapping her arms tightly around his neck, she buried her face in his shoulder, just like when they flew across the ocean back in her world. Back when she smiled and teased him, and when life felt easier somehow.

Maybe he could take her up over the ocean again. Maybe he could make her happy, after all?

"You really mean it, don't you?" She shook her head in disbelief. "You'd leave Nerifir for me? You'd spend the rest of your life in the human world?"

Determination grew in his heart. "I'll live longer than you. I'll protect you until the day you die."

"But then what? What would happen to you when I'm no longer there? You'll be alone."

"As I would be here." Sorrow tightened around his heart at the thought of her death. Even if she lived well into old age, it would still be too soon. The human lifespan was just so heartbreakingly short.

"No, Elex. Here, you're with your own kind. In your family

home. When in my world..." Her chest rose and fell with a sigh. "Humans aren't better than fae, you know? They may be fascinated by the extraordinary, but that wouldn't stop them from trying to destroy you, one way or another. There is not a point in human history when you wouldn't have to hide what you are."

She ran her hands through his hair, and he kept still, enjoying it way too much.

"I appreciate you trying to right what's wrong, Elex. But returning to my world is just not going to work at this point. Not for you, not for me."

Things couldn't remain the way they were, though.

"If we stay in Dakath," he said, "you can't continue living with the *salamandra*. I want you with me, living in my room, not working hard with them from sunrise to sunset."

"Hard work doesn't scare me. I never had it easy in life, in either world. I feel safe enough with the women. They found me, took care of me, accepted me as one of their own. They've been keeping the secret of who I am. I don't want to risk making it worse by going elsewhere."

"You don't want to live with me?"

She gave him a sad smile, stroking the side of his face tenderly.

"Maybe one day. When it's safer to do so. But not right now. The *salamandras* of the Sanctuary don't live with men. Even the king doesn't bring Zenada into his chambers for longer than it takes him to bed her. She's never spent a night away from us. If I move in with you, there will be questions, Elex. The king won't allow it."

He scoffed. "I'm not afraid of the king."

He wasn't going to let anyone stand between Amber and him, be they royalty or the gods themselves.

"But you can't fight the king on this. If he finds out I exist, it'll bring trouble to all of us." She flinched, her eyebrows moving close together. "I'm not sure what he'd do, but it wouldn't be good. They took a woman from the Sanctuary shortly after I got there. She was the one with the venom in her teeth. She fought ferociously, but they overpowered her, muzzled her, and took her away. Mother said she'd be executed. You see, Elex, King Edkhar eradicates anyone who is different and punishes those close to them. And I am more different than anyone in this world."

He pressed his forehead to hers, hugging her tightly.

"But how do I keep you safe when you're not with me?"

"For now, you'll just have to trust me with my own safety, I guess."

Eight

AMBER

I huddled under the covers. There were probably half a dozen of them on me by now, but I just couldn't get warm, shivering uncontrollably. The metal cuff on my ankle pulled at my leg. I bent my knee, dragging the cold chain under the covers with me.

When I closed my eyes, Elex's face was right there on the back of my eyelids. It was either the image of his cheeky smile with one of his dark eyebrows cocked. Or the one with that desperate plea in his eyes.

"I'll take you back to the human world."

"I'll come with you."

The skin on my arms pebbled with goosebumps at the memory of his words. These weren't just words, either. I knew he meant what he said when he offered to take me back to the human realm.

Elex had honor. He teased, joked, and flirted without shame, but when he was serious, he didn't play games. He meant what he said. If I'd told him I wished to leave, I had no doubt he would've taken me through the portal. He would've stayed with me in the human world, just like he said he would. And I knew he would've made every effort to build a life for us there.

That didn't mean that at some point in his long life, he wouldn't have grown to regret leaving Dakath. I couldn't possibly demand that from him.

But I also meant what I'd said. I didn't have much trust in humanity. I couldn't put my fate into the whims of the River of Mists, hoping it would deliver us to a better time period or that it wouldn't end up killing us outright during the next crossing.

Like I'd said to Elex, regardless of where we lived in my world, he would always have to hide what he was. And if he were discovered, he risked a whole bunch of horrible things being done to him, from tortures by the Medieval Inquisition to getting dissected and studied by scientists of the more modern times.

I didn't regret not accepting his offer. I'd come to terms that Dakath was now my home the night Ertee died. But his apology meant the world to me. It was sincere, and it was all that mattered.

Heat pulsed inside me, making my cheeks burn, but my body shivered. I rubbed my hands, trying to warm them up, and tugged the blankets tighter around me, pulling my knees to my stomach.

If Elex remembered his history lessons correctly, which seemed like he did, the war would be over within the next few days. Maybe he was right and things *would* get better in the peaceful times?

I couldn't imagine a brutal man like King Edkhar changing that drastically, but he was to marry this summer. Maybe his wife had a bigger influence on him than history gave her credit for? Maybe she would be the one who helped their son grow into the great king that Elex claimed he would become?

Hope bloomed in me. I'd had no one back in the human world, no one for me to even miss or mourn. In Dakath, I had Elex. I'd found a good friend in Zenada, too. The rest of the women treated me well, and most were friendly.

Maybe there still was a chance for a better life for all of us here?

Nine

ELEX

She didn't train the next day. He sat on the wall for two hours, waiting for her, but she didn't show up. He wasn't hiding, sitting there in plain view. Maybe that was what scared her?

Was she avoiding him again?

Maybe she needed time to realize he was not going anywhere. If so, he had to make it clearer to her, he was there to stay. He wasn't going to abandon her. He never had.

He sat in the same spot the following day again. Waiting. Her board with the painted "dragon eye" remained in its spot, hidden by the wall, but she didn't come.

Did she need all this time to think about their last conversation? He fucking hoped she didn't regret their kiss, because he fully intended for more of those to come.

When the king decided to have another "celebration" with the *salamandras*, Elex was sure he'd finally see Amber there. This time, his anticipation wasn't marred by fear. He'd claimed Amber as his at the event before. He could reasonably expect she'd be sitting on his lap today and every day. And he was looking forward to that.

Except that when the *salamandras* quietly padded into the Great Hall, their heads bowed, the golden lace lowered over their faces, Amber was not among them.

He knew it the moment he scanned the row of the women. Despite their identical clothes and poses, he would've recognized Amber even if there were a million of them.

His anticipation was immediately replaced by unease. Then, the unease grew into worry, bordering on panic. He shifted uncomfortably on his lavishly decorated perch like it was a bed of knives and arrowheads.

Amber wasn't here. And he didn't know why.

"Lord Elex," the king boomed from his throne, shoving the woman on his knee aside to see Elex better. "You'll have to choose another little lizard today. Mine says that yours is *indisposed*."

Laughter erupted from the king's mouth, along with the crumbs of the bread he was chewing. As if the concept of a woman getting sick was somehow comical to him.

Elex clenched his hands into fists, forcing himself to remain seated. Punching the royal face wouldn't help anyone right now.

"What's wrong with her?" He tried to keep his voice neutral, asking not the king but the *salamandra* in his lap.

Well trained, she just jerked her head lower and kept quiet.

The king dipped his bread into a bowl of gravy, speaking for her, "She's sick. Probably ate something she shouldn't have. Get another one. We have plenty left." He gestured with the bread at the small group of unclaimed women standing by the entrance.

"Come to think of it..." Elex stretched deliberately slow and yawned especially wide. "I believe I've overexerted myself during the weapon's training earlier today."

"Did you break or pull something?" The king took a bite of the gravy-soaked bread, the grease and crumbs dripping down his beard. "Do you need a healer, now that they're conveniently here?" He gestured at the group of the *salamandras* again.

"No. It's not that bad, just uncomfortable. But a soak in the water caves may help. If Your Majesty would excuse me, I'll head there right now." He got up from his perch and gave the king a gracious bow.

He was determined to leave, whether the king excused him or not. But he was relieved when the king waved at him with the dripping bread in his hand.

"Go. I need you well for your trip with the High General next week. A dragon isn't of much use either at a party or at war if he isn't feeling his best."

That obviously didn't apply to women as the king slapped his arm around the middle of the *salamandra* in his lap. She released a sharp breath, bending over. Her burned side couldn't have fully healed yet.

"Oh, you'll be fine." The king rubbed her back.

The woman giggled softly, clearly trying to please him.

Elex turned around and stormed out of the room, his jaw clenched so hard it hurt.

He'd never been to the *salamandras'* bedroom before, but he knew its position by the window he'd been watching from the outside. He also knew that it was on the same level as the kitchen, which he had visited to make the breakfast delivery arrangements for Amber and the *salamandras*.

He jogged down the winding staircase, past the window Amber had pushed him out of. It'd been a long and lonely night on the wall that he'd spent stewing in frustration. Now, he would've gladly let Amber push him out again, if only to make sure that she was well and alive.

Once he arrived at the floor with the kitchen, he grabbed the first servant he saw.

"Where is the room of the *salamandras* from the Sanctuary?"

"That way, off the side corridor." The servant gestured with some reluctance. "Only no one is allowed to go in there, my lord, not without the king's permission."

"I have permission," he lied.

The corridor was dark and narrow. The door was cracked and creaky. He had to duck his head when entering, to avoid bumping it into the low door frame.

"Lord Elex?" A woman rose from a perch she was sitting on. By the pendant with the Sanctuary symbol around her neck, he recognized her as the Mother of the *Salamandra* Sanctuary.

Her hood was down, exposing her face. She was old, he realized, visibly old, which meant she had less than a few decades to live in this world, maybe just a few years. A pattern of thin fissures, like cracks in the desert floor, had crinkled the skin around her eyes and already edged her face around the hairline. Sooner or later, it would take over her body completely, her own fire burning through it and breaking it apart from within.

Dropping her gaze under his scrutiny, she promptly lifted her hood over her head, then lowered the lace in front of her face.

"Are you here on the king's orders, my lord?" she inquired.

"Where is Amber?"

"She's unwell. I've let the king know. She was excused..." The woman sounded nervous, babbling away.

He moved along the narrow room, picking out the signs of a lifestyle he had never known before and never expected to see in a royal castle, the place of abundance and opulence.

Bare perches were hardly wide enough for a person to sit on. A pair of boots was tucked under each, most had holes gaping in the worn leather. Small baskets with women's belongings stood nearby. Linen shirts with faded embroidery and scratchy woolen dresses of washed-out colors were folded neatly on each perch. The fine silk and bright jacquard were obviously reserved for the king's parties only.

"My lord?" Mother followed him. "May I ask what you're looking for?"

A pile of blankets on one of the perches drew his attention. He mistook it for some spare bedding at first, but the sound of labored breathing came from under them. Looking closely, he noticed the pile move.

"Amber?" He kneeled, lifting the covers on one side.

Her eyes were closed, and she breathed heavily. The cloth on her head had shifted, leaving some of the red, wavy strands visible. Soaking wet, her hair was plastered around her face. Her head cloth was drenched, too, as was the plain linen shirt she was wearing.

"Why is she wet?" he demanded from Mother.

"It's not our doing, my lord." The woman's voice shook with fear. "She's excreting the moisture from her skin, it seems." She added hesitantly, "Amber is...um, not a gargoyle."

"I know." He leaned closer to the shivering woman under the covers. "Amber, can you hear me? Say something, my spark?" His voice cracked. His heart seemed to crack as well when she didn't answer.

She didn't move. Didn't acknowledge him in any way. But her body was rocking with violent shivers.

"She's cold, my lord." Mother took the blankets from him and tucked them all around Amber's thin frame. "She is always cold."

Kneeling by her perch, he propped his hands on its edge and dropped his head between his shoulders.

"What happened?" he asked Mother, not turning his head. "How long has she been like this?"

"About two days, my lord. We're not sure what happened. Yesterday, she could still talk. Though not everything she said made sense. But today... It seems she can hardly breathe."

"*What's* happening with her?" he gritted through his teeth. "What did she eat? Could she have been cursed?"

"She has a warded protection from curses."

Right. Amber had never taken off the ring he gave her.

Mother exhaled heavily. "We honestly don't know what this ailment is or how to help her."

Women were healers. If they didn't know what was wrong with Amber, if they couldn't help her, who could?

"Maybe if the king would be so kind as to allow the royal hag to look at her..." Mother suggested tentatively, letting the end of the sentence hang in the air for him to finish, fearful to impose her opinion on a king's man.

The hag. She should know what to do.

"Right. I'll see to that."

He had to figure out a way to make the king allow using the hag's skills on a lowly woman of the Sanctuary, whose kind the king clearly saw as disposable. But despite all his perceived strength, King Edkhar had one rather obvious weakness. His inflated ego and vanity opened a door for others to manipulate him. Elex had already used that royal weakness to bring the *salamandras* and Amber to the castle. He could do it again to get Amber well.

Something nagged at the back of his head, however, as he slid his hand under the covers and touched Amber's arm. It was hot but felt clammy with the sheen of moisture that covered her skin.

Mother's words from earlier rang in his head, *"Amber is not a gargoyle..."*

Then something that Amber told him long ago, back in her world, rose in his memory. *"If I was as hot as you, I'd probably be dangerously ill and would need to cool off by any means necessary."*

He jumped to his feet, ripping the blankets off her. "These have to go."

"Oh, gods..." Mother gasped. "With all due respect, she needs them, my lord. They keep her warm."

"She doesn't need to be warm right now."

"But she does." Behind the lace, Mother's eyes expanded in shock at her own audacity to argue with one of the king's men, but she wouldn't stop. "She can't keep warm on her own. My lord... Amber is a *human*."

The confession left Mother's lips with the finality of an executioner's axe. She knew it was a betrayal, and it pained her. He didn't envy Mother's choices: keeping Amber's secret or saving her life.

"I know who she is," he assured her. "But don't tell anyone

else. All right?" He slid the soaking wet shirt off Amber's limp body. "And don't tell anyone I took her."

He tried to lift the ill woman into his arms, but something was stopping him. He glanced down her body to find a metal cuff on her ankle. Amber was chained.

"What, by the Great Mother *Salamandra*, is this?" he roared. "Why is she chained?"

Mother's face paled behind the lace of her hood. Her hands trembled.

"It's... It had to be done, my lord... She'd be accused of spying if anyone saw her wander the castle after sunset at night."

"Get it off. Now!"

Mother fumbled through the fabric of her robe, searching through her pockets with shaking hands. He snatched the key from her the moment she produced it, unlocked the manacle around Amber's leg, then tossed it away with so much strength, it chipped the rock of the wall.

"Where are you taking her?" Mother panicked, rushing after him on his way to the shuttered window.

Anger burned through him, hotter than his fire. He didn't want to speak to this woman. But he needed her cooperation.

"I'll try to make Amber feel better, but no one can know where she is. Not even the king. Do you understand?"

"Not even the king?" Mother's hand flew to her throat, as if just the notion of disobedience to the monarch physically choked the life out of her.

"No one," he repeated firmly.

Propping his leg on the windowsill, he shifted Amber's slight weight in his arms to free a hand to open the shutters.

The fresh air rushed into the room as he unfurled his wings and leaped into the late afternoon sky. The thick clouds were already tinted with orange in the west. The day was heading to its end. He didn't have much time.

He moved his wings, rising higher, where the air was cooler. Amber's skin puckered with tiny bumps all over her arms.

How cold did she need to get to start feeling better? How cold would be too cold? What if he ended up freezing her up here in his attempts to cool her off?

"Amber, sweetheart," he tried to coax a wisp of awareness from her. "Tell me if I'm doing this right?"

But there was no reply from her. Her head lolled on his shoulder. It was only by a soft moan from her lips that he knew she was still alive at all.

He slowed down, taking them on a slow glide through the evening sky.

"This is the first time I've taken you flying in Dakath," he said to her, wishing she could hear him. "I should've done it earlier, so you could see the beauty of this world."

Sharp angles of the king's palace mirrored the spikes of the surrounding mountains. Black stone stood in a striking contrast with the bright orange sky. The clouds broke up the sunset into vivid colors of gold, burgundy, and magenta.

Far on the horizon, the brilliant green stripe of the valley came into view. Spring always came sooner there, taking its time to climb all the way up to the peaks of the mountains. The foothills were already tinted with red from the buds of the snow poppies breaking through the ground even before all the snow had melted.

"It's so beautiful, Amber," he whispered, kissing her forehead. "I wish you could see it."

Her braid had gotten loose from the knot she'd worn it in. He was surprised she'd kept her hair long. She seemed furious when he'd made it grow, and he'd half-expected her to chop it off right after.

He'd made so many mistakes. All he wished for was a chance to make it up to her, for everything.

"Please, get better, my spark. And I'll do everything to make you happy."

Regardless of who wore the king's crown, happiness was possible in this world. He and Amber would just have to find it.

A shudder ran through her body. He pressed his lips to her forehead again. It felt significantly cooler now and no longer wet.

The setting sun pierced through the clouds with sharp red needles of light, too close to the horizon. He had to go back.

Gliding through the sky in a wide turn, he laid course back to the castle. Instead of returning to the *salamandras'* bedroom, however, he aimed higher, to one of his own windows.

Salamandras were great healers. But no one knew Amber better than he did. Not even them.

He kicked the thick furs off the wide perch in his room but left the featherbed on, then carefully put Amber down on it. He didn't bring any of her clothes with them. She probably didn't have many anyway.

Instead, he took one of his long tunics made with the soft cotton from the valley and put it on her, carefully tugging the cozy fabric all the way down to her ankles. After a brief consideration, he also covered her with a silk sheet but left the window open for the fresh air to come in.

Would any of the things he had done help Amber? Did he do any of them right? Doubt bombarded him with questions. Urgency vibrated under his skin as the sun was sliding lower and lower behind the horizon.

Soon, Amber would be on her own. After the sun had set, he wouldn't be able to help her, even if she cried for help. Even if she was dying...

Ten

AMBER

Oh, it was freezing. So cold, my bones seemed to rattle, and my teeth chattered. I patted around with my hand in search of a cover. My feet were tangled in a sheet, but it was too thin to keep me warm.

I pried my eyes open. It was dark, with only the cool blue glow of the moon and the stars coming from an open window.

Where was I?

My throat felt dry, like sandpaper, making me cough. I shifted to my side, waiting for the bout of cough to subside. My nose was clogged, too, making it harder to breathe. I had a nasty flu once when I was a kid. This felt very much like that.

I finished coughing and dropped my head back into the poofy pillow. It was as soft as a cloud. This wasn't my usual hard, narrow bed. This one was at least five times as wide and covered by blankets as light and soft as a feather. A pile of them lay on the floor by the bed, along with the few soft pelts of thick, light fur. I grabbed one and dragged it over myself.

Clearly, I wasn't in the *salamandras'* room anymore. There were no other perches here other than the one I was lying on. It also had some real furniture, not just slabs of rocks. There was a recliner by the fireplace with a low table next to it. A trunk stood next to the bed. It also served as a nightstand. In the glow of the moonlight, I spotted a wide metal jug and a large bowl on top of the trunk.

My hand shook when I reached for the jug. Sitting up, I lifted it with both hands. Something sloshed inside it. Water. I brought the jug to my mouth and drank until my stomach was so full, I feared it'd burst.

Snuggling back under the furs and blankets, I turned to my other side and...came face-to-face with Elex.

He was sitting on the floor with his forearm placed on the bed. His spread wings shielded me from the breeze from the open window. His stone face frozen in a frown of concern. His eyes were open, their gaze directed at my head on the pillow. The sunset had caught him as he was staring at me.

He looked so worried, I wanted to reassure him somehow, whether he heard me or not.

"I feel like shit," I confessed with a weak smile. "But at least I feel something, right? I'm awake and alert now. I'll be fine, Elex."

The frown on his face didn't ease, of course. The deep crease between his eyebrows didn't smooth out. But if his concern was for me, I hoped he saw me awake, and I hoped it made him feel a tiny bit better.

I crawled closer to him and pressed my face to his forearm. It felt smooth and pleasantly cool against my feverish skin.

"Good night, Elex," I whispered, as a dizzy sleep started to take over. "And... Thank you. For whatever you did."

The next time I woke, it was bright. Sunlight flooded the room through the open window.

The snow had melted from most of the mountains. Only the

deep crevasses where sunlight didn't reach it still glistened with white.

"You're awake." Elex plopped onto the bed next to me while I squinted and blinked in the sunlight. "Are you cold? Hot? How are you feeling?"

He was wearing a pair of loose-fitting pants and a long burgundy tunic with gold embroidery on the sleeves and around the neckline. Without a belt or his usual dagger, his outfit looked rather casual, but his expression was far from relaxed. It was a mix of both concern and excitement.

Seeing his face was like a breath of fresh air after being cooped up in a hot oven somewhere. That was what it had felt like before. All I remembered was the scorching heat that had made me shake from head to toe.

"How are you feeling?" he asked again, brushing a sticky, sweaty strand of hair from my forehead.

"Both hot and cold." I drew the covers high to my face. My nose felt cold like an icicle.

Elex stared at me. *"Both?* How do I fix that?"

He looked so adorable with his wild tousled hair and his gorgeous dark eyes open wide in confusion, I couldn't hold back a smile, reaching for his hand.

"There isn't much anyone can do, Elex. I must've caught something."

"Caught *what?*" He laced his fingers with mine, and I promptly dragged his hand under the covers with me.

"A cold. Or a bug. A virus, I mean." I shrugged. With all the constant winds and bitter drafts in the castle, it was a miracle I didn't get sick sooner. "Did you know you had viruses in Nerifir? Or maybe I brought some with me. In which case, it's good you guys don't react to them."

It was a lot of words at once. My throat felt dry again.

"I need some water," I croaked, turning to look for the jug.

Elex beat me to it. There was a silver goblet next to the jug this time, and he filled it with water. With his arm around my shoulders, he lifted me into a sitting position, then shifted behind me, propping my body with his.

"Here." He brought the goblet to my lips. "I saw you drink last night."

I emptied the goblet quickly. He poured me another one, but I declined, thinking I should visit a bathroom first before taking in any more liquids.

"You saw me? So, you weren't sleeping when I woke up earlier? Were you worried about me?"

He set the goblet on the trunk by the bed, then hugged me with both arms from behind.

"I haven't been sleeping well since... well, ever since we got to Dakath. And yes, I was worried." He kissed my temple, drawing my back into his chest.

"Thank you for..." I looked around the room. "Where exactly are we?"

"It's my room in the Bozyr Peak castle."

"You live here?" It was the biggest bedroom I'd ever seen, hands down. It had not one, but two huge windows. One was shuttered, the other one wide open. "How am I here?"

"I brought you here last night. You weren't doing well. Mother of the Sanctuary told me you'd felt cold, but you were so hot to the touch... And you were unconscious." With his arms crossed over my chest from behind, he rubbed my upper arms with his hands. "It wasn't good, Amber. No one could tell me what was happening or what to do."

"So, what *did* you do?"

"You told me humans can't regulate their temperature very well on their own. I remembered you said if you ever felt hot, you'd need to cool off. So I took you flying."

"You did?" I turned over my shoulder to see his face. "I think I remember some of that. Or was it just a dream?"

"Depends." A corner of his mouth lifted in a teasing smile. "Did we have sex in your memories?"

"Um..."

"If we did, then it was most definitely a dream. There was no sex yesterday." His smile dimmed. "Just a lot of me begging and praying to all the gods of Nerifir. You scared me, Amber."

I stroked his hand on my shoulder. "Were you scared? For me?"

"I still am. Are you sure you're feeling better? Did I do it right last night? What can I do to stop it from happening again?"

"It's all good, Elex. You don't have to worry. I'm not a doctor, but I should be fine now. Once the fever drops and stays down, it usually takes a turn for the better. Just need to take it easy for a few days. Don't gargoyles ever get sick?"

"We do. If we get wounded or cursed. Or if we eat something we shouldn't, without wearing something with wards for protection." He tapped a ring on his left pointer finger. It was a large ruby in an elaborate dark-gold setting.

"Is that the replacement for the one you gave me?" I freed my hand with the lizard ring from under the covers.

"Yes. King Edkhar is generous to those he finds useful. I got the new ring shortly after I came to the Bozyr Peak."

"Do you want this one back, maybe? I don't have to worry about selling it now. And it was your great-grandmother's."

He touched the carved ruby on my finger. "It was. But I want you to have it. It fits you better than me, anyway."

I was ready to give the ring back if he took it. But I was glad that he didn't. I never had anything so beautiful in my life. And now that I didn't have to break it into pieces, I really enjoyed wearing it.

"You know, where I come from, a man giving a ring to a woman has a meaning." Why did I say that? There was absolutely no point in him knowing that.

"I know." He smiled.

"You do? How?"

"It happened in Ghata's menagerie quite a few times while I was there."

"Someone proposed at the menagerie?"

Talk about an unusual place for that. But then again, people liked and even actively searched for unusual places to propose.

He nodded. "I got a very good view of it a couple of times. In your world, a man gets down on one knee, opens the box with the ring, and asks the woman, 'Will you marry me?' Then she screams 'Yes!'" he squealed in a high-pitched voice, making me laugh. "Then, he puts a ring on her finger and they snap those flashing things, what do you call them? The ones that preserve images of the moment, kind of like our picture books or crystal balls?"

"Cameras? Cell phones?"

"Something like that." He nodded. "Then the woman calls someone on that *cell phone,* cries, and yells, 'Guess what? We're getting married!'"

The excited squealing in his voice made me burst with laughter all over again.

"That's very much how it happens," I said. "In my world, rings don't carry any wards or protection for the wearer. They only have the meaning people place into them. Sentimental value, nothing else. How do people propose in Dakath?"

"Wait. Just let me do this first." He piled up a bunch of pillows behind me to prop me in a sitting position, then got a silver tray with food from the low table by the unlit fireplace.

I realized he was going to feed me and stopped him by asking where the bathroom was first. He carried me to a spacious room by the entrance door to his bedroom. Once I was done, I washed my hands and walked out, holding on to the wall. My legs shook, and I was dizzy. It was a relief when Elex grabbed me into his arms again and carried me back to bed.

He placed the tray with food into my lap. "This was supposed to be breakfast, but it's more like a midday meal now."

The tray held the usual dishes that the *salamandras* got delivered each morning—a large bowl with red plums, a basket with round flaky pastries, fragrant coffee with mountain goat milk, a plate with cold cuts and cheeses, and a few small metal dishes that contained honey, cranberry jam, whipped cream, and cherry preserve. Several trays like that were delivered to the women's bedroom each morning.

The food looked and smelled amazing. Sadly, my appetite hadn't returned yet. My body felt like it had been put through a grinder, and my hand shook when I reached for a plum.

"How long did I sleep? What time is it?"

Sitting on the bed, Elex handed the plum to me. "It's almost noon already. You slept as long as you needed. I'm glad to see you're better, Amber. You have no idea how happy I am to have you awake and talking."

Shaking his head, he turned away. His chest rose and fell rapidly for a few breaths. When he finally faced me again, his eyes looked glossy.

It must've really upset him to find me passed out, hot and sticky with sweat. It felt rather scary to me, too, to know I'd lost my awareness for a while.

"I don't ever want to see you sick, Amber." He cut a pastry with a small knife from the tray, stuffed it with slices of cold cuts and cheese, then passed the sandwich to me. "Eat. Your hands are shaking. You need to regain your strength."

I took the chubby sandwich from him and bit off a little. It tasted good, but the sandwich looked so big.

"If I eat all of it, I'd probably throw up. Sorry," I said with a short laugh. "We humans are ridiculously delicate things."

"That you are," he agreed, continuing to fuss over me. "Do you want some coffee? It used to be piping hot, but it's barely lukewarm now. I'll have to take it back to the kitchen to brew a fresh pot."

"Can't you just warm this one up yourself?" Zenada routinely warmed up the rock of my perch to keep me warm through the night.

To my disappointment, he shook his head. "No. Only women gargoyles can do that."

"Then, it's fine," I said, waving my hand at the coffee pot. I really didn't want him to leave. "I don't want it hot, anyway.

Please don't go. Tell me more about the gargoyle magic. How is it different between men and women?"

"Are you sure?" He hesitated. "No one drinks cold coffee."

"Humans do," I assured him cheerfully. "We even add ice to it sometimes."

"Ice?" He made a face.

Dakath had great coffee, the kind that would be served in some fancy restaurants back in my world, in tiny cups with golden trim. Elex had every right to be a snob about it. Making an iced coffee out of this delicacy would likely be considered an insult in both worlds, his and mine. But I didn't really care about any of that. I just wanted him to stay here with me instead of leaving to go to the kitchen.

"Yes, ice." I nodded quickly. "But you don't need to get me any ice either. I'll drink it the way it is. Just keep talking to me."

"You want to talk?" He smiled, pouring some coffee from a narrow pot with a long handle on the side into a small metal cup inlaid with tiny garnets. "About gargoyle magic?"

I nodded again. It was as good a topic as any.

"Some say women's magic is weaker than men's," he said. "Because warmth is weaker than heat. But there is more than one way to look at it. A *salamandra* could easily warm up this pot of coffee, for example. The best I could do would be to set this entire tray on fire. A man would also break most of the furniture in this room by shifting into a dragon to make the fire in the first place. So you see, strength is not always the most useful thing."

He handed me the cup, then placed his hands around mine, helping me hold it. His hands looked strong and big compared to mine but were also deft and elegant at the same time. They could crush stones if needed but also use a tiny spoon to stir the milk into the coffee for me.

"You never answered my question." I remembered. "How do gargoyles propose?"

"Oh. It's nothing as specific as in your world. And if you are a Crown Prince, for example, you don't get to propose at all. By the time you meet your future bride, all is decided and asking her to marry you is useless and way too late."

The concept wasn't entirely new to me. Arranged marriages happened back in the human world too. I just never knew anyone who married that way.

"It's different."

I took a sip of my coffee. It tasted divine, either hot or cold. No wonder Elex had made a face at the train station coffee I'd given him back in Munich. It certainly paled in comparison.

I placed the cup back on the tray and asked for another glass of water.

"Does a prince have absolutely no say in who his future wife would be?"

"Not in Dakath." He helped me drink the water from the goblet again. "It's not a good idea for a prince to even meet his potential matches before the arrangement is finalized."

"Why not?"

"So as not to develop any preferences for one woman over the other before the selection is complete. A royal marriage is not a matter of the heart. It's best to avoid disappointment."

"I see." The meal, as little as I'd eaten, had exhausted me. I slumped back into the pile of pillows.

He put away the breakfast tray and adjusted the covers to make me more comfortable. I caught his hand as soon as he'd finished. Afraid he'd leave if I drifted to sleep, I kept talking.

"But what if you don't like the person chosen for you? What if she hates your guts? What if you two are extremely incompatible and drive each other crazy? Then what?"

He sat on the edge of the bed next to me.

"Then the couple just have to do their best to co-exist in the same castle."

"For centuries?"

He nodded.

That couldn't be fun.

"I read somewhere," I said, "that by marrying your spouse,

you're getting a partner to share twenty thousand meals together. That's a lot of miserable meals if you don't like the person."

He chuckled, leaning down to place a kiss on my forehead.

"Such is the life of royalty—great privileges combined with heavy obligations."

I hooked an arm around his neck.

"Don't leave. I'm so tired, I'll fall asleep again soon. But please, stay with me."

Maybe it was the sickness that made me feel so vulnerable. Or his taking care of me had disarmed me. But I needed him, even in my sleep.

"I'm not going anywhere." He kicked off his shoes and climbed on top of the covers behind me. Fitting his long body around mine, he spooned me from behind. "Sleep, Amber." He kissed my hair. "I'll be here when you wake up. I'll always be here."

I so wished for that to be true.

Eleven

⤴︎

AMBER

Spring was coming full force to the mountains. One late morning, I opened the shutters on both windows of Elex's bedroom. They were so tall, the windowsills weren't even a foot off the floor. I sat in a pile of cushions on the floor in front of a window, with a fur throw over my shoulders. The golden-yellow fur was short but warm, soft, and light like a feather. Elex had told me it was the fur of a gryphon, an animal I used to think lived only in myths.

But wasn't I living in a myth, too, now?

I'd been in Elex's room for five days now. After he had broken my fever in a rather unconventional but effective way, I'd been steadily recovering. My body had defeated the virus, or whatever it was that I had. And with Elex's care and attention, I actually enjoyed my recovery time.

The sun was high above the mountains. The sky was clear. I could see all the way to the valley from here. The snow poppies were in full bloom. The fields of them came up all the way to the black walls of the castle, making the mountains look as if splashed with red paint or...blood.

The door to the room opened, and Elex walked in. Wearing a long, ivory-colored caftan with colorful beadwork around the sleeves and neckline and soft fabric shoes instead of his boots, he looked as casual as a fae prince could in a royal castle.

He carried a tray with a steaming bowl on it.

"Mushroom soup for your midday meal." He beamed, joining me by the window.

I drew in the air flavored with the fragrant steam from the bowl. "Mmm, it smells good."

He kicked a floor cushion closer to the window, then sat next to me and placed the tray in my lap.

"It tastes amazing, too."

The pride with which he said that prompted me to clarify, "You didn't cook it yourself, did you?"

"No. But I supervised. And gave a lot of instructions."

"I'm sure the cook loved you for it," I quipped.

"As long as the result is worth it." He dipped a painted wooden spoon into the bowl, then attempted to feed me.

I laughed, taking the spoon from him. "Thank you, but I'll manage."

As my body recovered, my strength had been returning, too. I could walk without holding on to the wall now. And I certainly could hold a spoon without my hand shaking from strain.

"Aw." He made a face. "I kind of miss the times when you needed me to feed you."

I just shook my head at that, focusing on eating my soup without spilling.

It didn't escape me that Elex made sure I had soup every day. Gargoyles mostly preferred solid foods. Bread, grains, richly seasoned meats, candied fruit, and roasted vegetables were common in the castle. But since I had a hard time eating and keeping down most of those while recovering, Elex noticed I fared better with mildly flavored liquid meals. He'd been terrorizing the kitchen staff with his daily requests for soup ever since.

"Oh, Elex, you've outdone yourself with this one." I smacked my lips, savoring the hearty flavors of wild mushrooms with grains.

"Really?" He grabbed my wrist, stealing a spoonful of the soup from me. "Not bad." He nodded with approval.

The breeze from the window played in his thick, wavy hair. The ivory fabric of his caftan complemented his darker skin so well. Sunshine danced in his onyx eyes. He was so breathtakingly beautiful, it made my heart ache.

Since he was still holding my wrist, I pulled it my way, bringing him closer.

"Thank you." I kissed the tip of his nose. "Thank you for everything."

He moved my braid behind my back over my shoulder, looking a little awkward. "Just get better, Amber. And stay better. I can't stand seeing you sick."

He released my arm, letting me finish my soup. My braid fell over my shoulder again, draping over my chest. I still hadn't gotten completely used to having long hair. It was weird, but in a nice way. I loved the color, the shine, the length... Except that the shine had dulled lately. After all the sweating and thrashing during my fever, I felt like the sickness was clinging to me no matter how hard I tried to wash it off using a cloth and the water feature in the bathroom.

"I wish I could take a shower."

Elex climbed to his feet. "I'll take you to the water caves."

I shook my head. "People will see me walking through the castle."

We couldn't let anyone see me. All this time, I'd been hiding in Elex's room. He'd asked Mother not to speak of me to anyone. The women kindly kept my secret. The king hadn't asked about me yet, and I hoped he never would. For him, I was just another faceless red robe, and I wanted to keep it that way. But if people saw me strolling through the castle, accompanied by the king's favorite, there would be questions.

I sighed with regret. "I can't go."

"I'll take you that way." He gestured at the window.

"We'll fly?"

He grinned, taking his caftan off. "Of course we'll fly."

Now he was wearing only a pair of thin cotton pants that left little to the imagination. They were even more scandalous than the sweatpants I'd made him wear back in my world.

I tried to move my gaze away, but I just couldn't. Fully dressed or not, this man commanded all my attention whenever he was in the room with me.

"But inside the caves?" I asked, clearing my throat. "Aren't there always people in the pools and waterfalls?"

"I'll take you to an outdoor waterfall. It's outside the caves, higher up the mountain. People don't usually go there."

That sounded tempting.

"All right." I shrugged off my fur throw, standing up. "Let's go then."

Opening his wings, he lifted me up, one arm under my back, the other one under my knees. I gasped a little as he leaped off the windowsill and into the open sky beyond, but I no longer felt the need to cling to him with all my limbs. I trusted him not to drop me.

Wrapping one arm around his neck, I leaned against his shoulder. I was wearing nothing but a thin cotton shirt of Elex's. However, pressed to him, I felt warm as we soared through the air in a wide spiral toward a mountain peak behind the castle.

Elex flew over the crest, then descended to a small pool hidden between the rocks.

"The water here is a part of the stream system in the caves," he explained. "It's hot, too, but flows outside of the mountain."

Steam rose from the surface of the pool, shrouding the water and the surrounding rocks in a milky mist.

Elex set me gently on the ground. "No one will see us here."

He toed off his shoes, then swiftly shoved his pants down his hips. Wrapping my arms around me, I admired the picture he presented. In the wisps of the mist that curled around him, he looked every bit the mythical creature he was—a true vision.

With his head down, he peeked through the dark curls falling over his eyes and caught me staring. A corner of his mouth lifted in a cocky grin.

"I like the look in your eyes, Amber. Are you enjoying the view?"

I glanced aside quickly, but it was hard, so hard to look away. My gaze drifted back to his tall figure that looked like it was carved from the finest gemstone.

"Come here." His voice softened as he came closer. "You must be getting cold, standing there. You need to get in the water."

Lifting my shirt, he took it off me, then took me into his arms and waded into the pool with me. The warm water enveloped my naked body, ripping a shiver of pleasure from me.

"Ahhh, this is so good." I stretched my limbs, floating out of Elex's arms.

He smiled, standing next to me.

"The hot springs are definitely the best part of Dakath I've seen so far," I gushed in delight.

"There are many wonderful places in the Dakath Mountains," he argued. "Only you won't see them from the window next to the palace kitchen."

"But that's the only place I'm allowed to be."

"Not for long." He sounded resolute.

I snapped my gaze to him. "What do you mean?"

"You're not going back to the *salamandras*, Amber. I can't let you live like that—"

"Oh, but it's okay for *them* to live in total poverty?" Floating suddenly didn't feel that fun anymore. I lowered my feet to the rocky bottom and stood up, facing Elex. "Do you know that the women go hungry all the time? There is never enough food at the Sanctuary. The villagers put curses on their well. So, even getting enough drinking water often is a problem. You see them wearing fine clothes in the king's hall, but they constantly mend their everyday shirts and stockings because they have no means to get anything new."

His features shifted into a grim frown. "The Sanctuary is under the protection of the king. It's the crown's responsibility to provide for the women."

"Sure it is." I scoffed. "Only the king's 'protection' is limited to pimping the women out to his buddies. He doesn't care about them in any other way."

"It's not right," he agreed with a somber expression. "But their wellbeing is not your responsibility."

"Whose responsibility is it then? Tell me, who is going to make it right? The *salamandras* took me in. They clothed me and fed me. Many of them are my friends."

"You don't owe the *salamandras* any loyalty." He remained firm. "They didn't treat you well. You said it yourself that they removed your hair against your will. For gods' sake, Amber, Mother had you chained to the perch—"

I tried to ignore the sting in my chest at the reminder of her mistrust.

"She used the simplest of locks," I said with a laugh and pulled a hairpin from my hair. "I could've unlocked it any time I wished. I hadn't bothered because I had no need to roam free at night."

The muscles in his jaw flexed. "That doesn't change the fact that she chained you like an animal."

I held back a reply for a moment, waiting for a flare of irritation to subside. In a way, he was right. But he didn't see the whole picture.

"Mother is scared, Elex. For as long as I've known her, she's been either worried or terrified. Often both. She's been going through life, balancing on a tightrope, trying to please the king and those in power while also doing her best to keep the women in her charge alive."

She had failed at that one. I closed my eyes tightly, thinking about Ertee and Isar again. The thoughts of them never stopped hurting.

Not wishing to argue any longer, I went quiet. Stepping aside, I started unraveling my soggy braid.

"I have to wash my hair," I muttered, changing the subject. "That may take some time, since I've never had long hair before."

"Just give me a minute." Elex flapped his wings, rising out of the pool. Water sluiced down his body and rushed in a stream back into the pool.

"Where are you going?"

"I'll be right back."

Waiting for him to return, I stood in the warm pool, raking my fingers through the dark, steaming water.

Far on the horizon, the brilliant green of the valley blended into the red of the snow poppies that dripped down the mountainside. Black peaks of the mountains framed the valley like long, sharp fangs. One of them stood out by being taller and sitting aside from the rest.

With a flutter of his wings, Elex came back. He brought a few jars with soaps and oils from the caves. His gaze followed mine to the lonely mountain as he landed in the pool next to me.

"That's the Desolate Peak." He set down his loot of jars and vials along the edge of the pool at the deeper end.

"Why do they call it that?"

"Probably because it's standing all on its own." He shrugged and picked up two of the jars from the ledge. "Here. I wasn't sure if you wanted to smell like flowers or berries."

I took a sniff from both.

"Mmm. Both smell wonderful. You choose." Either flowers or berries would be much better than whatever it was I must be smelling like, after days of sweaty fever and then recovery.

I'd unbraided my hair and now it was floating behind me, the weight of the wet tresses pulling at my roots.

"How do people do it?" I tipped my head back, then sideways, trying to figure out the best way to tame all that heavy mass.

"Let me help." He stood in the water behind me, then scooped some of the shimmering paste from one of the jars. "How about this one?" He brought his hand under my nose.

The pink paste smelled like honey and cranberries, with a hint of citrus.

"It's nice." I nodded.

Gently but firmly, he started massaging it into my scalp.

"Mmm." I tipped my head back, letting him do whatever he wished with me now.

He lathered and rinsed my hair, the entire length of it.

"Now, take a breath and hold it." Cradling me with one arm, he pinched my nose with the fingers of the other hand and dipped me under to rinse my hair.

I closed my eyes, gripping his hand, but didn't panic. He brought me up again, turning me in the water to face him.

"Were you scared when I did that?" he asked.

"No." I smiled, blinking droplets of water out of my eyes. "Not at all. Why would I be?"

He stared at me with a faint smile playing on his lips. I didn't know what he was thinking, but it seemed to mean something to him.

"Should I have been scared?" I asked.

"A while back, if I did that, you would've clung to me, sputtered, and yelled like a wild cat. Damn, you would've slapped me, too," he chuckled.

"That was *a while back*." I shrugged. "Now I know you wouldn't let me drown. Just like I know you wouldn't drop me when we fly."

"You trust me." It wasn't a question, but there was a challenge in his voice, like he dared me to disagree.

I didn't argue. I just stared at him, hit by the realization of how much he was right. I literally put my life into his hands without a second thought now. There was no doubt in my mind, no inner debate of talking myself into it. The trust came naturally. And it was...weird.

"I do," I mumbled, flabbergasted.

"It took a long time to happen." He grinned.

It wasn't long at all. I'd known Elex only for several weeks. So much had happened in that time, however, that it felt like forever.

"Hmm." I poked at the fragrant suds from my hair floating on the surface of the pool. This was new, this discovery of my unconditional trust in this man. I had no idea how to feel about it. I released a sigh. "The last time I trusted a man, I almost got shot."

"Was it back at the portal in your world?"

I glanced up at him. "How did you know?"

"The man in the leather jacket shouted your name. He knew you. Which didn't stop him from sending armed people after you."

I kept chasing the soap bubbles in the water.

"I... I didn't have much experience with men when I met Chris. I was too young to have much experience in anything, really. He seemed to care about me. And maybe he did, in some way, at some point in our relationship. But it was never unconditional. I always felt I had to do what he wanted and be what he wished to earn his affection."

"Did you steal me from Ghata for him?"

I nodded, refusing to meet his eyes. "Chris was the one who got that job for me. Yes."

"I see," he said softly.

There was no judgment in his voice, yet I felt the need to clarify, "We weren't together anymore."

"But he still had some hold over you, didn't he?"

"He wanted to," I admitted. Somehow, things were easier to see more clearly from a world away. "Chris never really let me go even after I left. He just allowed me to play at independence for a little while. Kind of giving some slack to the leash while knowing he could always yank me back whenever he wished." I rubbed a hand over my face. "One thing is for sure, it feels good to know I'll never have to face that man ever again."

I had nothing in this world, not a penny to my name, but here I felt more free than ever before.

"He'll never find you here," Elex assured me. "He's as good as dead to you now."

It was so good to hear.

Elex slid his hands up my arms, and I stepped into his embrace. It felt as natural as coming home. He pressed his lips to my temple. "I'll have to leave tomorrow, my little spark."

I leaned back to see his face. "Leave? Where?"

"Just for a little while." He stroked my wet hair soothingly. "The king wants me to fly down to the foothills of the Bozyr Peak, to the place where the battle will take place in two days."

I winced at the reminder of the war. "Why do you have to go there?"

"He wants me to survey the area and to explain to the High General the entire battle, step by step."

"Because you know how it'll go?"

He heaved a heavy breath. "Not in as many details as the king demands. I learned about the war, of course, but I realize now how superficial my knowledge is."

"Well, it has to be different *reading* about something as compared to actually *living* through it."

"Exactly. So, the king wants to test my memory. The High General is going to make sure that the maneuvers I remember match with the location and the landscape. He also hopes that going to the area of the action may jolt my memories, to give him more details for his planning."

I resented the king even more now that he was taking Elex away from me.

"When are you leaving?"

"Tomorrow morning. It'll take a whole day. We most likely will have to spend the night out there, too. In which case, I won't return until after the battle, the day after."

My heart thundered with worry, and I tried to breathe through it in small, measured breaths.

He'd be fine. He had to be fine.

He glided his hand up my back.

"You'll be safe in the castle. The king and his men will leave the day of the battle, too. Just stay in my room. I'll have meals delivered for you. It'll be just for a day or two."

"I'll be fine." I nodded.

It wasn't me I was worried about.

"Promise me to stay safe," I wished to say. But that would be demanding a promise from him that wasn't in his power to keep. A war was going on in Dakath. He was putting himself in the middle of it. That carried a risk. A risk no promise would minimize.

"It's all right." I swallowed around a thick lump lodged in my throat and turned away, hiding my face. The devastation raging inside me would surely be reflected in my expression, and there was no need to upset him with how I felt.

"Hey." He cupped my cheek, turning my face back to him. "You look like you're going to miss me," he murmured, his thumb stroking my skin.

"Maybe I will." I focused on his chest, tracing the edge of his pectoral with the tip of my finger.

It was both exhilarating and terrifying to admit, but Elex didn't just gain my trust. Little by little, he'd been taking over my entire being.

I'd felt something similar before, like a part of me was dissolving into the man I was with as our lives merged. The big difference this time was that I didn't feel less because of that. Elex gave as much as he took. With him, it wasn't giving up but gifting. It made me fuller, not emptier.

I slid my arms around his neck, pressing my body to his. He kissed my temple, then my cheek, and finally my lips.

This kiss, just like the one before it, wasn't meant to happen. I wasn't supposed to come to Dakath. But here I was now, and I couldn't bring myself to regret it anymore.

"I'll miss you too, Amber," Elex whispered against my lips.

"Somehow, my happiness is now directly dependent on whether you're next to me."

He slid his hands down my back. Cupping my backside, he lifted me out of the water and placed me on the smooth rock at the water's edge.

I shivered as the cool air chilled my wet skin.

"I'll keep you warm, my spark," he vowed, spreading his wings around us. "I'll always keep you warm."

His wings curled around us. Heat rolled off his body in waves as he leaned over me. He kissed between my breasts then down my stomach.

"Elex...I..." I gripped his hair.

"Let me taste you." Hooking my legs over his shoulders, he dipped his head between my thighs.

I gasped with a moan as his mouth connected with my sensitive flesh. His tongue was hot, almost too hot to bear, making me squirm.

"Wait...just give me a minute." I yanked at his hair, not letting his head come any closer.

His body was so hot, I had to give mine some time to adjust. He stuck his tongue out, reaching to flick it over my most sensitive spot. The heated touch sent a wave of shivers through me, a wave of pure pleasure.

"So...good," I moaned, loosening my grip on his hair.

Unrestrained, Elex lapped at me in earnest. The heat of his tongue was everywhere, inside and out. His lips closed over me as he sucked, gently at first, but with ever-increasing intensity.

I let go of his hair completely, surrendering all control to him. Tossing my arms over my head, I let the pleasure take me.

Heat surged through me from the spot where his mouth was making love to me. It spread through my entire body, from the tips of my fingers clasped over my head to my toes propped on his shoulders.

He increased the pressure, moving his tongue faster. I lifted my hips, pressing into his mouth.

"More... Oh..." Orgasm tingled up my thighs. Pleasure exploded through my core. Speechless, I could only gasp for air as the most intense climax rocked my body.

Elex gently massaged my thighs. Kissing between my legs, he took me through the swells of bliss, one by one.

"Oh, wow. You..." I let my arms fall at my sides. My legs draped weakly over his shoulders like two cooked noodles, boneless.

He pulled himself up along my body. His full lips glistened, stretched into a happy grin.

"Come here." Cupping his face, I placed a kiss on his warm mouth.

I slid a hand between us and found his hard length. It was almost too hot to touch as I carefully wrapped my fingers around it. He eagerly thrust his hips into my hand.

"You feel like you're about to burst into flames, darling," I murmured.

"You have no idea," he growled with a tortured groan.

"Can you...um, cool it off a bit, please? I'm worried this thing would give me blisters...from the inside." I giggled awkwardly, but there was no other way to put it. I did worry about his fire dick burning all my delicate places.

He rose over me on his elbows. His arms shook with strain.

"I'll try," he gritted through his teeth. Leaning his forehead to my shoulder, he stilled.

Gargoyles regulated their body temperature at will. At the moment, however, Elex seemed too wound up to cool off on his own.

I thought about the ways to help him.

"Think about the snow. Cold, white snow. Ice. Ice cream. A blizzard milkshake. Do you have something like that in Dakath? Drinking it too fast can give you a brain freeze. Maybe it could give you a dick freeze, too?" I stroked his shoulders soothingly, feeling rather sorry for him. With a gargoyle woman, this wouldn't be an issue. But poor Elex had to deal with a delicate human, highly sensitive to extreme temperatures. "Do they make ice at the castle? Maybe we could make a cold pack for your crotch. Would that cool it off? Or will it just melt the ice, steaming up the place?"

"Amber!" He threw his head back with a strangled laugh. "Can you just...shut up? Please. It's not helping."

I pumped my hand along his length. It felt hot but far more manageable now.

"But I think it very much is." I wiggled my eyebrows at him.

He laughed again, shaking his head.

"Oh, I love you."

He said it so casually, as if he'd said it a million times before.

Or did it just slip off his tongue unintentionally?

I stilled, halting my breath. He kept quiet, and I ventured a glance at his face.

"I meant what I said." He held my gaze.

Instead of a reply, I guided him inside me. Heat spread through me from where our bodies connected, not painful but invigorating. Like licks of fire, my desire sprung back to life. He thrust deeper inside me, and I wrapped my legs around his hips, bringing us closer.

Once again, he was making love to me when we both knew he'd be leaving in the morning. Only this time, it wouldn't be for good. It wasn't forever. Because our forever now had a chance to be spent together.

He found my lips as he pumped harder into me. I raised my hips, meeting his thrusts. He slipped a hand between us.

"With you." He pressed a finger where I needed him most.

"Oh yes..." I rubbed hard against him.

I gripped his arms, falling over the edge. And he fell with me.

"Amber, my spark..." he panted, dropping his head to my shoulder again. His chest rose and fell rapidly. "You're burning inside."

It really felt like I was on fire. It spread through my body, making the air around me shimmer like over a hot desert floor.

But I didn't feel sick or feverish. I felt powerful. Life coursed through me, inextinguishable.

I laughed, exhilarated. "You set me on fire, my dragon."

He kissed my face. "I don't know how I'm going to survive a whole day without you tomorrow."

"Make sure you do." I looked at him sternly. "You *have to* survive to come back to me."

He smiled, kissing the finger I wagged at him. Grabbing me, he slid back into the water. As I floated on the surface, my head resting on his shoulder, he played with my hair.

"I've lived for over a hundred years," he said. "But there's only a handful of memories of me in existence right now. And you have most of them."

People who would know him in the future weren't born yet. And those who knew me in my world in the past weren't here.

Here, in the present, there were just the two of us, he and I.

Twelve

AMBER

"Amber!" Mother's voice was followed by the rapid knocking on the door to Elex's bedroom. "Open up, please."

There was urgency in her voice and worry. Always worry.

Elex left that morning. I was alone in his room. He'd brought me breakfast and said he'd arranged for my meals to be delivered for the rest of the day. I didn't think Mother was the one bringing me my midday meal. But she certainly sounded like she had something important to say.

After tying a cloth over my head to hide my hair, I padded to the door and unlocked it.

"Can I come in, please?" She snuck by me into the room, without waiting for my answer.

"What's going on?"

Once I locked the door again, her shoulders relaxed somewhat. She lifted the lace of her hood, folding it back, then walked toward the windows, taking in the lavish furnishings of the room.

"It's nice here." She stroked the carved mantelpiece over the fireplace.

Flames danced cheerfully inside it, making the room warm even with one of the windows open. I didn't want to close it. It was still rather chilly outside but sunny. The mountains dripped with flowers, making for the most wondrous view.

Elex wasn't supposed to come back until tomorrow morning, but there was a tiny hope that he might return earlier. Deep inside, I thought he'd love to see the window open when he came home.

Mother regarded my outfit that consisted only of a pearl-white caftan embroidered with multicolored beads and golden thread.

"Nice," she repeated.

"Is everything all right?" I asked, wondering what brought her here.

Elex had been able to keep me in his room for the past few days. According to him, the king never asked about me again. I doubted the king really cared about the whereabouts of any of the *salamandras* of the Sanctuary or even knew any of them by name. He certainly never asked me for mine.

Mother knew where I was. But unless Elex updated her on my wellbeing while getting my food from the kitchen, she had no other means to know I was getting better. She had never sent anyone up here to enquire about my health and never came here herself, until now.

She folded her hands in front of her and straightened her shoulders.

"King Edkhar invited you to share the midday meal in the Great Hall."

My heart dropped, a chill spreading through my chest.

"What?" I plopped down on the perch, my butt sinking into the furs and featherbed. "But why? How does he even know about me?"

Not meeting my eyes, Mother stared outside through the open window.

"You are to get dressed now and attend with the rest of us," she said in a weird mechanical voice.

"No." I shook my head. "There is no need for me to be there. The king doesn't care—"

"The king has given his order. If you don't come, you'll get all of us killed for disobedience."

"But how did he order it? He doesn't know me. To him, I'm just another faceless figure in a red robe."

Mother marched to the door and opened it.

"Clothes," she ordered, reaching out. Someone, probably another *salamandra* in the hooded robe, handed her the see-through shirt and the pink dress I'd worn to the king's midday celebration before, along with my dress slippers and the well-worn red robe.

"Get dressed, now." Mother threw the clothes on the bed for me. "Unless you want to go just the way you are?" She tilted her head with the question.

Showing up in public wearing Elex's clothes would mean nothing but trouble. Mother knew it, of course. Folding her arms across her chest, she waited patiently.

"Why does the king want me?" I asked.

"He doesn't necessarily want *you*," Mother explained slowly. "He requested all *salamandras* to be there today. A big battle is coming. The king and his men wish to have one last celebration before that."

"All *salamandras* will be there?" I clarified.

"Yes."

That made sense. The king wished to unwind before the big fight. And in his true fashion, he chose to do so with an orgy.

I made a quick calculation in my mind. There were more women than king's men the last time. A few *salamandras* went unclaimed. With Elex, the High General, and a few others gone, even more women would be left without a partner. If I stayed at the back of the crowd, kept quiet, and attracted no attention, no one would choose me. The men had picked their favorites already. Without Elex there today, I'd just show up and leave quickly.

"Fine," I conceded as if I had any choice on the matter. "I'll go. But I won't sit in anyone's lap."

"That is neither up to you nor me, child."

"No," I protested. "Lord Elex has claimed me. No one would dare take me while he's gone. He's the king's favorite."

She inclined her head again, and I took it as a confirmation of my words. Slipping out of Elex's caftan, I promptly changed into the clothes Mother had brought me.

The sooner it started, the sooner it ended.

With any luck, I'd be back here in a few minutes.

As the women filed in into the Great Hall, I kept to the back of the line. The mood was a little different among the *salamandras* this time as they knew what to expect. Some of them peeked through the lace at the men reclining on the perches. One or two even gave them a small wave and a few giggles.

There clearly had been some couples formed, which was great for me. There was less need to create new ones.

As the row of women formed along the wall, I took half a step back, which hopefully took me out of sight for most of the men present. Before any man summoned his chosen to his perch, however, Mother marched in front of our line. She stopped right next to me.

"Here she is, Your Majesty." She placed a hand on my shoulder.

I froze. My head rang as if I'd been punched. My stomach hollowed.

Did she just expose me? But why?

I tried to shuffle further back, but Mother gripped my shoulder, not letting me move.

The king perked up in his throne.

"Is she really human?" He flicked his wrist, urging me closer.

I didn't move. I couldn't even if I tried. My feet seemed to grow into the rocks of the floor and my legs went so weak, I feared they wouldn't hold me.

Mother shoved me forward.

"Go," she hissed under her breath. "Or you'll get us all killed."

I stumbled forward, tripping over my feet. But I wouldn't take a step on my own toward the man in the crown.

"You told me she's been with you for a few weeks now," the king enquired.

Mother bowed so deeply, any lower and she'd be kneeling. "For well over a month, Your Majesty."

"And despite all that time, you failed to teach her obedience." He snapped his fingers impatiently.

One of his men jumped from his perch, grabbed my arm, then dragged me to the king.

"Sit." The king yanked on my hand, and I plopped down on his knee.

"A human." The king ripped the hood off my head.

I glared into his eyes, without the golden mesh of the lace between us.

"Hmm." He didn't seem to be bothered by the resentment that surely was conveyed in my expression. Instead, he examined my face closely, as if I were a doll. "There is absolutely no glow in her skin." He pressed a finger to my cheek that burned with indignity as fear shook my body. "Even her blush has no shimmer. And her eyes..." He pinched my chin between his thumb and his finger. "They're rather dull, too. How boring."

Mother cleared her throat.

"My king, she is the only human in all of Dakath. And possibly, in all of Nerifir."

"Yes, yes, that is exciting. Why is she wearing this?" He tore the cloth off my head, and his eyes widened. "Would you just look at *this*..."

The king unraveled my braid from the back of my head.

"Take it apart." He shoved the end of the braid into my hands. I gripped it in my fingers, unsure of what to do.

"You'll get all of us killed," the words Mother had said more than once echoed in my brain.

What was happening? What was at risk here? And how could I protect anyone?

"Can you do at least *one* thing you're told," the king complained impatiently. "Let loose your hair. I wish to see it."

With stiff fingers, I tugged at the tie at the end of my braid, then undid it completely.

The king raked his fingers through the wavy strands, spreading them over my chest.

"Bright like fire." He clicked his tongue approvingly. "A day before my final victory, the gods sent me a human with the hair of royal color." He looked around with a self-assured smirk. "The gods want me to win."

His men cheered, raising their wine goblets. With the king's permission, they started choosing their women. Once every one of them had a *salamandra* perched on his knee, the king dismissed the rest of the women.

Even without looking at the exiting *salamandras*, I felt Zenada's stare at me as she left the room with the unclaimed.

Thirteen

AMBER

The king kept inspecting his "gift from the gods." Holding my chin, he turned my head this way and that. His fingers then trailed down my throat.

"Not a speck of fae shimmer anywhere," he muttered under his breath. "Yet, technically, she looks so much like us."

Technically.

I rolled my eyes—the gesture that probably would earn me a few stern words of worse from him, except that the king was no longer looking at my face.

He tugged at the laces of my robe, opening it. Sliding the robe off my shoulders and down to my elbows, he effectively trapped my arms at my waist. Next, he dipped his hand into the neckline of my shirt.

I jerked my arms back, shaking off my robe completely to free myself, then slapped my hand over his, stopping him from progressing any further.

He shot me a surprised look.

Arching a reddish eyebrow, he snarled into his beard. "You want to play, little human? That may be fun, some day. But I'm not in the mood right now." He swatted my hand away, as if it were a pesky bug. He then undid the clasps of my dress and shoved it down my arms in a similar fashion as he'd done with the robe, trapping my arms. "Now, stay put and let me look."

I bit my lip so hard it bled as he ripped my shirt open. Then, his rough hands were on my chest.

"These are nice," he murmured, kneading my breasts and rubbing my nipples. "Though I prefer them bigger. Maybe the hag can do something about that."

Repulsion surged through me in a foul swell, making my stomach roil. Speechless from shock and burning with shame, I twisted my torso away from him, evading his hands.

"Sit still I said." He turned me back to face him, but I couldn't look at him, keeping my head turned away.

Olanna, another woman from the Sanctuary, was straddling the thighs of the man on the perch next to the king's throne. Her dress was also undone. The ties of her shirt were open. Leaving her breasts exposed. The man played with her pink nipples as she ate cherries from a small metal dish. Olanna looked completely unfazed by his attention. Absorbed by her meal, she allowed the man to use her body however he pleased.

Clearly, I was expected to act the same.

"How much are you like us?" the king mused. "Would you feel wet and hot inside like *salamandras* if I fucked you?"

He pinched my nipples, then rubbed them with the pads of his thumbs. The caress was firm but gentle enough to cause an echo of an unwelcome physical reaction in my body. I winced and squirmed in his lap, trying to shift away.

The king took it as a sign of excitement.

"You liked that?" He smirked.

"No," I bit out.

His eyes flashed with cold anger. He grabbed my chin again, forcing me to look at him.

"Don't you *ever* say 'no' to me, woman," he snarled in my face. "If I hear it again, I'll personally cut your tongue out."

118

The force with which he said it left no doubt he'd do it. I drew in a shaky breath, fighting the fear that gripped my throat.

"That's better." The king's voice was thick with satisfaction.

I closed my eyes, wishing for it to be over. It had to be over sooner or later. Everything had its end.

He hiked up my shirt and shoved his hand between my thighs. His touch was rough. It hurt. The pain spurred my anger, making me forget about caution. Choking with disgust, I grabbed his wrist and twisted his arm as far as the dress around my elbows allowed it.

I already balanced precariously on the very end of his knee. Yanking on his arm threw me off balance. I tipped sideways and fell off his leg, crashing to the ground.

Baring his teeth in a snarl, the king launched after me.

But then, someone laughed. One of the king's men was laughing so hard, he grabbed his sides. The others joined him. They pointed their fingers at me, slapped their thighs, and laughed so loud, the crystals suspended under the dome-ceiling danced and clinked.

The king glanced around. As he realized the merriment was at my expense, not his, a smirk parted his beard. Leaning back in his throne, he snorted a laugh, too.

"Get up, you clumsy human." He poked at me with his foot. "Go tell Mother I want you cleaned up and brought to my room after this meal."

I didn't mind the humiliation. I couldn't care less if the entire world was laughing at me as long as I could leave here. I scrambled to my feet, grabbed my robe from the floor, and fled.

Instead of searching for Mother as the king ordered, I ran straight to Elex's room. Once inside, I locked the door, then pulled out a satchel from one of the trunks.

My midday meal had been delivered while I'd been in the Great Hall. The tray sat on the small table by the window where I usually ate. I grabbed from the tray everything I could safely pack into the satchel—flat bread, plums, cheese, and cherries. Then I forced myself to eat some of the stew in a bowl. Once I left the castle, who knew when my next meal would come?

The dish was tasty, but I could barely swallow a few spoonfuls. Everything inside me vibrated with urgency. And fear. I was shaking with fear at how easily everything could be taken away from me—my dignity, my body, and any sense of security.

I couldn't let it happen. I had to get out of this castle as soon as possible.

My plan was simple. Once past the castle walls, I'd head down to the valley. Making it on my own would be hard, but not impossible. I was not the same woman whom the *salamandras* had found by the river weeks ago. I might not know all about this world, but I'd learned the most important thing—I knew the dangers to avoid.

I also had a very important advantage over everyone in this kingdom—I could move at night unimpeded.

Since I had no spare clothes of my own, I packed some of Elex's in my bag. I didn't dare wear my red robe, but I took it with me. It was still chilly outside, especially at night. I could use it for sleeping if not for anything else.

In one of the trunks, I also found Elex's cloak. Warm and soft, it enveloped me like a cloud. I closed my eyes, inhaling his familiar scent. I'd find Elex somehow. Once I was far away from here, once the war was over, I would find a way to send him a message. And this time, I had no doubts that he would come for me.

Throwing my bag over my shoulder, I padded to the door and pressed my ear to it. All seemed quiet out there, so I cracked the door open just a little. The corridor behind it was deserted. The king's men would still be in the Great Hall with him and the *salamandras*. The servants and the guards would be having their own midday meal, taking a break from running around all day on royal orders. That didn't mean someone couldn't be around to see me. I had to be careful and fast.

Slipping out through the door, I hurried to the tower and the winding stairs inside it. Then I went down to the floor with the kitchen. Taking the side corridor, I tiptoed by the bedroom of the *salamandras*. Most of them were with the king in the Great Hall. But the few that went unclaimed might be inside, along with Mother.

Thankfully, I made it past their bedroom undetected. Then I turned left, toward the small door down the corridor that led outside.

Before I got sick, I'd used this route daily for sneaking out of the palace to practice shooting my bow and arrows. Past that door and to the right, a section of the inner castle wall had crumbled, neglected like so many other things in this place. I would climb over it, then make my way to the main gate in the outer wall that would be open at this time of the day.

All I had to do was to get out of the castle.

"Amber."

Mother's voice wasn't loud—it never was—but the sound of it had the effect of a whip cracked in the silence. Startled, I froze in my tracks.

She stood in the corridor behind me, her hands clasped in front of her, not a single fold of her robe out of place.

"You have nowhere to go," she stated the simple truth.

Only at this point, it wasn't about me going *somewhere* as much as it was about me escaping this place.

I shook my head. "I can't stay here. Please don't try to stop me."

Even one on one, I couldn't fight her if she chose to stand in my way. As a gargoyle, she had far superior strength. But I might be faster. I took a tentative step toward the door.

Mother didn't move.

If I ran, would she chase me?

"Please don't do anything you may regret," Mother implored. "King Edkhar is a very powerful man. It's unwise to anger him."

I gritted my teeth at the mention of the king.

"Well, now that he knows I exist, he sure wouldn't like to lose his *present*, would he?" Sarcasm saturated my every word. Bitterness at her betrayal burned through me like acid.

She went quiet for a moment.

"I had to tell him," she said. "I've kept your secret for far too long."

"Was it such a burden to keep it?" I clenched my fists, willing my voice not to shake.

She blew out a breath, taking a step in my direction.

"You don't understand..."

I promptly moved back, keeping my distance.

"No, I don't. Why would you tell him who I was? Why *gift* me to him? Why hurt Zenada's feelings? Why?"

Her shoulders rose defensively, her face pinched into a frown.

"The Sanctuary is accused of harboring a venomous one, which is a great offense to the crown. The king has every right to burn our Sanctuary to the ground, along with all its inhabitants..." Her breath hitched. She shut her eyes briefly, swallowing hard before looking at me again. "But he chose to be merciful."

"Merciful? That's him being *merciful?*" I gestured in the general direction of the Great Hall.

She planned it all along, I realized. She'd always kept me as a bargaining chip in her back pocket, "a gift" to please the king when all else failed. That was the reason she had told me not to use the cream that stopped the hair growth before we had left the Sanctuary. She knew that the king's fascination with redheads would make her "present" to him more appealing if he could see my hair color.

"The only reason we live, Amber, is because I keep persuading the king that we're worth more to the crown alive than dead. That is the *only* reason, my dear," she said softly.

The sadness in her blue eyes made her look more vulnerable than I'd ever seen her before. She'd just shoved me into the lap of a man I loathed, and I couldn't even be angry at her right now. All I felt was pity.

"Single and widowed *salamandras* without a family to take

care of them have no place in the kingdom," Mother continued. "We are a burden. We own nothing. We have no means to support ourselves. We rely solely on the mercy of our monarch for our existence. And that's what I have been doing most of my life— keeping the women of the *Salamandra* Sanctuary alive."

"By whoring them out to the king and his men." I glared at her from under my brow.

"By any means necessary. We entertain the king. That's our purpose. Zenada knew her time was limited—the king gets bored easily. She knew it when she won his attention from the *salamandra* before her. Now, it's your turn."

"Oh, no." I shook my head, backing away from her. "I'd rather die."

"Then you will kill all of us with you. The king is ruthless in his retaliation. Is that what you want?"

I stumbled with the answer. Of course I didn't want the women dead. But neither was I ready for the sacrifice demanded from me.

Either way, I got no chance to reply.

The sound of rapid footsteps rushed down the hall behind Mother. Then Iolena, one of the *salamandras* of the Sanctuary, turned around the corner and into the corridor where we stood. She was out of breath, her eyes flickering anxiously from me to Mother.

"They're here, Mother..." she panted. "As you requested."

The king's guards stomped into the corridor after Iolena. Mother stepped out of their way as they rushed to me.

"Shit..." I spun on my heel and ran.

I didn't make it far.

A guard grabbed my braid and yanked me backwards. I fell on the hard stone floor. Pain shot up my back from the impact, but I ignored it, trying to scramble to my feet. The guard lifted me under his arm, as if I were a misbehaving toddler.

"Take her to the water caves. On the king's orders." Mother went ahead of the guards, leading the way.

"Let me go!" I kicked at the guard's shins.

Another guard calmly collected my legs and held my ankles as the two carried me down the corridor, up the tower stairs, and to the water caves.

Tears sprang to my eyes from my utter helplessness. But Mother's double-betrayal hurt the most.

"Will you let Iolena wash you?" Mother inquired inside the caves. "Or should I ask the guards to help her with that?"

It was bad enough that the guards were staying to watch me bathe. The last thing I wanted was for them to touch me, too.

"I'll do it." I bit my lip, taking off Elex's cloak, then my dress and shirt.

I kept my head down but could feel the guards' stares burning holes through whatever was left of my dignity as I walked into the water.

Keeping her shirt on, Iolena walked in after me and unbraided my hair.

"It didn't take much time to grow. Just about three weeks." Mother didn't sound surprised at seeing my hair. I wondered if she'd learned about it during my sickness. I'd been too out of it back then to ensure it was covered at all times. "Does human hair always grow so fast?"

I didn't reply to her. As Iolena washed my hair, I closed my eyes, trying not to think about Elex doing it for me just yesterday. But the memories rushed in anyway.

Where was he now? Making sure the king won his useless war?

As much as I wished to have Elex with me, however, I knew it was a blessing that he wasn't here. He couldn't fight the king. And at this point, I believed he *would* fight for me, even if it cost him his life. It was best for him not to know what was about to happen.

Tears trickled from under my closed eyelids and ran down my cheeks.

"I'm sorry, Amber," Iolena whispered into my ear softly.

I bit my lip, shutting my eyes so tight my vision turned white. It wasn't Iolena's fault. She just did what she had to do to survive. And if I wished to live, I'd have to do that too.

By running her heated hands through my hair, Iolena managed to get it almost completely dry in a few minutes. After that, Mother had another *salamandra* bring new clothes for me.

These were even worse than what we all had to wear to the king's parties before. I got underwear this time, but it was just a tiny pair of shorts made from material so thin, it concealed nothing. Next was an equally translucent, long shirt. Open in the front, it was only held together by one tiny bead-button below my breasts. The dress that went over the shirt was slightly more opaque, made from thin pale-yellow silk. Its neckline, however, was cut so low, it completely exposed both my breasts.

"What's the point of wearing any of these?" I asked flatly.

"The king likes some teasing," Mother replied in an even voice.

Iolena helped me put my robe on, then lifted my hood over my hair and lowered the lace primly over my face.

With all the revealing clothes underneath, the robe felt like a travesty. But that probably was what turned King Edkhar on. He seemed to have a thing for the stupid robes.

With Mother walking in the front, the guards on each side of me, and Iolena behind me, there was no way to run as I was escorted to one of the castle's top floors I'd never been to before. At least a dozen guards in the king's red-and-gold uniforms stood on each side of the double doors of what must be the entrance to the king's rooms.

I stopped, refusing to move a muscle. I didn't want to go through these doors. But what else could I do? Run? It wouldn't make any difference. I knew it wouldn't, but I still wished to try.

"May we have a moment, please?" Mother dragged me aside, out of the earshot of everyone present. "Amber, I know you hate me right now."

I winced. Did I hate her?

I certainly severely disliked her right now. I despised her meekness, her subservience to power, and her compliance with injustice.

But I *understood* her. I understood her reasons for doing what she'd done. Most of her life, she'd been balancing on a thin blade, making sure her *salamandras* were fed and alive. She wasn't entirely heartless, but she was often helpless.

That didn't make her betrayal any easier to bear. I didn't think I could ever forgive her.

"Sooner or later," she continued, "you may learn to see things the way I do."

"I hope not," I bit out.

"A king is a much better patron to have than any lord, trust me. Something great may come out of it for you." Mother's voice lifted. "Children are rare among fae. Many of us go through life without ever giving birth. But I've heard humans are far more fertile."

"No, Mother." I cringed openly, guessing where she was going with that.

She grabbed my hand, speaking in a fervent whisper, "Just think about it. Bastard children are often accepted by their parents and included in the line of succession. If you bear King Edkhar a child, you'll be the mother to the Heir to the Crown."

Just the idea of that possibility made my heart sink into such a dark pit of despair, I didn't think I could ever climb out of it.

I pinned her with a glare and squeezed through my teeth, "I pray to your gods and mine that it will never happen."

Fourteen

AMBER

The guards shoved me through the doors into the room that was shaped like the Great Hall and almost as big as it, too. The opulence of the furnishings rendered me speechless. I took it all in, almost forgetting for a moment about the reason I was here.

The room was at the top of one of the main towers of the castle. It was round with a high domed ceiling. Just like in the Great Hall, colorful crystals dangled from the thin golden chains suspended under the dome.

The walls consisted of tall windows between the thick support columns. Every one of the windows was closed with solid wooden shutters.

The light came from a giant fireplace located across a wide perch the size of a theater stage. There was enough space on the bed for an entire army of gargoyles to have an orgy or for the king to have sex in his dragon form if he so wished. The perch was piled so high with furs and cushions, one would probably need a ladder to climb up on it.

The monarch of Dakath stood by the fireplace. He wore a

long, fire-red caftan and a pair of embroidered fabric shoes—a casual look for a king. Though it didn't make him appear any more approachable and didn't help me relax in any way.

With my spine straight and stiff like an iron rod, I pressed my back to the closed doors, wishing I could just seep through them like a ghost and get out of here.

The king glanced at me over his shoulder. "Well, come here, human."

I remained where I was, not moving an inch.

He blew out a breath. "Should I get the guards in here? To move your limbs for you?"

I knew he would do it too. He would get his men in here to maneuver my body like a marionette on a string, to force me into any position of his liking.

Not wishing to have anyone's hands on me, I peeled my back from the doors. Drawing in a deep breath, I willed my feet to move in his direction. I stopped a fair distance away from him, but he made the last few steps for me, coming closer.

Lifting the lace of my hood, he studied my face. I stared back at him.

The king was a good-looking man. If I didn't know how ugly his soul was, I'd call him beautiful. His red hair shimmered with gold, spreading in waves over his wide shoulders. A gold crown with sparkling rubies sat atop his head. His beard reached down to his chest, with two thin braids made on each side of his mouth. A dozen or so golden clips decorated each braid, glistening in the light from the fireplace. The vivid green of his eyes reminded me of precious stones—emeralds.

If it was just about the looks and under different circumstances, having sex with King Edkhar wouldn't be a chore. What repulsed me was his heart, or the lack of it. In addition to his cruelty, he also lacked character. King Edkhar was vain, insecure, and a coward who partied in his castle with a few chosen men as the rest of his army fought his battles for him. Not the qualities I could admire in a person.

There was no warmth in his eyes as he stared at me, just cold curiosity, as if he was examining an object in a museum.

He stroked the side of my face with the back of his fingers, tilting his head. "So incredibly plain."

I glanced aside, resisting an eyeroll. Calling a woman plain wasn't going to win her heart. But then again, it wasn't my *heart* the king was after.

He took my hood off slowly, clearly enjoying the process of "unwrapping his present."

I peered at the slivers of light filtering between the shutters on the windows, desperately hoping the sunset would stop him. The sky behind the shutters was turning a warmer sepia color with the sun dipping toward the horizon, but there was still plenty of time for the king to do whatever he wished with me.

He knew that, too, and didn't hurry. Slowly, he untied the strings of my robe, then slid it off my shoulders.

His expression heated at the sight of my nipples barely covered by the see-through material of my shirt in the low neckline of the dress. I swallowed hard, feeling nothing but dread pressing heavily on my chest.

But feelings weren't necessary to go through with this. In fact, the less I felt, the better.

Could I force myself to think about it as some sort of business transaction? After all, wasn't that the only interaction I vowed to have with men after Chris? A straightforward business transaction that didn't involve my heart. Except that was before I met Elex.

My heart was no longer mine. No matter how hard I'd tried to hold on to it, Elex had taken it. What we had between us now was so beautiful and new, I hated to damage it in any way.

I couldn't let the king have me, but maybe I could keep him busy with something else for a while? Just until sunset.

I swallowed the bile rising in my throat and managed a smile, frantically searching for a topic of conversation to strike with him.

Only what could one talk to King Edkhar about?

"How is the war going?"

"What do you do for fun, other than stuffing your face with food and burning women?"

"So," I tossed a look around the room. "This is where the mighty King of Dakath spends his nights?"

"Mm," the king hummed, caressing my left breast through my shirt. "If you manage to please me, I may let you enjoy yourself, too."

"Tempting," I said tersely, unable to keep the sarcasm out of my voice.

His eyes flashed with warning, and I bit my tongue, stopping the words "but I'll pass" from leaving my mouth. That would be too close to a "no"—the word he'd threatened to cut my tongue out for.

He clicked the closure of my dress open. "Do you know what they say about your kind, human?"

I said nothing, trying not to cringe as he let his hands roam all over my body.

He didn't need an answer, anyway, as he kept talking. "They say humans can bond with fae, any kind of fae. Do you know what a fae bond is?"

I knew of it. Elex had mentioned a bond before. But the king clearly didn't need an answer to that question either, not giving me a chance to reply.

"It gives men power," he said with a greedy glint in his eyes. "It makes them stronger. But the bond is rare, and it doesn't happen between the different kinds of fae. A siren can't bond with a gargoyle. A gorgonian can never form a bond with a werewolf. But humans... Humans are a blank slate, ready to bond with any of us."

He dragged his hand up my front, getting a feel of my breast on the way.

"Do you realize what you can give me, little human?" he murmured. "None of the current monarchs in Nerifir are bonded. Not a single one of them. I could be the only one. All I have to do is make you fall in love with me."

"What?" I nearly choked on the word. Everything I'd tried to suppress inside me came out with it—sarcasm, resentment, the shock at his audacity to believe that I could ever, ever love him.

He gripped my throat, not too hard as to hurt but firm enough to make it clear who was in charge here.

"Apparently, human love transcends magic. That's the one worthy quality you have. So, make yourself useful. Love me. Make me strong, and I'll make sure you'll never go hungry again."

He offered to trade food for love. Did he realize how ridiculous he sounded? I'd laugh in his face if I wasn't so terrified of this man and what he was capable of.

Incredibly, he seemed absolutely serious about what he'd said.

"No one can love on command," I croaked against his hand on my throat.

"I know that *feelings* take time." He grimaced at the word "feelings" like it was a bad joke. "But I'll give you all the time you need. From now on, you're staying in my room, day and night."

The king let go of me and walked to one of the wall pillars with a massive metal ring mounted on it. With his hands off my body, I could finally draw in a full breath, crossing my arms over my chest.

He lifted a thick chain attached to the ring.

"Do you see this, my pet? This is for you." His voice filled with pride, as if he presented me with a precious gift. "Isn't it pretty? Look." He worked his hands to the end of the chain where a golden, bejeweled collar dangled. "It's the exact copy of my crown. See?"

He lifted the collar higher for me to see the rubies and the sharp peaks that were just like those on the upper edge of his crown. On the collar, the peaks would cut under the chin of the person wearing it.

According to the king, that person would be me.

I moved my throat in an attempt to swallow, but the inside of my mouth was so dry, it didn't work. I stiffened like a wild animal about to be chained.

"You're not putting me on a leash."

"But of course I am. You don't think I'll let you roam here freely while I'm in my stone form at night, do you?" The king glanced over his shoulder at the shuttered window. "The sunset is close enough. We may as well put this on you now."

He strolled toward me with the collar in his hand.

I stepped away from him as he approached. If he put the collar on me, the sunset no longer mattered. He would finish in the morning anything I might manage to prevent him from doing tonight.

"N-n..." The word "no" stuck in my throat.

"Come here, my pet," the king cooed. "And I'll make you the queen."

"The queen of what?"

He laughed so loud and so suddenly, I jumped, startled.

"Not the real queen, of course," he mused. "Lady Amree will have that title soon enough." He rubbed his chin in thought. "I'll have to make sure to put you elsewhere once she arrives. You can't stay in my rooms with my wife present. The lady has a temper. She's maimed quite a few of her maids in anger."

He laughed again as if there was anything funny about his bride hurting her servants. So much for my hopes that his future wife would be able to inspire him to change for the better. These two seemed to be very much alike.

I kept walking away from him, backwards, and he stalked toward me, holding the collar, like a hunter with a snare in his hands.

"She'll bear me a son," he boasted. "So I'll have to put up with her, at least for the time being. But until Lady Amree arrives, you'll be the queen of my bedroom, my rare find. You'll be the only one allowed to bestow pleasure on me. Come now, be a good little pet, and I won't punish you."

I leaped to the doors. He moved after me. The chain snapped, stretched to the limit. It yanked the collar out of his hands. One of the sharp peaks nicked his finger. The king growled in pain, shaking his hand.

"Get over here. Now!" he roared, launching after me.

I slammed my back against the locked doors. There was nowhere to run. Twisting to avoid his hands grabbing for me, I sprinted across the room.

My toe hit the platform with the perch, making me stumble. The king caught me by my shirt. The flimsy material tore in his fingers like paper, leaving me only in my transparent, lace-trimmed underwear.

With a shove on my back, the king tossed me onto the perch. I sank into the mountain of furs and silk bedding. Frantic to get free of them, I flailed my arms and kicked my legs.

The heavy weight of the king's body crashed on top of me, shoving me back into the suffocating pile of bedding.

"You want to fight me? You human brat!" the king growled, pawing at me through the silk of the sheets. "You dare defy me? You know what happens to those who do? Fight me, and you'll end up dead. Unlike the venomous ones, you're not even worth keeping in the dungeon."

He grabbed my hair, pressing my face into a pillow. I managed to turn my head just enough to gasp in a breath of air.

He hiked up his long caftan, rummaging through its folds for the closure of his pants.

"I'll fuck you until the sun goes down." Words left his mouth with rugged breaths, strangled by anger. "And when it does, I'll leave my cock in. You'll spend the night pinned with my stone-hard cock to this perch. So that I can fuck you again first thing in the morning."

I fought against his hands that pried my legs open. But he was so much stronger than me. He swatted my hands away like annoying flies.

"Fight me, wretched human," he gritted through his teeth. "See how long I'll let you live if you land but a single blow."

Hopelessness suffocated me more effectively than the silk cushions. Tears streamed down my face, soaking the bedding under me.

I closed my eyes, sending my thoughts to my one and only happy place—Elex. I tried to imagine being with him, hidden from the cruelties of the world in the safety of his arms and wings.

If I shut my mind from what my body was about to go through, maybe I could survive it?

A loud crash thundered through the room. Pieces of wood, large and small, flew everywhere. Some shot up to the ceiling and sent a rain of crystals down.

The king leaped off me.

The crystals kept raining from the ceiling as I rolled off the bed, on the opposite side from where the king was.

He grew in size. His clothes ripped to pieces, replaced by golden-red scales. His crown turned into horns. The rings on his fingers merged with his claws as the king transformed into a dragon.

Another dragon had burst through the window. He gripped the windowsill with his black, curved claws. The crimson glow of the sunset glistened off his black shiny scales. Scarlet-hot rage burned in his eyes like flames of fire.

"Elex!"

I'd only seen him once in this form before. Back then, it terrified me. Now, a wave of tenderness rushed over me.

A burst of fire came from behind me. The king-dragon stretched his neck, sending a fiery blast at Elex. At once, the air in the room heated. The stone floor scorched. I cowered behind the king's perch.

The black dragon lowered his head and opened his mouth. Flames churned in his throat, ready to blast.

"Elex, no!" I yelled, shaking in terror.

He couldn't harm the king. If he killed him, he'd end his own bloodline and cease to exist. But the obsidian dragon looked furious enough to risk it all—his kingdom, his family, and his own life—to annihilate the man who wronged me.

The king jumped behind me. The movement of his massive body made the stone room shake. He glanced at me with a smirk. The great mighty dragon-king was hiding behind me. He used me as a shield against Elex's fire.

The black dragon paused. I was in the way. If he aimed at the king, he'd burn me.

"Guards!" the dragon-king roared.

"Coward," I scoffed under my breath.

The doors burst open, and the guards barged in. Every single one of them was armed. Some carried swords, others had bows and arrows. All weapons glistened with the red of Nerifir iron, aimed to kill.

At the sight of them, my heart plummeted with despair. We didn't stand a chance against so many gargoyles.

Elex lowered his head to the floor again, aiming at the guards this time. I drew my head into my shoulders, bracing myself for another blast of unbearable heat.

But nothing came.

The shouting stopped suddenly. Just as did the clanking of weapons and the stomping of feet.

The sun had set.

Fifteen

AMBER

I froze in a crouch, my shoulders drawn up to my ears, my face hidden behind my arms. The sudden silence proved more deafening than all the noise before it. I shook so badly, my legs gave in and I plopped down with my butt on the floor.

The sensation of cold stone under my barely covered ass jolted me out of my shock. I scrambled to my feet.

Run!

It was my first instinct. Run the hell out of this room and as far away from this castle as possible.

Before I even made a step, however, I turned to Elex.

He was glorious in his dragon form. An obsidian masterpiece, with a subtle glow of red inside his stone, as if life pulsed inside him like fire—like love itself.

I walked over to him on my shaking legs and dropped to my knees. With his head low to the floor, it was at my chest level in this position. His mouth was open, ready to release a blast of lethal fire when the sunset had turned my dragon to stone.

His prominent eyebrow ridges were drawn together into a frown of rage. His sharp teeth were bared in warning. But when I touched his face, I knew he was worried more than he was angry. He was terrified for me.

I hugged his big head.

"I'm okay, Elex," I whispered, knowing he could hear me. He wouldn't fall asleep so soon, not after everything that had just happened. "You came just in time." I exhaled a shuddering breath. "Thank you... Thank you for coming for me."

Gusts of wind blew through the broken window. I was practically naked, but with him, I felt warm. I could sit like that all night, just hugging him, warmed by his stone. But the longer I sat, the calmer I got. And with the calm came the clarity of thought. I was able to think past this moment and beyond the castle walls.

I couldn't stay here. Now was my chance to flee the castle, just as I'd tried to do before. I had one and only advantage over the much stronger, magical gargoyles—unlike them, I could move at night. I had to use this advantage to the fullest.

"I need to go." I gave Elex a kiss on the cheek, just above the row of short horns that decorated his jawline in this form.

I found my robe. Of all the clothes I was wearing when I got to this room earlier, it was the most practical one. I put it on and tied the laces at my neck.

In the room full of statues, I felt their unmoving eyes follow my every step. It was unnerving. The awareness of their stares prickled with unease along my spine.

I yanked a sheet off the king's perch, then came up to the red dragon.

"You've seen enough." I threw the sheet over his head, then tied it around his eyes.

It finally fully registered with me what it meant to be the only one capable of moving around right now. The only one in the whole of the Bozyr Peak. In the whole of Dakath. And I had time, not enough to waste it, but enough to use it to my full advantage.

Looking around, I took in the scene in the room. As large as it was, the two dragons took up most of the space. The guards spilling through the open doors were still men, not dragons. But there were a lot of them. And they were armed. Come morning, all of them would attack Elex. I had to tip the scales in his favor as much as I could.

Unfortunately, the guards' weapons turned to stone with them. I couldn't take them away or break them off. I wished I could toss all the statues out of the window. But they proved too heavy for me to even move, not to mention lift.

The sunset had caught them in motion, however, as they had rushed in to aid their king. The first guard had his right foot off the ground, as he'd been running. His statue was now balanced only on the left. Pressing a shoulder under his ribs, I gave him a firm shove. He tipped over, then crashed to the floor with a loud thud.

Sadly, nothing broke. Even the sword in his hand remained without a crack. It must take a much harder impact to damage a gargoyle. But he was lying on the floor now. It would take him a second or two to get up in the morning. A second or two before he'd gather his bearings to attack Elex. A second or two for Elex to act first.

Next, I shoved every guard I could down on top of the first one. It would create a pile of bodies and weapons in the morning that would take some time to untangle.

I didn't stop there. Yanking some furs and blankets off the king's bed, I spread them all over the pile, tying the corners around the guards' eyes, to their swords, or to their ankles. I grabbed as many cushions as I could and stuffed them everywhere into the pile—anything to add to the future confusion.

"This will be a nice knot of gargoyles for you to unravel at sunrise, assholes," I muttered under my breath, stepping back to admire my work.

Satisfied with the contraption I'd created from the guards and the bedding, I moved on to the king.

He looked so ridiculous with the sheet wrapped around his head, I snorted a laugh, picking up the chain with the collar he'd tried to force on me.

"This is the only crown that suits the type of king that you are," I said, wrapping the chain around the red dragon's neck.

The chain looked thick enough to hold a gargoyle. Maybe it wouldn't hold a dragon for long. But when he came back to life, the king would have to deal with it first before he could deal with Elex. Every second I could give Elex might mean a lot to him at sunrise.

"There you go." I threaded the chain through the collar, then snapped it closed. "A king. Leashed."

I didn't think he'd be sleeping yet, either. He must be furious at his favorite who dared going against him. And now his "little human pet" humiliated him.

I wished to make him even more furious. So that the rage would burn through him, keeping him awake through the entire night. I wanted him to have not a moment of rest until the morning, for the rage and fury to consume all of his energy, so he'd have little to spend when it came to fighting Elex again.

Stepping closer, I crossed my arms over my chest.

"Look at you, the mighty King of Dakath," I mocked. "You're at my mercy now. How does it feel to be weaker than a wretched, lowly human? You know I can do anything I want to you right now. I can use a knife to chip off one of your scales to keep it as a souvenir. I can find some paint and color you pink, head to toe. Or I could pull my underwear over your stupid head to have you wear it as a crown all night." I leaned closer. "Guess what, I'm not going to do any of that. My time is better spent elsewhere. But you *know* that I could. I, a human and a woman, have the power to do anything I wish to the King of the Dakath Mountains right now. You're my bitch, buddy."

I slapped his cheek with my hand. Not hard. I knew I couldn't hurt him physically even if I tried. But I hoped the indignity from the slap and the humiliation from my words would burn hot enough to last him until morning.

Tonight, I gained a powerful enemy in the King of Dakath.

But after what he had done to me and the others, it couldn't be any other way.

I went back to Elex one last time. His black eyes remained unmoving, but I sensed his ever-present concern for me deepen.

The elegant curves of his eyebrow ridges ended in a pair of short horns on each side of his head. A second pair, thicker and much longer than the first, was growing on top of his head. Below them was the slit of his ear. I leaned to it, hugging his head tightly.

"Don't fight them," I whispered, hopefully for only him to hear. "There are more guards in the hallway outside of this bedroom. Too many for you to win this fight. Fly away. Leave the castle. I won't be here, either. I'm leaving now for the valley. Find me. I know you can because you found me here tonight somehow."

I closed my eyes for a moment, afraid to think about what would've happened had he not come to my rescue just in time.

"God, I'm so glad you found me, Elex. Please, find me again."

I stroked the smooth scales on the side of his face, then ran my fingers along his jawline, tracing the base of the short horns there. I kissed him in the corner of his scowling mouth.

"I love you. I know I should've said it earlier, back when you told me you loved me. But these three little words have gotten me in trouble before. It's so hard for me to finally say them again. But that's exactly how I feel about you, Elex. I love you."

Sixteen

AMBER

After a brief stop in Elex's room to get some clothes to wear under my robe, I hurried to the floor with the kitchen.

I entered the *salamandras'* room to grab my bow and quiver. I only had six arrows, but they were made with iron, capable of killing a fae.

The *salamandras* sat on their perches, their heads bowed, their hands primly folded in their laps. I felt a twinge of regret, leaving them behind. Most of them were the victims of their circumstances, and I would've loved to take them with me, to free them all somehow.

"Maybe, one day," I whispered, passing by Zenada.

Her eyes were closed, her features withdrawn. I yearned to hug her goodbye, but I feared my hugs might not be welcomed by her anymore.

The last time I saw Zenada was when the king had chosen me over her. We'd had no chance to speak since then. I just hoped she knew that what happened wasn't my choice. I didn't want the king in any way or capacity, and I never intended to cause her any pain.

"I'm sorry," I said, unsure whether she could hear me. "I hope we'll meet again." And I hoped for the sake of us both, it'd be under much better circumstances.

I padded out of the women's bedroom and went into the kitchen to find some food for the road. After searching through cabinets, crates, and baskets, I packed some bread, fruit, and cheese into my satchel, filled a metal flask with water, then hurried to the side door for the second time that day.

I kept looking over my shoulder, half-expecting someone to jump on me from behind, but no one was chasing me this time. There was no danger of anyone stopping me. I truly was the only person not made of stone in the castle right now.

It was hard to believe, but there was no need to rush or cower.

I stopped on my way to the door and glanced back down the corridor that led to the tower stairs.

Something the king had said when assaulting me earlier snapped to my mind.

"Unlike the venomous ones, you're not even worth keeping in the dungeon."

If there was anything lower than the kitchen and the women's accommodation in this place, it must be the dungeon. And there was no one to stop me from finding it.

Leaving the corridor with the door to my freedom, I went down the tower stairs. It took longer than I'd thought. The stairs seemed to spiral further and further down into the mountain until they finally led me to an arched wooden door in a solid, wrought-iron frame. This had to be the lowest floor as the stairs ended here.

I inspected the door, looking for the lock to pick. But when I pushed at it, the door moved, opening with a soft sound of well-oiled hinges. I entered the wide corridor with a low ceiling.

Torches illuminated the crudely hewn walls and floor. Their

flames flickered. It appeared they were expected to go out some-time after sunset, which made sense. Why light the place when no one walked here at night?

Afraid they would go out too soon, I removed one with the strongest flame from its holder on the wall. Holding it in front of me, I headed down the corridor.

Arched openings on either side of the corridor lead to what I assumed must be the king's holding cells. They had no bars or even doors. But the walls opposite to the entrance held all possible kinds of restraints. Thick chains, leather belts, collars, and mana-cles of all sizes hung from the rings mounted into the rock.

The first couple of dungeon cells were empty. The chains dangled uselessly. The keys to them hung on the hooks by the entrances. I sensed the cells were unoccupied not due to the king's benevolence but, as he'd said himself, one had to be "worthy" to be imprisoned rather than just being killed on the spot. The king wouldn't keep anyone alive at the crown's expense, unless there was a purpose for that to him.

I stumbled in my step when I came upon the first occupied cell. A man was sitting by the wall here. His head dropped on one shoulder. He must have been asleep when the sunset had caught him. If he were dead, he wouldn't have turned to stone; he would've burned to ash like Weyx had.

A giant lizard was collared in the next cell, with a chain running from its collar to a thick ring on the wall. The chain was stretched tight by two royal guards, bringing the lizard's head up and making its neck bend back unnaturally. All four legs of the lizard were also manacled and chained to the metal rings in the floor.

The third guard wore a long chain mail apron and gripped a knife in his gloved hand. He stood right in front of the lizard, with a bucket of clear, shimmering liquid positioned at his feet.

It took me but a moment to recognize the gold-brushed ridge running along the lizard's back.

Isar!

My heart leaped with joy. She was alive.

The despot king wouldn't dispose of someone as lethal as Isar, especially not during the war he was so eager to win.

It took me a minute to figure out what was happening in this room before the sunset froze the scene for me to decipher.

Clearly, King Edkhar kept Isar alive. The liquid glistening in the bucket was her venom. The cuts around her mouth must have been left by the knife in her jailer's hand. He'd used it to pry her mouth open and drain the venom from her teeth as she bit into it. The thick metal glove on his hand and the chain mail apron were his protective gear against her teeth and poison.

"Oh, Isar..." I stepped to her as my mind worked feverishly on a way to help her.

The keys to her restraints were on the hooks by the door, but the locks on her chains had solidified into stone, just like the guards' clothes and weapons had. I kicked at a chain with all my strength, but it wouldn't break. The stone at night wasn't any weaker than the metal during the day, it seemed.

I stared at the bucket, half-filled with poison. I'd seen Isar's venom corrode the rocks in the yard in the Sanctuary during her arrest.

Without any protective gloves, I crouched by the bucket and examined it for any drips around the handle. Not finding any, I propped my torch into the elbow crook of one of the guards. "Hold this for me, will you?"

I took the bucket and splashed some of the viscous toxic liquid on each metal ring on the floor. Even if it did nothing to the metal of the ring, I hoped the venom would weaken the rock the rings were mounted into. I also dripped some of it over the rock wall with the ring that held the chain of Isar's collar.

"Isar." I touched her cheek, praying she could hear me. "Sorry, I can't do much for you. Sorry if this doesn't work. But if it does, if you get free, run away. Leave the Bozyr Peak. The door to the dungeon is unlocked. Get up the tower stairs to the next floor, then use the side door past the kitchen to get out. And don't go to the Sanctuary, either..." I bit my lip, agonizing about the best way to tell her about Ertee. Was there any good way to break the news like that? "There is no one left at the *Salamandra* Sanctuary. Ertee..." I pressed my forehead to the side of Isar's face, unable to look into her eyes, even as they were nothing but stone right now. "Ertee is not there, Isar. Ertee is gone... She's dead."

I stroked the side of her neck, hoping she'd feel my heart hurting for her loss, wishing it would soothe her pain somehow.

"The final battle of the war is tomorrow," I whispered to her. "Use the time to get as far away from here as you can."

There was still some poison left in the bucket. Lifting it again, I strolled towards the first guard. The glee on his face while he was pulling at the chain attached to the *salamandra's* collar told me he wasn't just a man doing his job. The asshole really enjoyed the suffering of another being.

"Hey, want a taste of this?" I splashed the venom from the bucket into the guard's face.

I didn't know if I could've done that if he were a living, breathing person of blood and flesh, screaming in pain. I was glad he was currently of stone. So, no screams came. His gleeful expression didn't change, even as the poison hissed, slowly corroding the surface and releasing thin, white tendrils of smoke.

"Look at you." I turned to the remaining two guards, both looking just as pleased with themselves as the first one. "Three men against one chained woman. How pathetic." I moved the bucket in my hands, swirling the remaining poison in it. "Is this what you want from her? Her venom? Well, have it, then."

I splashed the shimmering liquid onto the faces of each guard. It bubbled and hissed, dripping down their noses, cheeks, and chins.

I stared at them for a while, watching the smooth surface of the stone turn porous as the poison ate through it. Would it kill them? I had a feeling it would. If not, I had no doubt Isar would finish them the moment she freed herself.

I didn't feel sorry for them.

I felt angry.

"I'm a thief," I said solemnly. "I've stolen, forged papers, and lied. But I've never killed before." I turned the empty bucket upside down and slid it over the head of one of the guards, leaving it there. "Now, you've made me a murderer."

Seventeen

AMBER

Eager to get as far as possible from the Bozyr Peak, I walked swiftly, without stopping for rest. By sunrise, I had made it about one-quarter of the way down the mountain.

At first, I'd followed the path the *salamandras* and I had taken to the castle when we first came here. Once it reached the lowest point of the ridge, I turned off the path and headed toward the valley.

Gargoyles didn't use the walking paths often. Rocks, big and small, littered my way. The path frequently disappeared completely, absorbed by the mountain, only to reappear a few steps farther down. Nighttime didn't make it easier to search for my way in the dark. I tripped, skidded, and fell more times than I cared to count. But I didn't stop. I had to cover as much distance as I could before the sunrise would bring the kingdom back to life.

I had no doubt the king would search for me as soon as he was able. He wouldn't want to make me his mistress or his pet anymore. I'd burned that bridge by insulting him. But an arrogant, petty man like King Edkhar would certainly want to take his revenge on me for the humiliation I'd put him through.

With the Battle of the Bozyr Peak happening today, I just hoped the king would have his hands full with other things for a while.

Mindful of the impending battle, I took the course toward the Desolate Peak for a while, circling away from the location of the battleground. The Desolate Peak was easy to spot, even in the dark. Its sole needle jutted sharply into the starry night as if painted with black ink against the indigo sky.

As the darkness thinned and the skies lightened with the new sunrise, I searched for a place to hide. It had been an intense day and a grueling night of walking. I was exhausted. The upcoming day could be even more challenging, and I needed some rest before facing it. Caution also dictated me to stay out of sight while the gargoyles were awake.

The slope of the mountain had plateaued. The path curved around high, sharp rocks that rose straight up into the air like pillars. The valley was hidden behind the next wide ridge. All I saw around were rocks, dirt, and patches of blooming red poppies that looked like splashes of blood between the rocks.

For once, I was glad to have my robe on. It was almost the same color as the poppies, allowing me to hide among them. Tucking the robe around me, I found a dry spot between the rocks and squeezed in there.

The ground was chilly. But I was too tired for the cold to keep me awake for long. I propped my bow and quiver with arrows behind the rock, shoved my satchel under my head, and soon drifted into an uneasy sleep.

A warm splash of sunlight on my face woke me up. I squinted at the sky, raising my hand to shield my eyes. The sun broke through the thick, gray clouds, shining straight above me.

It must be around noon, way too soon for me to start walking again. I was still too close to the castle. A flying dragon could spot me. But I was hungry and thirsty, and most importantly, I had to pee.

I grabbed some cheese and bread from my satchel, along with a couple of plums, then ate hurriedly while scanning the skies above me. After washing the food down with water I'd brought with me, I ventured to climb out from my hiding spot.

Grabbing my bow and arrows just in case, I left my satchel hidden in the place where I'd slept. Finding a "bathroom spot" wasn't hard on the deserted mountain. After I was done, I straightened my clothes and went back to my sleeping spot but didn't climb back in.

A flock of birds rushed from the horizon. I shielded my eyes from the sunlight and...froze. These weren't birds. But dragons. Hundreds...no, thousands of them were flying from the valley toward the Bozyr Peak.

An even larger mass separated from the king's castle and the surrounding mountains behind me. Their massive wings obstructed the sun like storm clouds as they flew to charge their enemy.

The final battle at Bozyr Peak was about to begin. And judging by the massive size of both armies, it was sure to spill way out of the area where I'd thought it was taking place.

I needed a better place to hide. Somewhere where the dragons' fire wouldn't reach me.

Gripping my bow, I yanked my satchel from between the rocks and swung it over my shoulder and across my chest, next to my quiver of arrows. Leaping from rock to rock, I spotted a deep crevasse just off the path. It was dark and probably wet in there, but I'd be completely out of sight in there.

A thunder of dragons flew over me. The wind from their

mighty wings rolled like an avalanche down the mountain. I grabbed on to a rock with both arms, just to stay on my feet.

The king's dragons from the mountain collided with the mass of the army approaching from the valley in a thundering, fiery crash.

The sky turned red with fire. Black smoke obscured the sky. Soon, the stench of burning flesh drifted through the air with violent gusts of wind.

"What are you doing here?" A voice boomed above me. A huge shape plummeted from the sky toward me. "Shouldn't you be with the others?"

A charcoal-gray dragon grabbed me with his giant claws and swept me into the air with him.

Up here, the world made even less sense than below. Clouds of smoke mixed with the clumps of real clouds. Blasts of fire ripped through both, tearing smoke and mist into shreds, then leaving more smoke in their wake.

A dragon roared to our right. His mouth was wide open, the flesh inside burning. These weren't *his* flames, but the fire of someone else, another dragon who bested him. His great wings flapped in the air erratically before his eyes glassed over and he crashed onto the sharp rocks below.

With cold fingers, I gripped onto the claws of the dragon carrying me through this hell in the sky.

"There," he snarled above me, jerking his head at a spot on the ground below the clouds.

As the smoke parted, I spotted a group of *salamandras* standing on a small patch of even ground on the side of a mountain.

"Go." The dragon released his claws, letting me drop next to them as he flew by. "And stay put. There's no place for deserters in my army."

The dragon turned his head my way briefly, giving me a stern look with one silver-gray eye. The other eye wasn't there. Only a jagged scar marred its place.

The High General had been away with Elex. He either hadn't heard about what happened in the king's chambers in his absence, or didn't recognize me, which was entirely possible. He saw the robe before the person, just like the king did.

Dropped by him from some height, I rolled on the ground and under the feet of the *salamandras* and their Mother.

"Amber." Mother's chest rose with a deep breath. Bitter disappointment rang in her voice. From the ground, I couldn't see her face behind the lace of her hood, but I knew it also held a disappointed expression.

Now, however, was not the time to discuss our differences or my yet another attempt to escape.

I scrambled to my feet, adjusting my satchel across my chest, as well as my bow and quiver over my shoulder. Despite the High General's mad dash through the war zone up above, I managed to keep my things with me. It had been impossible to lose them as they were clutched in the claws of the High General with me.

"What are you all doing here?" I stared at the women in confusion. None of them had any weapons. With their threadbare red robes blowing in the wind, they seemed more vulnerable than ever on this desolate mountainside with the battle of mighty dragons raging just over our heads. "It's not safe for us here."

Mother clutched her hands together. "It is our duty to help the king win the war."

"What? How are you going to help him fight an army of dragons?" I gestured at the fiery chaos churning up above. "Trust me, you don't want to be up there."

A dragon plummeted from the sky. His massive body hit the ground just a few feet down the mountain from us. His glossy, chocolate-brown scales cracked. Blood sprayed the rocks, misting the red robes of the women closest to the edge of the platform where we all stood.

One of them jumped aside with a gasp. It was Iolena. Despite the lace of her hood, I could see how pale she'd turned.

"See? Even they can't survive it!" I wildly gestured at the dead dragon, whose body already started to shrink, turning into a man. "You being here is useless. It's suicide, plain and simple."

Mother tilted her head, looking uncharacteristically serene.

"Don't underestimate the power of women when we come together," she said softly, then added, leaning closer, "Pray that we win. And pray to every god you know, Amber, that the king will be in a benevolent mood after his victory."

She turned her face up to the sky where the clouds of smoke and fire had thinned somewhat. The dragons appeared to regroup. The Rebel Lords' army that came from the direction of the valley pulled back. The king's dragons from the mountains were holding their line slightly behind us.

"Our turn, *salamandras*." Mother's voice shook slightly, but she steadied it. "Form the crescent."

I retreated to the mountain, giving them space on the platform. Holding hands, the women shifted to form a semi-circle, their backs to the mountain, their faces turned to the enemy army that went into a new attack. The rebel dragons were fast approaching again. But this time, the king's army held back.

"Our Great Mother *Salamandra*..." Mother started. Her voice changed completely. Any shakiness was gone. Her words flowed smoothly, filled with strength. "Take our healing power. Combine our strength. Together, we are unstoppable..."

Others joined her in the chant that appeared to be some strange mix of pep-talk and prayer, peppered in with words that sounded so ancient, I didn't understand their meaning.

The women raised their hands to shoulder height. Their palms open, they placed each hand flush against the hand of the person standing next to them, palm to palm, forming an uninterrupted connection from one end of the semi-circle to another.

The air shimmered around their interconnected hands. The view of the mountains around them distorted as waves of heat rolled from the group. It concentrated inside the crescent. The shimmering streams rushed from their joined hands, churning into a twister in the middle.

The twister grew taller as the dragons approached. Heat scorched my face. I pressed my back to the mountain, trying to get away from the women and whatever they had brewing in their midst.

The *salamandras'* power was not fire but warmth. The magic that Zenada had so generously shared with me was meant to comfort and heal, not kill. When combined, however, the warmth turned to heat, scorching the air above the mountain.

The twister of the shimmering energy thickened over the women's heads. It grew into a sphere, larger than the platform they stood on.

With a loud cry, the women thrust their hands forward, launching the churning heat orb toward the approaching dragons. It floated through the air, almost invisible against the clouds. The moment it connected with the first dragon, the ball of energy exploded.

There was no fire and no smoke. The sphere just expanded momentarily, eerily quiet and lethally devastating. The dragons were scattered all over the sky. Some managed to stay airborne, but many were hurled against the rocks. Hundreds of them hit the ground, both above and below us.

I gaped in shock and horror as the air erupted with cheers. The king's army roared triumphantly. Now, they surged ahead, launching the attack at the rebels still in the air.

The effort to create the heat explosion took its toll on the women. They staggered and swayed on their feet. Some sank to their knees, propping their hands on the ground for support. I rushed to them.

"Hey, guys, are you okay?" I grabbed Iolena around her middle, before she would've collapsed to the ground. "You really need to get out of here. Now."

The battle above us no longer had a front line. The fighting was everywhere. The king's dragons chased the rebels. The rebels fought back. I had no idea how they could even tell who was who.

One fight broke up especially close to us for my liking.

"Let's go. Quickly." I tried to help Iolena move.

She shook her head, sinking to the ground. "Please... I just need a minute."

Their power was warmth, not heat. It was meant to nurture, not to kill. What the *salamandras* had done for their king went against their nature. And it cost them. None of them could walk. Most could hardly move at all. Mother stood on one knee, her head bowed, her breathing shallow.

I couldn't leave them here on their own. Weak, their powers depleted, the *salamandras* were sitting ducks, a perfect target with their red robes standing out against the surrounding black rocks.

And there was not a single king's man anywhere around to protect them.

"Well..." I frantically scanned the sky. The danger appeared to come from every direction now. Blasts of fire scorched the rocks all around us. The rebels clearly thirsted for retaliation against the women. I yanked the bow off my shoulder. "Get better soon, ladies. I'll do what I can."

I plucked an arrow out of my quiver and nocked it.

Six arrows. Against an army of dragons.

That would have to do, because that was all I had.

Eighteen

AMBER

Dragons were swarming the sky as far as the eye could see. There were so many of them, their wings blocked the sun, turning day into night. The air heated from their fire, turning spring into scorching summer.

One of them shot a blast of fire as he passed by. The flames hit the mountain just a short distance up from the recovering women.

Another dragon swerved our way. The burgundy of his scales lightened to sandy brown on his belly. His eyes were rimmed with the lighter color, too, which made them easy to see, even from a distance.

"Well, come on, buddy," I whispered, raising my bow with an arrow nocked.

Taking aim, I breathed in and out. Slowly, rhythmically. I waited for the world to fall away with all its distractions. The noise of the battle, the roaring of the dragons, and the fiery blasts no longer existed. It was just the iron tip of my arrow and the gold-brown eye of the approaching dragon.

Closer... Just a little bit closer.

I smoothly glided the arrow, following the dragon's flight. His head was turned, aiming for the *salamandras*, which made the angle just right for me as he flew by.

His mouth opened with a ball of fire curling over his tongue. He spewed it out in a blast. I waited for him to blink. Then I let the arrow go. It sang through the air, then sank right between his eyelids.

"Fuck..."

Did I actually do it?

I watched, stunned, as he rolled through the air, his wings flailing. Blood poured from his eye. But it was the blood that remained in his body that killed him. Each pumping of his heart spread the poison of Nerifir iron through his body.

He crashed onto the rocks below, then rolled down the steep mountainside. I turned away just as the dead dragon started to transform into a dead man. I had no desire to watch that transformation to the end.

"We can do it, ladies!" I shouted enthusiastically, facing the platform where the women were.

It was engulfed in flames. The *salamandras*—every single one of them—had turned to ashes. Wind blew the gray ash from the platform. The morbid tendrils of it joined the smoke above, filling the air with the stench of burned flesh.

"No..."

It'd happened so fast. The dragon I'd just killed had managed to release a single blast of fire. And that was all it took. One blast of the dragon's fire at its full power, and dozens of living breathing women were now nothing but gray ash drifting in the wind.

"No." I dropped my bow. It proved useless. It didn't save them.

I didn't save them.

More airborne dragons pivoted my way. Clearly, they didn't want anyone to leave this mountainside alive, including me.

Struck by shock and weighted down by sorrow, I didn't move.

But when their shapes grew bigger as they approached and the flapping of their wings grew louder, the instinct of self-preservation kicked in. I scrambled up the mountain, trying to get away.

The climb was steep. I used both hands and feet. Yet it was futile. I couldn't hide. My red robe, clearly visible against the black rocks, betrayed me. Both the satchel and the quiver dangled on my side, getting in the way. No matter how hard I tried, I couldn't escape.

I pulled my head into my shoulders, waiting for a fiery blast to incinerate me any minute.

A dragon's claws closed around me, instead. Their sharp tips scraped the rocks, snatching me off the mountain.

The ground grew distant as the dragon took me higher. I couldn't look away from the scorched platform where the women had been just moments ago. They fought for their king. And now they were gone.

King Edkhar used them, without ensuring their safety. The royal asshole didn't even give them a single dragon for protection. All they had was me. And I failed them. I did what I'd been training for. I killed a dragon. But I still failed. People died. So many...

Tears rushed from my eyes. Wind smeared them on my cheeks.

Everywhere I looked was devastation and death. Dead dragons littered the rocks below me. Huge and intimidating when alive, their bodies looked far more vulnerable as they turned into men upon their death. Pale, tanned, black, gray, and brown, they lay naked, impaled on the sharp rocks. Their perfect, beautiful fae bodies were broken and crushed.

What was this war for? Who needed it? Did it matter who won and who lost in the end? What did any of this prove?

Nothing made sense.

My grief brewed into anger.

"Let me go!" I slammed my fists into the claws of the dragon who had captured me. "If you're taking me to your king, you may as well drop me down right now. I'd rather be dead than come back."

"I won't drop you. I made you a promise to never let go." The dragon's voice sounded strangled. But I recognized it, nevertheless.

"Elex?"

He found me.

"You're alive. Thank God," I breathed out, gripping his claws tighter.

The relief was intense but short-lived. Anger burned brighter than ever, refusing to subside when faced with the horror saturating the sky.

"Do you see this, Elex? All of it? Take a good look. Count the bodies. This is all the king's doing. This is the war you wanted him to win."

Wind swept through the mountains. It carried the pungent stench of death. I buried my face into my hood, but it helped little.

Spreading his great wings, Elex glided along the mountain ridge. He wasn't taking me to the valley, I realized. But he also kept away from the castle. Instead, he headed toward the tall spear of a mountain jutting out into the blood-red evening sky like a rugged sword. The Desolate Peak.

Circling it, he flew toward an opening in the side of the mountain—a cave. Just before flying in, he shifted into a man to fit through the smaller entrance.

"Amber. How are you?" He set me down on the ground inside the cave.

Anger kept boiling inside me. Uncontrollable.

"How am I? How do you think?" I shoved against his chest, shaking with tears streaming down my face. "Did you see the *salamandras* burn? All of them! Every single one... Do you know why? Because the king told them to be there. He needed their help. Then he left them on that mountain to die..."

"I saw. I'm so sorry." He tried to pull me closer, but I flexed my arms, pushing with my fists against his chest.

"Did you know it would happen? Was that the king's strategy all along?"

"I had no idea." He shook his head, his expression sincere. "The records have no mention of the *salamandras* taking part in the Battle of the Bozyr Peak."

They all died today. And history kept not even a mention of their sacrifice.

"This is the man you protect," I cried. "This is the king you wish to keep on the throne. The king you'd die for—"

"No." He grabbed me by my upper arms. "*You* are the only one I'm willing to die for, Amber. No one else. Do you hear me? Only you."

He reached for a kiss, but the anguish inside me could not be extinguished by tenderness. It burned way too bright.

I needed a torrent of stronger sensations.

Unclenching my fists, I splayed my hands on his bare chest— smooth, strong, and solid. The contact was one stable point in the hurricane of darkness and ashes that raged inside me. Elex was my rock. He kept me grounded and sane.

I kept one hand on his chest, tugging at the ties of my robe with the other.

"Help me," I said.

He yanked at the ties, ripping them off. I dropped my satchel and my quiver to the floor, then shrugged out of my robe, letting it drop to the ground, too.

"And these." I fumbled with the laces of my pants, *his* pants, that I took from his room. I'd had to tie the laces all around my waist to keep the pants on and roll the bottoms up a few times. They looked like harem pants on me.

"Come here." Hooking his fingers under the laces, he yanked me to him. He buried his face in my shoulder, breathing in my scent mixed with his from his clothes I was wearing.

With another hard yank, he ripped the laces apart, then tore through the waistband. The pants slid down my legs, and he ripped his shirt off me.

His black eyes grew darker at the sight of my see-through underwear that were meant to entice the king. With a growl, he tore through the paper-thin fabric, tossing the shreds at my feet. Grabbing the back of my neck, he pivoted me around, my face to the wall.

"Is this what you want, my spark?" he gritted through his teeth, pushing against my back. "Is this how you want it?"

His hard-as-steel erection pressed against my back. One hand gripping my ass, he grabbed my breast with the other, grinding himself against me.

"You want me to fuck you. Hard. Until you can breathe again. Is that it?"

That was exactly it.

I was suffocating. Smoke, ash, and fire permeated every cell of my body. The air was strangling. Fear pressed on my chest. Despair gripped my throat. I needed Elex's hands on me to banish them all.

He had to fight the bad for me. With me. Then, maybe, some good could return.

My arms spread, I gripped the cold rock of the cave. With an arm around my middle, he lifted me off the ground, shoving me up against the wall. He kicked my legs open with his knee. Then his hard, hot length pressed between my thighs.

It burned as he entered. I hissed but didn't shrink away, embracing his invasion. He slid in easily—I was ready for him. But he burned. All of him. His body glowed brighter with the fire inside him. And the part of him buried in me, burned me from the inside.

Fire spread through my body like lava. I clawed at the rocks, moaning in need. He cupped a hand between my legs, shielding me from the wall as he pounded hard into me. His fingers pressed against me, rubbing me just the right way with each violent thrust.

He fucked me from behind. And I growled and snarled like a feral animal in heat. So, so much heat. The air seemed to waver and steam around us. The rocks glowed, ready to melt. I, too, felt like I was melting, evaporating into the ether.

My head was spinning as I came. Violent shudders rocked through my entire body. Elex's roar filtered through a haze in my brain as he pumped his release into me.

I stayed splayed against the wall. He leaned against me, holding me in place. His chest pushed into my back with his fast, shallow breathing.

Pressing the side of my face to the wall, I closed my eyes. There was numbness inside me now, fragile like the first ice on a river. But it was better than the earlier turmoil. Like this, I could think. And when Elex finally moved us away from the wall, I could finally breathe.

He folded his wings. Turning with his back to the wall, he slid down to the floor, taking me with him. I sat sideways, my butt on the floor between his spread thighs, both of my legs draped over his left knee.

"Is it over now?" I asked, resting my head against his chest. "The war? Is it done?"

He wrapped one arm around my shoulders and rested the other one on my naked thigh. Sweat was cooling off my skin, sending a shudder through me. Instantly, Elex's body felt warmer. He leaned away from the wall for a moment to free a wing from behind his back, then wrapped it around me like a blanket.

I stared straight ahead, not speaking and feeling nothing. He slid a finger down my throat.

"Your skin releases moisture when you're hot. Or is it when you're cold?"

What was he talking about? I couldn't focus on his words or on any one thought.

He touched the tip of his finger with his tongue. "It's salty."

"Sweat? Is that what you mean?" I smiled. Yes, somehow, I

could *smile* after everything that had happened today. Who knew?

"That's how you regulate your body temperature, right? You can do it to some degree."

I nodded.

"I knew it," he said. "I figured that must be what your body was doing when you were sick." He trailed his finger along my collarbone. "It's not a very efficient way, though, is it?"

"As compared to gargoyles, no, it isn't," I agreed. "But that's all we humans have."

"Now, you also have *me* to keep you warm." His wing draped over my legs felt like a heated blanket.

I stroked its leathery surface. It felt soft and silky, like fine suede. Warm. And so very comfy. I appreciated the warmth. And I really, really appreciated Elex chatting about a lighter topic, unrelated to what had happened today, to put my mind at ease before finally answering my earlier question.

"The war is over, Amber. It really is, now."

I drew in a shaky breath. "The king won?"

"He did."

I stared at my hands. They were covered in dirt and grime from the smoke. The fingers were scratched from climbing up the mountain when trying to escape the dragons. Or maybe that was from gripping the wall while Elex fucked me?

"Just as you wanted," I said.

"Right," he echoed.

"Only it doesn't feel right, does it?"

His chest rose and fell with a deep sigh.

"He's not my king, Amber. I don't serve him. I certainly don't want to die for him. And last night, I came close to killing him myself. But if King Edkhar dies before his son is born, I would cease to exist. My life is tied with his, whether I like it or not."

"I understand. It's self-preservation—"

"It's more than that, my spark. Can't you see? All of this around us. The injustice, the death, the pointless violence. All of it will come to an end eventually, if we just allow history to take its course."

He'd said that before. And just like then, his assurance wasn't enough.

"What will happen until then, though? More people will die. More cruelties will happen. Have you not seen enough?"

I paused, shutting my eyes for a moment. I hated arguing with him. I saw his point, and I knew he saw mine. Neither of us could do anything about the current situation. But I needed him to know everything I'd seen and lived through since coming to his world.

"Elex, the king has a dungeon, deep below the castle. It's a dark, gloomy place. I went there last night. He has one of the *salamandras* from the Sanctuary imprisoned in there. Remember I told you about her? Her crime is that she was born with venom in her teeth. The king's men had been draining it from her..." I held my breath, trying to push the images of Isar's torture out of my head or I would scream. "I tried to free her. I hope it worked. But the dungeon is a vile, horrible place, Elex."

He stroked my hair, falling silent for a few breaths. His voice sounded hollow when he finally spoke.

"I know. I spent a few days in King Edkhar's dungeon myself. They tried to torture me too, before I proved I was of the royal blood."

Shock sliced through me like a sword. "They did? And you never told me?"

He exhaled a sad laugh. "It's not a fun topic to talk about."

"Did they hurt you?" Anger against anyone who dared to harm him bubbled inside me, making my voice sound low and rough.

He pressed his lips together firmly before replying carefully. "They didn't inflict any new injuries."

That didn't mean they didn't hurt him in many other ways. Clearly, he was sparing me the details. I understood he didn't feel like rehashing his "not fun" memories. Compassion tightened around my heart.

"Elex, I'm so sorry." I leaned my forehead to the side of his face. "They tortured you on King Edkhar's orders. And you still agreed to serve him after that?"

"I didn't do it for the king. Not even for myself. But for the better life I want for Dakath one day."

I said nothing to that. His commitment to his kingdom was admirable. No one could fault Elex for loving his homeland so much. I certainly wasn't going to do that.

"But I'm not serving him anymore," he said with determination.

"You're not?" I tilted my head back to see his face. "Is it because the war is over? He doesn't need you anymore?"

"No. It's because of what he's done to *you*." His jaw moved and his eyes glistened dangerously. "I could ignore the king's lack of ethics, his ruthless politics, his crimes against me, but the moment I saw him on top of you..." His throat bobbed with a swallow and he drew in a long shuddering breath. "It was all I could do not to kill him this morning."

As much as I would've loved to strangle the king with my own hands by now, I was glad the bastard escaped with his life. And that was our tragedy. The life of the man I loved depended on the life of the one I hated so fiercely.

"What did you do at sunrise?" I asked.

"I did what you told me to do. I left. You're all that matters to me, Amber. And since you said you wouldn't be in the castle, there was no need for me to stay, either. I spent the morning searching for you."

"And you found me." I snuggled against him. "Tell me, how do you keep finding me?"

"Well, that is a curious thing, sweetheart. I have this little spark burning right here." He placed my hand on his chest, over the spot where his heart was beating inside. "The spark is not of my fire, yet it feels just as close to me. It's a part of me. It hurts when you're hurting. It glows warmly when you're content, like you are right now. It burns, driving me wild with lust when you want me," he murmured, pressing his lips to the top of my head. "And it flutters against my ribs like a trapped firefly, not letting me rest, when you're scared. It was rather quiet this morning, though. I could hardly feel it at all."

"I slept this morning, hiding."

He nodded. "That's why it took me longer to find you. But you were scared last night, Amber. I *felt* it. I couldn't spend a night away from you. I had to come back."

Gratitude for him filled me. "Thank you so much for coming for me." I kissed his chest and didn't move away, leaving my face pressed to his warm skin. "Was the king mad at sunrise?"

"Was he ever!" His chest vibrated with a chuckle. "I wish I could've stayed longer to watch them all struggle this morning. But even the little I saw was extremely entertaining."

"You saw what I did?"

"I sure did. At sunrise, the guards all tumbled over each other. It was just one huge pile of limbs, weapons, and bed sheets." He laughed. "The king thrashed around on the leash you put on him, while trying to shake off the blankets you tied over his head. It's a shame I had to leave, really."

I laughed, too, now. The darkness was still there inside me, but it no longer consumed me. Among all the death and devastation, I felt fully alive again.

Nineteen

AMBER

"Do you want a plum?" I offered Elex the fruit I had in my satchel.

He'd refused any of the bread and cheese I'd offered to share with him before. And now he was shaking his head again.

"Are you not hungry at all?"

He took a drink of water he'd brought from a creek outside of the cave. "I'll be fine without food for a while. There's no need to waste it on me. Not until we at least know where your next meal will come from."

I sat cross-legged on my robe spread in the middle of the cave. The sun was setting, leaving us no choice but to spend the night here. But my thoughts went to our future beyond tonight.

The war had been looming over all of us like a dark shroud. Now that it was over, however, the shroud didn't disappear. There was no relief. The fact that the king had destroyed his opposition and was free to do whatever he wanted didn't feel like a victory to me.

"What's next, Elex? What are we going to do now?"

He sat down behind me and pulled me closer, my back to his chest. We remained naked. His clothes were gone wherever he had last shifted to his dragon form. Mine lay mostly torn to pieces by the wall where he'd ripped them off me.

"Now, we get to figure out our own future," he said.

"What will it be?"

"Whatever we want it to be. We can go far away from the Bozyr Peak. Live in a small village somewhere, where no one knows us. Or I can build you a home on a mountain peak far away from here, where no one can find us. We can also go elsewhere in Nerifir. I'd stay away from the Lorsan Wetlands—gorgonians can kill with just a look. But the Sarnala Plains are nice, especially this time of the year. Or we can live on an island in the Olathana Ocean and listen to the sirens sing under the stars. Their voices are magical, the most beautiful thing you'll ever hear. But we can only listen to them when I'm in my stone form. And I'd have to hold you tight, so you can't get away. The sirens' voices sometimes make people follow them to the bottom of the ocean — Well," he interrupted himself. "I don't like the idea of moving to the Olathana Ocean, after all. Let's not do that."

"Let's not," I laughed.

Though, I wouldn't mind hearing a siren sing at least once. When I'm securely held in Elex's arms, of course.

Hugging me from behind, he stroked my side. The tips of his fingers touched the underside of my breast, sending a rush of tingles through my lower belly.

"Elex? That spark in your chest you were talking about, remember? The one that tells you how I'm feeling?"

"Hmm." He nuzzled just below my ear, then kissed my neck gently.

"What is it doing right now?"

"It pulses hotly, telling me you like my hands on you." He circled my breast with his fingers in a slow, deliberate caress that felt like teasing.

I squirmed, needing more.

"But you're off a little." I pressed his hand to my breast.

"How about this?" He pinched my nipple, pulling and rolling it between his fingers. "Does that feel better?"

"Ohhh..." Breath rushed out of me. Hot, thick desire spread through my body.

"And this," he murmured, sliding his other hand between my legs.

"Is that spark..." I struggled for words as his fingers smoothly slipped in and out of me. "Is it telling you how much I want you right now?"

"Oh yes, it is."

"How is it doing that?"

"By making me want you even more. Just like this." He slid me backwards, closer to him, until my butt pressed against his hard, scorching hot length. "I feel what you feel, my spark."

"It's so hot," I gasped, but made no move to shift away.

"It always is when you're around. Do you want me to think of something cold and icy again to cool off?" I heard a smile in his voice.

"No. Don't."

I wished to take him just the way he was—hot, hard, and massive. I pressed myself to him, letting his heat seep through to me.

"It doesn't hurt, Elex. It only turns me on more."

He moved me to face him, then kissed me, lowering me onto the robe.

This time, there was no frantic desperation. He made love to me slowly, thoroughly, kissing every inch of my body. Until I, too, felt the fire course through my veins.

He made me come with his mouth and tongue first before thrusting his burning hot shaft inside me. By the time I came again and he pumped his release into me, the sun was already low over the horizon.

He rolled to his back, then pulled me on top of his chest.

"Try to get some rest, sweetheart." He kissed my lips, wrapping his wings around me. "Tomorrow, we'll figure out which way to fly."

Tomorrow sounded just fine by me. Tonight, I was truly exhausted.

I yawned, curling against his chest. His body solidified under me, growing as hard as rock as the sun sat. His wings stiffened, forming a firm cocoon around us both.

"Good night, Elex," I whispered with another yawn.

I placed my bent arm under my head since Elex was too hard to use him as a pillow. But he remained nice and warm, helping me fall asleep quickly.

The sound of footsteps woke me up.

Footsteps!

Alarm shot through me, jerking me fully awake.

It was dark in the cave. No sunlight filtered into our cocoon of Elex's wings. He remained in his stone form. Hard and dark, as he should be. It was night. Yet someone was walking out there, through the passages beyond our cave.

Then, the light appeared. But it wasn't from the sun. A pale, yellow spotlight moved along the surface of Elex's wings that proved semi-transparent, even in their stone form.

"Another one," a male voice stated.

I held my breath, afraid to make a sound, praying that Elex's wings completely concealed me from view.

The newcomer moved around the cave, the sound of his footsteps circled us. He appeared to be alone. At least I only heard one set of footfalls. But he kept talking, as if to someone.

"Would you look at that?"

He paused by the wall, probably standing over the pile of my discarded clothes. The shirt and the pants I'd worn were Elex's. It wouldn't be hard to assume he'd taken them off before the sun set. My robe was on the ground under us, and I hoped it looked simply like a blanket.

I kept quiet. There was no reason for the man to think Elex was hiding anyone inside his wings.

"Hm," sounded right above our heads.

Then, I felt a firm tug on my braid.

Chills trickled down my spine. The freaking braid had draped over Elex's shoulder with its end sticking outside from under his wing. I instantly regretted never having cut it off after all.

"My lady?" Another tug came, not strong enough to be painful but firm and persistent. "At least I assume you're a *lady*," he added. "Come out here."

Well, did I have a choice? Not really. He could literally pull me out from under Elex's wings by my braid. The fact that he waited for me to come out on my own had to be a good sign. At least, I hoped it was. Still, I lingered, clinging to the illusion of safety, tucked against Elex's chest, warm and comfy.

Another tug came. "I insist. Or would you have me break the gargoyle's wings to free you?"

I couldn't let that happen.

"No, don't." I pulled myself up Elex's body and poked my head out through the opening between his wings. "Please, don't hurt him."

The man dropped my braid and stepped around Elex to face me. Dressed in black, he was tall, dark-haired, and pale. A few silvery strands glistened in his short, dark locks in the front. A large black bird, a crow or raven, was perched on his shoulder. That must be whom he'd been talking to.

In one hand, the man held a lantern with a thick candle burning inside it. In the other...my decimated underwear dangled from his finger.

"Get out." He gestured impatiently. "I have questions to ask you."

"Um..." I shifted out a little more, placing an arm over my

bare chest. "Could you pass me my clothes, please?" I pointed at the pile by the wall.

"None of them are in a much better state than this." He lifted the remnants of my underwear in his hand. "I doubt they would be of any use to you now."

He tossed the shreds of the see-through fabric out of the entrance to the cave. It fluttered into the dark night sky like a remnant of a sexy dream before disappearing from view.

He put his lantern down on the floor, then pulled out the silver pin that held his long cloak at his shoulder.

"This will have to do for now."

He removed his cloak and held it open for me.

The distance between me and the garment was about a foot or two. I'd have to climb out into the open, naked, before I could have it.

He sensed my hesitation and blew out an impatient breath.

"Fine. I won't look." He turned his head aside and demonstratively shut his eyes.

I climbed out from the tunnel formed by Elex's wings.

"Thanks." I awkwardly stepped into the cloak, allowing the stranger to drape it over my shoulders, then took the silver pin from him and fastened the fabric at my neck.

His cloak smelled like the wind—literally, a breath of fresh air in the world saturated with ashes and smoke. Though, I sensed the cloak's owner was far from a benevolent savior.

He stepped away from me and folded his arms across his chest. As he gave me an assessing look, I did the same to him.

His hair was darker than Elex's. Aside from the thin silver strands in the front, it was ink-black. His skin was light, but without the freckles or the ruddy undertone of King Edkhar's. I couldn't tell the exact color of his eyes from this distance, but they were light, too, gray or blue.

"Who are you?" he demanded. "And what are you doing in one of my caves?"

"Yours?" I squinted. "How is it yours?"

"All of the Desolate Peak is mine. No one comes here, not even the king."

Why didn't Elex say anything about that? Probably because he didn't know it himself. Things might be different here a thousand years from now, the time when Elex grew up.

"Who are you?" I asked the stranger.

He tsked, shaking his head. "I asked you that first."

I eyed him suspiciously, not saying a word.

He exhaled in exasperation. "Listen, this game will go nowhere if we just keep asking questions without giving any answers. What's your name?"

That one was easy enough to answer without giving too much away. Maybe it'd help me get some information from him too?

"I'm Amber."

His features pinched in concentration, as if searching through his memory. "That doesn't tell me anything."

"Why should it?"

"Well, you are awake and made of flesh at night. That alone makes you special in the Kingdom of Dakath. Special enough to make you famous."

"I haven't been here for long. And I prefer not to broadcast my existence everywhere."

"Hmm." He gave me another one of his penetrating stares. "Clearly, you're not a gargoyle. You have hair instead of snakes on your head, which makes you not a gorgonian. I don't think you're a siren, either. It's way too far from any large body of water up here in the mountains. A werewolf, maybe? You seem snarky enough to be one."

I snorted a laugh. "I wish I was a werewolf. I could certainly use some sharp teeth and claws."

He picked up his lantern and lifted it to his eye level, then took a step closer. His eyes grew bigger as he studied my face.

"No. You're not a fae at all. By the Wings of Death, you're not from this world, are you?"

I dropped my gaze down, wondering how much I could tell

him. I didn't trust him, not even a little bit. But the sun wasn't up. The night was deep. Elex lay on the floor, helpless and vulnerable. I had to make sure this man didn't get any ideas about harming him or me.

However, he didn't need my answer this time.

"You're a human, aren't you?" He narrowed his eyes at me.

It was useless to deny it at this point.

"Yes, I am."

"Hm." He took his chin into his hand, regarding me with new interest. "I've heard of your kind but haven't met one before."

I shifted my weight to another foot, keeping close to Elex. "Yeah... Well, nice to meet you."

"We should talk," he determined. "Come with me."

He headed to the dark entrance of a side tunnel with the confidence of a man who was used to his orders being followed.

"Come where?" I didn't move from my spot.

He glanced over his shoulder.

"You have nothing to fear, my dear. I just want to talk. And I prefer to do it from the comfort of my chair. Not in this dark, tiny cage that reeks of sex." He wrinkled his nose in disgust.

My face heated. Was the scent that obvious?

"Give me your promise that I won't get hurt," I retorted.

He made a face. "I'd rather not. What if you trip on the way and twist your ankle? I don't want to die a horrible death over you being clumsy."

I widened my stance, rooted in place. "I'm not going anywhere without a promise from you."

He huffed in irritation but didn't leave me.

"I'll tell you what." He came closer, peering straight into my eyes. "I *promise* I have no intentions of harming you tonight."

A swirl of air rose from him to me. It curled around us, shimmering in the light of his lantern. I felt a faint breeze against my skin. He had given me a promise, sealed by magic.

Only how much was his promise really worth?

He said he had no intentions to hurt me. That didn't guarantee I *wouldn't* get hurt or that he wouldn't get the intentions later.

He obviously was aware his promise wasn't that reassuring because he kept talking, trying to convince me.

"Look at it this way, Amber. I didn't invite you to come here. You and your..." He twirled his hand over Elex. "...um, *gargoyle* dropped by on your own. You have no clothes. Very little food by the looks of it." He scowled at my deflated satchel. "I am in the position to help you. *If* I feel so inclined."

I wasn't opposed to having a conversation with him. I was burning with curiosity to find out more about this man who lived in a mountain and didn't turn to stone at night like everyone else did in this kingdom. Also, getting help would be nice. Unless this was a trap, of course.

"What's your name?" I asked.

"Voron," he answered promptly.

Giving him a warning stare, I crouched by Elex's head. He looked so peaceful and relaxed under the arch of his wings. But that was the reflection of how he had fallen asleep, not of what he might be feeling right now. I was sure he was awake and fully conscious inside his stone. He was probably freaking out about me leaving with someone I'd just met.

I stroked the stone waves of Elex's hair.

"This is Voron, my love. He is..." I glanced up at the man with the lantern. "What are you?"

He pointed a finger up at the ceiling of the cave, but I had a feeling he meant much higher than that. Higher than the mountain. "I'm a sky fae."

"Sky fae? Really?" I gawked at him, now fully understanding *his* shock at seeing *me*. "I've never met one of you before."

My desire to speak to him grew.

"Just give me a minute." I turned to Elex again. "Voron is a sky fae who lives in the Desolate Peak. If I'm not back by sunrise, find him and kill him, would you, darling?"

I moved my eyes back to Voron, making sure he'd heard every word. He arched an eyebrow, looking either impressed or amused.

I picked up my quiver with arrows. My bow remained back on the mountain where I'd dropped it. But at this distance, I didn't need a bow to jam an arrow into Voron's neck if I had to. Then I shoved my feet into my boots and stood tall to face the sky fae.

"Did you hear what I said to Elex? If something happens to me, he'll make you pay."

"Elex?" A flash of interest burned brighter in his eyes. He bent over, bringing the lantern closer to the stone face of my resting gargoyle. "*Lord* Elex? The king's favorite?"

Dammit. I cursed myself for letting the name slip. Voron might live here, but he clearly wasn't entirely isolated from the court life.

"Have you been to the Bozyr Peak?" I asked.

"No. But I try to stay informed."

"How?"

"I have my sources," he replied evasively, then straightened and headed to the tunnel again. "Are you coming now that my life has been sufficiently threatened?"

"Fine." With a last look at Elex's sleeping form, I followed the sky fae out of the cave.

Twenty

AMBER

Spreading its wings, Voron's bird leaped from his shoulder and flew ahead.

From the short, narrow tunnel, we entered a much wider one. It had a long red rug on the floor and a high, arched ceiling which made it look more like a hallway in a castle than a mountain tunnel. Rows of stone statues on each side of the tunnel strengthened that illusion.

Upon a closer look, I realized these weren't just statues, but gargoyles in their stone form.

I stopped in my tracks, feeling their eyes on me.

"Why are they here?"

Voron turned back over his shoulder, then glanced at the stone people on either side of us.

"They live here." He shrugged.

"With you?"

"Yes. Though I'm often just as confused as you are why anyone would want to put up with me." That was said with a hefty dose of sarcasm but not a trace of self-deprecation. Arrogance was strong in this man.

"Are they the king's men?" I asked cautiously.

All of them would come to life in the morning. If they served King Edkhar, it was best for Elex and me to be out of here at the first light of day.

"No," Voron bit off. The resentment in his steely stare at my mentioning the king gave me hope. "These are *my* men. The king didn't want them."

"He didn't? Why?"

"Look closely, Amber." He touched the shoulder of the gargoyle closest to us. "This man has no wings." He slid his fingers along the arm of another man, whose wings were out but their tips barely reached his elbows. "This one's wings are too small to carry him in flight. And this one..." He touched yet another statue, passing by. "His are the wrong shape. He can't fly far."

The wings of the third man appeared to lack the hard spines. The leather membrane hung loosely from the main bone of the wing that was its leading edge.

"And this one?" I pointed at a man who appeared to have perfectly shaped wings, proudly displayed over his shoulders.

"His magic is too weak to lift him. You do know it's not just the wings that make them fly?"

I knew that gargoyles cared about the type and strength of the magic they possessed.

Voron proceeded down the hallway.

"King Edkhar loves perfection. The men he finds lacking have no chance to succeed in his kingdom."

"So, they come to you for help?"

He exhaled a laugh. "No. I'm not their *rescuer*, dear Amber. Most of them were here before I came along."

That left me only more puzzled, but the hallway ended, and we entered a wide, tall cave that could rival King Edkhar's Great Hall in size. Instead of the crystals, however, bats squirmed silently under the high ceiling. Steady streams of them flew in and out through the cracks in the rock.

The view of the star-studded sky blinked outside the mountain.

Keeping a cautious eye on the bats, I followed Voron down the red rug across the room to a huge fireplace with a log burning inside. To my relief, there were no bats directly over this area. The creatures clearly preferred darker corners of the giant cave.

"Some wine?" Voron inquired, heading to a round table set between two high-backed armchairs in front of the fireplace. He lifted a crystal carafe with blood-red liquid glistening in it and gave me a questioning stare.

Wine seemed like a great idea. My nerves had been strung tight for days and my throat felt parched right now.

"Please." I nodded.

He paused with the carafe in his hand.

"You said you haven't been in Nerifir for long, didn't you?"

"Yes. Why?"

He calmly poured the wine into two tall crystal glasses. "You obviously don't know not to accept food or drink from a fae."

I lifted my left hand and wiggled my fingers. Elex's ruby ring caught the light from the fireplace, breaking it into a myriad of marvelous sparkles.

"I've got that covered."

"Oh," He raised an eyebrow in that curious expression of his. "Is the ring warded?"

"Yes, it is." I plopped into one of the armchairs by the fire, not waiting for an invitation.

Without Elex next to me, the night chill had found its way under Voron's cloak I was wearing. I stretched my legs toward the fire, soaking in the warmth radiating from it.

The large cave was dark and empty, save for this cozy area by the fire. In addition to the two armchairs and the table with wine, there was a thick rug on the floor. A large, painted trunk stood at the wall near the fireplace. With its lid open, a folded fur throw and an embroidered pillow came into view. A tall basket on the other side of the fireplace held hundreds of tightly wound scrolls with a stack of leather-bound books sitting on the floor next to it.

Voron must have a bed somewhere else, and there had to be dining and living areas for all the gargoyles. But this here clearly was his own personal space. I imagined him reading here in complete silence and solitude as the rest of the kingdom turned to stone at night.

"It's not a bad set-up you have here," I said, glancing around. "Despite the bats."

Voron scowled at the animals swarming in the corners of the ceiling above.

"Well, they have their uses," he admitted. "We've learned to co-exist."

I swirled the wine in my glass, admiring the colors of the liquid. If Voron meant to trap me by adding something to it, why warn me by telling me I shouldn't accept it?

Just in case, I waited until he had taken a sip from his glass first before taking a drink, too. The wine was light, warm, and a little tart, with a hint of sweetness. It slid easily down my throat. Way too easily. I made a note to pace myself.

Voron stretched his long legs in front of him, crossing them at the ankles. "So, Amber. What brought you into this wretched world?"

I smirked. "Not *what,* but *who.* Elex did."

"He stole you." He nodded, as if stealing people was a natural thing to do.

"No... Kind of... Well, actually, I stole him first." I shrugged awkwardly. "It's a long story."

He waved a hand, his elbow propped on the armrest of his chair. "I have time."

"Yeah, but I don't."

Before the sun was up, I had to figure out whether he meant help or threat. And act accordingly, hopefully, before Voron's people woke up.

"Fine," he conceded. "Let's get to the point, then. Why are

you here? Shouldn't you and your dragon be in the Bozyr Peak? Celebrating the victory with the king?"

"I've nothing to celebrate." I scoffed. "The king never showed me any kindness. And he was cruel to anyone who has."

"He was cruel to your friends?"

I'd been too careful to call anyone my friend. But despite my mistrust and caution, a few people in Dakath had found their way into my heart, along with Elex. To some degree, I grew to care about all the *salamandras* of the Sanctuary. Now, they all were dead because of King Edkhar's neglect and indifference. Or because of his spite. Did he send the women to that mountain to punish them for my actions?

I winced, rubbing my chest against the burning guilt rising inside. "King Edkhar is cruel to many people."

"Hm," Voron hummed noncommittally, taking another drink of his wine. "But isn't Lord Elex related to the king? Some say he's his bastard son..." He let the end of the last sentence hang in the air, as if inviting me to elaborate.

"Elex isn't his son. God forbid having a father like that," I muttered into my wine.

"But Lord Elex possesses the royal magic, does he not?"

I squinted at him. "You really are well-informed about life at the castle."

I expected another brush-off reply about some vague sources of his, but he rested his stare on me, explaining calmly, "A gargoyle named Trusad joined us a few days ago. He's painfully young, barely twenty, and still so very naïve. He came to the Bozyr Peak to offer his life to the king. Only, you see, Trusad was born without wings. Every now and then, it happens. The gods single a man out for some unknown purpose. The gods might have their reasons, but people are ignorant. Trusad was ostracized in his village."

"That's just cruel of the villagers."

Voron shrugged. "What is a dragon without wings but a lizard?"

I shot him a glare. "You're cruel, too."

My words didn't seem to faze him.

"Maybe I am. But I took Trusad in when King Edkhar kicked him out after a few days of keeping him in the dungeon below the castle. Such is the hospitality of the great king," Voron said sarcastically. "Anyway, Trusad happened to be in the dungeon when Lord Elex used royal magic against his jailers. Trusad didn't see it with his own eyes. He was in another cell, but he heard enough to understand what happened. Lord Elex is of royal blood. It's very easy to tell with gargoyles."

"Is it more difficult to tell with sky fae?"

"Yes. Our magic is far more complex," he dismissed, rather haughtily.

I chewed on my bottom lip. It was safe to assume Voron was honest about his source. He could've just as easily told me he learned about Elex from a servant, and it would've been believable enough. There was no need to make up such a detailed story.

"People can be related by blood," I said. "But it doesn't mean they're alike."

"Oh, that's so true," he said with a bitter smile that made me wonder what other stories this man might be hiding. "The royal blood, however, always comes with some claim to the throne."

"Elex is not interested in the throne."

Voron set his wine glass down. "He should be."

"King Edkhar isn't looking for someone to pass on his crown to any time soon. And even if he was, Elex isn't his heir."

"But he's the closest one the king has for an heir right now. And he certainly shouldn't wait until there's more competition."

I stared at him incredulously. "What do you want Elex to do? To start a riot? Hasn't there just been one? The rebels lost."

He flicked his wrist dismissively. "They were destined to lose. They had no cause."

"I heard the reason for the war was an insult to a woman's honor," I said.

"No." He moved his head from side to side. "Men don't fight

for women's honor, even if they say they do. In such cases, we fight only for our egos. But a bruised ego of one or two isn't enough of a motivation for the rest. The Rebel Lords never had a bright enough spark to give their armies a sufficient fire for the fight. That's why they lost."

I sipped my wine, watching the dancing flames in the fireplace.

"So, all of this was just a dick measuring contest? That's all there was behind this war?"

He smiled at my choice of words. "Behind any war, really."

"But how would a new rebellion be any different?"

"It wouldn't if you just replace one king with another. But it all depends on what kind of king Lord Elex would be."

"He'd be great."

I knew it in my heart. I might be way over my head at the very idea of plotting to overthrow the king. I had no clue what I was doing here. But one thing I was absolutely certain about—Elex could be the ruler this kingdom so badly needed.

"Elex was born to rule this place," I said passionately. "He has Dakath's interests at heart. Always has had. There is nothing he loves more than his kingdom."

Voron rested his chin on his hand.

"Oh, I bet there is something that he loves even more, Amber. Maybe not *something* but *someone*. Isn't that why he ended the day making love to you in my cave instead of playing politics in the Bozyr Peak?"

Elex loved me. I didn't doubt that. But was he making a sacrifice by planning to leave the castle with me? After all, the Bozyr Peak was his home. And the crown was his birthright.

Except that he couldn't have it now. Could he?

"Elex can't be the king, Voron. And it's not because of me. In fact, for Dakath's prosperity in the future, King Edkhar has to remain on the throne."

With both elbows on the armrests, he steepled his fingers. "And why is that?"

Was it the wine that kept me talking? Or was it that sharp intelligence shining in Voron's eyes? He seemed to have an answer to every question, and I wondered how he would handle the cave-in if I threw it at him.

I put my glass next to his, then leaned over the table toward him.

"Dakath does have a bright, prosperous future ahead of it. But King Edkhar has to stay where he is for that to happen. He is an asshole, don't get me wrong. Nothing good will come from this guy but his son, King Elex."

"Elex?" Voron echoed.

"Yes. My Elex... I mean *Lord* Elex was named after that particular ancestor of his."

"So, he's from the future." It wasn't a question. Voron didn't sound that surprised. By now, he must've connected all the dots, from my confession about Elex taking me from my world, which meant he'd crossed the River of Mists and traveled through time, to my referring to someone who hadn't even been born yet as his ancestor.

"Right." I turned to stare at the fire again. "You see how it complicates things? King Edkhar can't die. If he does, it would wipe out Elex's entire bloodline, including him. He just wouldn't exist. And Elex can't take the throne, because, well, he can't be his own great-grandfather, can he?"

"No. That wouldn't work," Voron agreed. "He can't father his own ancestor."

His chin on his hand, he stared into the flames with me.

I wondered why he was interested in all of this, anyway. True, he hadn't displayed much respect for King Edkhar during our conversation. Maybe he cared about his men at the Desolate Peak more than he liked to admit and hoped for prosperity and recognition for them under the new king?

"Anyway..." I took my glass again and emptied it in one sip. "Sorry for intruding on you. Elex and I will be gone first thing in the morning. If you do feel *inclined*, a clothing donation will be greatly appreciated. All I have to wear at the moment is the red *salamandra* robe. And I'm getting really, really tired of wearing it."

"Unless..." Voron refilled my glass, then handed it back to me, indicating he wasn't finished with the conversation. "Unless we won't kill King Edkhar."

We?

He really was into this, wasn't he?

"Well, yeah," I said. "*We* are not killing him."

"The king doesn't need to die. He just needs to lose his crown." He flicked his wrist, waving his hand as if knocking the Crown of Dakath off the king's head already.

"And how would you suggest we do that? Jail him?"

He tilted his head back, rubbing his chin.

"You see, the reason you want King Edkhar to stay alive is for him to have a son. But he doesn't have to be a king to father one. Challenge him, defeat him, lock him in one of the towers of the Bozyr Peak. Let him marry his betrothed. Or don't marry them. Make her visit him until the future comes true and she bears him a child. Then, you can take the baby and do with the parents as you please."

I stared at him, speechless.

"Huh... That simple, is it? These are real people you're talking about. King Edkhar may have deserved every consequence he'd be bringing upon his head. But how about his future wife? She is set to marry a king, and you want to reduce her marriage to some kind of conjugal visits in a tower? And the baby? You think it's okay to kill his parents—"

He stopped me by lifting a finger.

"I didn't say 'kill.' Though..." he added casually. "I have to admit, I'd prefer them both dead by that point."

I didn't know much about the king's future bride, Lady Amree, other than what the king had told me about her, and it wasn't good. But I couldn't agree with this plan.

"Voron, we're talking about real people here," I repeated. "Living, breathing, feeling people."

He waved his hand at me.

"Well, you see, that's the difference between you and me, dear Amber. I prefer to view them as political figures. Kings and queens are just game pieces on my board. And to me, this looks like an excellent plan. All you'll have to do to go along with it is to find the moral reasoning that suits you." He heaved a sigh. "Honestly, ethics only hinder politics."

"Elex would never agree to this."

He glanced at one of the openings under the ceiling where the sky had grown lighter. The bats had settled into the corners. Only the last few were still making their way in.

"I guess we could ask Lord Elex himself soon."

He leaned back into his chair, his glass of wine dangling in his long, elegant fingers.

Curiosity finally got the best of me. "What's *your* story, Voron? How did you get to Dakath? And why are you staying here?"

He rolled his head my way on the high back of his chair. His hair was in disarray, yet it didn't look messy. It was black, like the feathers of his bird that perched on the back of his chair. The white strands in the front looked like streaks of moonlight at night.

Voron was a beautiful man, like all fae. But there was something unsettling in his cold gray eyes. It made staring straight into them difficult.

"You want to hear my story?" he asked.

"I'd love to."

"Why?"

I had to admit, I was curious. He was the first non-gargoyle I'd met in Dakath. And the way this kingdom was—inhospitable to outsiders—he and I were probably the only two people in the entire Dakath Mountains who didn't turn to stone at night.

"Don't you think I should know more about the man I may be plotting to overthrow the king with?" I quipped.

A smile played on his lips as he finished his wine.

Something stomped out in the hallway, then more stomping and clanking came.

Voron got out of his chair.

"My story will have to wait for another day, dear Amber. I'm afraid we're out of time. The sun is here. Your gargoyle is waking up. And so are mine."

Twenty-One

AMBER

"No." Elex shook his head. "King Edkhar can burn in a thousand fires, for all I care. But his bride is innocent of his crimes."

I gave Voron an I-told-you-so look. He sat in the entrance to the small cave where Elex had spent the night. We had come here after breakfast to have a conversation out of earshot of Voron's men. As predicted, Elex had a problem with Voron's ruthless plan.

I half-expected Voron to ridicule Elex's morals or ethics in retaliation, but he just stared out into the morning sky, twirling between his fingers a long-stemmed poppy flower that he'd gotten from God knew where.

Elex sat across from Voron, at the opposite end of the entrance to the cave, with his back against the wall. He had me on his left thigh, his arm securely wrapped around my waist like a seat belt.

He hadn't found me by his side in the morning and had been all set to do as I'd asked him. Naked and fuming with rage, he was on his way to murder Voron when I'd run into him on my way back to our cave. Now, he wouldn't let me out of his sight or out of his arms.

The men of the Desolate Peak had found some clothes for us. Elex was dressed in one of Voron's white frilly shirts and a pair of black velvet pants. And I had an outfit that must've belonged to a teenage dragon, because it almost fit me. The brown suede pants were just a little loose at the waist but the belt fixed it. In addition to a soft cotton tunic, I also got a breast plate constructed from embossed strips of leather. The strips were held together by vertical lacing. When I'd adjusted and tightened all the laces, the whole thing hugged my torso like a corset.

I bit into the jam-filled pastry. One of Voron's men had made lots of these for breakfast. They were so good, I had to take one with me after the breakfast had ended. Voron clearly made sure his men ate well.

"How are you their leader, Voron?" I asked when the conversation had stalled after Elex's definite rejection of Voron's plan. "You said you came here when they already had a group formed. Didn't they already have a leader then?"

He winced, obviously not enjoying reminiscing about his past.

"I'm not their savior, Amber. Never was. My men are the ones who rescued me. I haven't been their leader for long. I was far too young to lead anyone when I first came to Dakath."

"How young? Were you a child?"

That bred even more questions. Unfortunately, Voron didn't look inclined to answer any of them. He spun the flower in his hands, staring away before turning to Elex.

"That's not to say that my men don't need *a true* leader," he said. "They are an army without a general."

"But aren't *you* their general?" I asked again.

He brought the poppy to his nose and inhaled deeply, then stroked its crimson petals with his long fingers.

"I have no cause for them to follow. I've no goal in Dakath, no aspiration. I'm content just where I am. But they aren't." He tipped his head back toward the tunnels where his men were going about their daily routine. "They need a purpose. And *you* can give it to them." He pinned Elex with his steel-gray stare.

Elex's chest rose with a deep breath, but he said nothing as Voron continued, "You are of royal blood. You could be the just, noble king Dakath needs. And it needs one *now*. Not a century or so into the future." He tossed the flower out of the cave, then leaned toward Elex and me. "The future isn't written in stone. Otherwise, we'd all be just moving along like puppets in a play. The future is not a detailed picture. It is but a sketch, left for us to fill it in with color and substance. It can be tweaked. You have the power to make life better for your people, Lord Elex. Use it. Why wait?"

Elex returned his stare. "What's in it for you, Lord Voron?"

The sky fae smiled, reclining against the wall again. "Let's say I feel like I owe a debt to my men for saving me so many years ago. I can't repay them, but I wish for them to have a better life."

"Is that it?" Elex sounded skeptical.

Voron's smile stretched wider. "There may be one more thing. I'll give you an army in exchange for a royal favor."

"I'm no king."

"You may be one day. I won't collect on the promise until you are."

"What kind of favor?" Elex didn't look enthusiastic about that request.

Voron vaguely waved his hand in the air. "I haven't decided yet. I just want you to promise that you will fulfill a wish of mine, any wish, once the time comes."

Elex laughed, shaking his head. "I'll give you no such promise."

Voron jerked an eyebrow up. He looked disappointed but not overly surprised. Really, what fae would agree to tie their life to a promise like that? It was way too vague.

No fae would. But I wasn't a fae.

"Will you take *my* promise instead, Voron?" I asked.

"Amber. No." Warning sounded in Elex's voice as he held me to him tighter.

"Human promises don't come with the grim consequences like the fae's do," I reminded them both. "Nothing binds us to fulfill a promise but our honor. I'll make the deal with you, Voron. But you'll have nothing to hold me to it. You'll just have to trust that I'll fulfill my part of the bargain."

Voron's calculating stare focused on me. Of course, he didn't trust me. Why would he? He barely knew me. This was a gamble for him. But I hoped he would take the risk. After all, wasn't it just a game for him, and we all were his game pieces?

"Well…" His eyes measured me as if assessing my worth. "I said I needed a *royal* favor. I see no reason why it couldn't come from the queen rather than from the king."

The queen?

I shot a glance at Elex over my shoulder. His eyes held a promise of their own, a promise I didn't need him to voice. No matter what happened, we were together, he and I, either as vagabonds, hiding in some distant parts of Nerifir or, as it might be, the royalty of Dakath.

Voron chuckled, rubbing his hands together. "It's a deal, dear Amber. Your man now has an army if he wishes to use it."

Elex huffed a breath, not pleased by the pressure.

I stirred in his arms, racking my brain for a compromise.

"Can we maybe wait with the attack until after the king's wedding and the baby's arrival?"

Voron frowned at my words.

"If you do anything at all, it has to be now, while the king's men are drunk on wine and yesterday's victory. If you wait, they'll sober up. The king will replenish their ranks after the losses of the last battle. You'll miss your chance. Remember, my people can't fly. They can't meet the king's army in the open without risking being slaughtered by the king's dragons from the sky. You have to give them every advantage there is."

"How long will it take them to make it to the Bozyr Peak castle on foot?" Elex asked.

"Hours. They'll be there by noon if they head out now. They stand a much better chance in an indoor fight, as they'd be fighting men, not dragons, in the castle's rooms."

"They'd never make it inside," I sighed. "They'd be slaughtered at the castle walls."

Elex rubbed his jaw. "I control the magic of the Bozyr Peak. If I get inside, I can open all its gates, drop down the bridges, and blast the shutters out of the windows. All at once."

Hope bloomed in my chest. Maybe it could be done? I thought about the crumbling part of the inner castle wall I'd used to get out to practice my arrow shooting skills.

"If you fly me over the outer wall, I'll help you sneak in through a side door by the kitchen."

"No, I don't want you to get involved," Elex declined quickly.

"I'm very much involved already, don't you think?"

He shook his head adamantly. "I want you to stay away from the castle, Amber, in a safe place."

I tilted my head, asking sweetly, "And what *safe place* would that be, darling? Tell me. How safe do you think I'd be anywhere away from you? Whom would you trust to keep me safe more than yourself?"

"Amber," he groaned, because he knew I was right. There was no better place for me than at his side.

Hugging me with both arms from behind, he buried his face in my shoulder. I felt the turmoil raging inside him. His need to keep me close fought with his fear of putting me in harm's way. But I felt the same way about him. I needed to be where he was.

Placing my hands over his, I laced our fingers together. "I'll stay out of your way, promise. And I'll take care of myself. I'll keep out of danger. I won't rush into a battle. You won't have to worry about me."

I kept feeding him promises like candies. He knew I wasn't

facing the risk of death if I didn't keep them, but I hoped hearing them assuaged his worries anyway.

With a deep breath in, he loosened his tight grip around me a little.

"Here is what we'll do," Elex sounded firm and determined, taking charge. "We'll attack today. King Edkhar will lose his crown, but he'll keep his life. As will his bride. Until their son is born, they'll be held as guests at the Bozyr Peak if they cooperate, or as prisoners if they don't. You..." He cupped my face with one hand. "You will come with me to the castle walls, but will stay out of the castle until it's safe to come in. Do you understand? The fight will take place inside."

I nodded.

He caressed the side of my face, staring into my eyes intently. "You'll hide in the same spot where you used to shoot your arrows. This battle will take place on the ground, not in the air. That section of the castle's wall is inaccessible by land, there'll be no action there. It'll be the safest. Stay there, out of sight, until I come for you."

The intensity of his focus and concern zapped through me, making my spine stiffen and my chest tighten, but I nodded again, managing a reassuring smile.

"I'll be fine," I said, and repeated, "you don't have to worry about me."

God knew he'd have plenty of things to worry about today without me adding to that.

Bending his leg, Voron hung his arm over his knee. "Having the former king and his wife as guests at your castle is a bad idea. They'll plot against you, and sooner or later, they will strike."

"Then, I'll kill them both," Elex said simply. "If they try to hurt me or mine, I'll retaliate without mercy."

I was against murder, but it was safe to assume that even if defeated, King Edkhar wouldn't accept the part of a house guest in his own castle that easily. He'd need to be watched closely.

"As you wish," the sky fae conceded. "If that's the moral

ground that makes you comfortable enough to accept over-throwing the king, so be it."

"Either way, we're getting ahead of ourselves," Elex said. "Neither the castle nor the crown are mine yet."

With his arm around my middle, he got up. Caught in his grip, I hung like a rag doll with my feet dangling above the ground.

"Um... Darling. I know you'd like to schlep me around like your favorite teddy bear. But could you please trust me to walk on my own two feet?"

"Sorry, my spark." He set me on the ground.

Voron got up, too. Shaking the dust off his black velvet pants, he gave us an amused glance.

"I need to talk to your men," Elex said.

The sky fae nodded. "That you do."

"Who are you?" A red-haired gargoyle asked.

Thousands of Voron's men were tightly packed into the spacious cave under the Desolate Peak. Thousands more filled the adjoining tunnels. A large number of them clung to the mountain from the outside, peeking through the large cracks and wide openings in the rock.

Voron stood back, not saying a word. He'd made it clear this wasn't his war or his battle. If Elex wanted his men to fight and die for him, he was the one to convince them to accept him as their leader.

"I'm Elex, the Crown Prince of the Dakath Mountains," he boldly introduced himself with his rightful title.

"Prince?" The gargoyle narrowed his eyes suspiciously.

"That's Lord Elex," someone shouted from the crowd. "The king's favorite."

Elex smirked. "No longer a favorite. Not after I went against the king yesterday." He moved his gaze over the many faces turned to him. "I have a rightful claim to Dakath's throne. And I need your help to take it. I want you to storm the Bozyr Peak with me."

A murmur rolled among the men.

"And why would we do that?" another gargoyle asked. This one was shirtless with only two leather belts crisscrossing his broad chest.

"Because you are warriors." Elex raised his voice. "Strong and capable. Warriors who, until now, have been denied every chance to prove yourselves in battle. I'm giving you that chance."

A man with a russet brown beard tamed into braids scoffed, "One battle to get you on the throne? Then what?"

Elex met his stare straight on.

"Then, you can do as you please. If you wish to remain in my royal army, I'll gladly keep you. Under my rule, you will be judged based on the kind of men you are, your loyalty and your courage, not on the size of your wings or the lack of them. That is my promise to you."

The murmur among the men grew louder as a wave of magic spread through the room, sealing Elex's promise.

As his words echoed through the giant cave, I watched the faces of the men he tried to rouse to go into battle for him. Some stared at him gloomily. Suspicion was still clearly visible in the eyes of many. But there was also hope. A spark of excitement lit up their faces as the magic of Elex's promise drifted through the air.

The man with the belt-crossed torso spat on the floor, then folded his arms across his wide chest. "When do you want to storm the castle?"

"Today."

Shocked sounds rolled through the crowd.

"We'd head out right now," Elex clarified.

"Now?" Several men exclaimed at once, their astonishment resonating through the crowd.

Elex took a wider stance. "Why not?"

The man with the braided beard shook his head. "Isn't that too soon?"

"What's your name?" Elex asked him.

"Gabrik."

"How much time have you spent in the Desolate Peak so far, Gabrik?"

"A hundred and twenty-four years."

"Has it not been enough? How much longer do you need to stay here before you take a chance to leave? A few more days? Months?" Elex propped his hands on his hips with a teasing glint in his eyes. "Should I come back in a year or two?"

The man grumbled something under his breath as others laughed.

"The sooner we attack, the higher our chances to win," Elex explained, his expression turning serious again. "King Edkhar thinks the war is over. I don't want to give him any time to recover from yesterday's battle and to replenish his army."

At the sound of King Edkhar's name, men cursed and spat.

"I want him alive," Elex warned. "You have every right to hate him for the way he's been treating you. But this is very important. The king has to stay alive."

Twenty-Two

ELEX

He would have reached the Bozyr Peak in minutes had he flown. But he chose to hike on foot alongside his men. Only when the king's castle walls rose above them did he unfurl his wings.

"I'll sneak in to open all the doors and gates," he told Voron. "Lead them to the main gates of the castle, then have them spread out once inside the walls."

The sky fae nodded, adjusting the ruffled cuff of his silk shirt.

Elex had been a little surprised to see Voron come along. He'd expected him to stay behind and let the gargoyles fight their wars on their own. But the sky fae must have grown too bored after the years spent in the gloomy Desolate Peak to miss out on the action.

Like the rest of them, Voron had walked, though he certainly could have flown instead. Sky fae came in all shapes and sizes. Some had tails, horns, or even hooves. Those who looked like Voron were called "highborn." All the highborn had wings. Elex imagined Voron hid his, just like gargoyles did.

Voron had kept up with the marching pace Elex had set

without a complaint. And now, he took his orders without pushing back.

Elex searched his army for the bearded man, Gabrik. He spotted him nearby and gestured for him to come closer. The man proved resilient, keeping to the front of the line all the way from the Desolate Peak. Elex needed his caution to counteract the sky fae's coldblooded determination.

"Voron will take half of the men south around the castle," he said to Gabrik. "Take the other half and circle the Bozyr Peak from the north. Spread out and use every door, window, and gate you can find to get in the moment they open. But stay away from them when they're closed. My opening them won't be safe for anyone nearby."

Amber stepped forward, adjusting the new bow on her shoulder, Voron's gift. She had mostly kept up with the gargoyles. Elex had only managed to talk her into allowing him to carry her once for a short period of time during their long, grueling hike.

"I'll show you a way to sneak in," she said.

He nodded somberly. The last thing he wanted was to drag her back into the hornet's nest of the king's castle. But he agreed it was best for them to stay close to each other.

He drew her slender body into his, wrapped his arms around her, and took off. He flew low, staying in the shadows cast by the surrounding rocks and avoiding the lookouts.

The main gate in the castle's outer wall was closed. It usually was kept open during the day to let in the merchants from the valley or to allow the female servants to move in and out of the castle a little easier. Only the many gates in the inner wall were usually closed and guarded during the day.

The lack of guards at the locked main gate told Elex it wasn't closed out of extra precaution today, but probably because no one cared to open it that morning. The king and his men must be celebrating heavily. And the guards and servants would be busy catering to them.

Once he reached the spot where Amber used to practice with

her bow and arrows, he flew over the castle's outer wall. No one stopped them. Clearly, King Edkhar felt confident after his victory, letting the security slack.

"There is a breach over there," Amber said, leading him to the spot where the inner wall had crumbled. The remaining part of it was so low, there was no need for him to use his wings. They climbed over it, then she led him to a similarly dilapidated wooden door low on the side of the castle.

"Lots of things need to be fixed around here," Amber observed.

They certainly did. It hurt him to see the signs of neglect and ruin in his family home. King Edkhar's resources had been clearly spent elsewhere.

He placed his hand on the door. The warm touch of the castle's magic was like a handshake of a friend. He used a tendril of it to turn the lock open. The hinges didn't screech when he shoved against the door.

"I put some lard on these," Amber explained, touching the metal scrolls of the hinges. "They're pretty rusty and used to be very noisy."

A smile tugged at his mouth, tenderness spreading through his chest with warmth. He wished he could kiss her. Only a kiss could cost them both their lives. Just past the narrow passage behind the door, life boiled over with the noises of running feet, clanking of dishes, and yelling between the servants. It was the time of the royal midday meal, which was at full swing, by the sound of it. The king prided himself on his celebrations, and the end of a decades-long war would be a great cause to celebrate hard.

Keeping an eye on the end of the corridor, he drew his sword. He planned to blast all the doors, gates, and windows open at once, not leaving anything to chance. But for that, he had to get to the middle of the castle, to use the magic at its core.

"Be safe," Amber whispered, gripping her bow so tight, her knuckles paled.

The pleading look in her eyes made him forget about everything for a moment. Grabbing her chin in his hand, he kissed her, all danger be damned. She half-whimpered, half-moaned against his lips, then staggered back when he let her go, her hands fisted in his shirt on his chest.

His voice was coarse, his throat tight when he told her, "Stay close to the wall. Out of sight."

She nodded before quietly slipping behind the door and heading back toward the crack in the inner wall. A part of him stayed with her. But he could focus a little better, knowing she was in relative safety out of the castle that was about to be attacked.

The servants scurried out of his way when he exited the corridor. They either hadn't heard about him attacking their king or didn't know what to do about the king's former favorite. Startled, they kept quiet, letting him through.

That wouldn't last long. Sooner or later, someone would let the guards know he was in the castle. He had to hurry.

He ran up the tower stairs to the floor with the Throne Room. Located in the very heart of the Bozyr Peak, this room was used by his father for all formal functions and many family celebrations. Elex had yet to see King Edkhar use it for anything. But the royal guards were there. Six of them were lined up along the wall by the carved double doors.

"Get him!" Pointing their weapons at him menacingly, they moved his way.

He touched the nearest wall, calling on the magic of the mountain that the royal castle was carved into. It tingled under his palm with a burst of sparks between his fingers.

"Stand back," he warned the guards. "Unless you wish to burn to death."

They hesitated, but only for a moment. These six must've not heard about what he did in the dungeon the day he became the "king's favorite." Either that or their memory was short.

He met their first attack with his sword, not wishing to waste the magic on the guards. Using the magic depleted his strength, and he still had a lot of gates and windows to open. He managed to stab a guard through his heart and slashed another one across his chest. The remaining four swarmed him, with more guards running down the hall to their aid.

Someone hit the back of his legs, dropping him onto his knees. He splayed his hands on the floor and sent a swell of fire in a circle around him.

The guards didn't get a chance to scream, instantly bursting into flames. The stench of burned flesh filled the hallway, drifting from the piles of their ashes on the floor.

He shoved the Throne Room's doors open. The large room was completely deserted. The high throne platform with stairs carved into it stood empty. The throne had been moved to the Great Hall with the *biqirelle* crystals under the ceiling where King Edkhar preferred to spend most of his time, drinking with his men and "celebrating" with *salamandras*.

The black granite floor of the Throne Room was inlaid with blood-red garnets that made the image of a flame curled into a circle in the middle of the room. Here, the magic was the strongest.

In the center of the circle, Elex got down on one knee and pressed both hands to the floor. The stone vibrated, both with magic and from the approaching footsteps outside of the room— the king's men were coming.

He took a deep breath, reaching deep through the castle and into the mountain it was carved into. Across time and through distance, he merged with the long line of his ancestors—his family.

The magic coursed through his veins, seeping through his fingers. Sparks scattered along the floor like gemstones. Through the rock of the mountain, he drew the ancient flames toward him. Then forced them out along the floor and through the walls.

The fiery explosion thundered under the tall ceiling, shaking every wall of the castle. Flames shot through the doors, incinerating the king's men who were rushing in. Window shutters exploded everywhere. The echo of the crash resonated through all floors of the Bozyr Peak as every single window, door, and gate burst open.

Sunshine flooded the Throne Room. Screams and the clanking of weapons sounded from the lower floors as his people moved in. The Bozyr Peak was under attack by the men who'd been banished from here before, found lacking and useless by their king.

Now they'd returned. With a vengeance.

Elex tried to get up. His legs refused to hold him, sending him back to his knees. Using the Dakath magic had consequences. He'd never reached the limit before. And now it seemed that he had.

With his hands on the floor, he breathed deeply, gathering his strength.

He felt a tug against his fingers. The power flowed away from him, following the call of another. Elsewhere in the castle, King Edkhar wished to tap into their family magic, too.

Closing his eyes, Elex willed the power to remain in his command, defying the king's call.

Generation after generation, royal matches were carefully selected to breed more powerful monarchs. With three generations between them, Elex was that much stronger than his great-great-grandfather.

His arms shook. His teeth clenched, he held on to what was his by birthright, not letting the king use Dakath power against the men storming the castle.

His vision dimmed, his head spinning. Red sparks appeared out of nowhere, dancing before his eyes. Finally, the king's pull on the other end ceased.

And Elex crashed, collapsing to the floor.

Twenty-Three

AMBER

An explosion boomed through the air. The mountain shook. I cowered under the wall. Splinters of wood, rocks, and metal rained down, hitting the walls and getting stuck in the stone.

I knew it was Elex wreaking havoc. I hoped it was him. But my mind just couldn't comprehend how one person, no matter how royal or magical, could cause so much noise and devastation.

The battle cry of his men announced the attack of the castle. From every door and any window they could reach, the men of the Desolate Peak were storming in.

My back pressed to the outer wall, I looked up at the black mass of the castle. All its shutters were gone. The windows gaped open, like sightless eye sockets. Against the bright, sunny sky, the black walls and towers of the king's castle appeared especially dark and evil. With no glass in the windows, the Bozyr Peak looked like a skeleton of a building. Soulless and neglected.

A large shadow stretched across the rocks, moving from the castle. Instinctively, I grabbed my bow and drew an arrow out of my quiver.

A dragon flew above me. With the sun directly behind him, I didn't recognize him. I couldn't even tell what color his scales were.

Until he flew past the sun. Then, I knew exactly who he was.

King Edkhar's crimson scales reflected the sunlight, blinding me for a moment. I hid my eyes behind my arm. And when I looked at him again, the dragon-king swerved off his course, soaring my way.

He'd seen me.

No, no, no... I backed away from the approaching dragon.

Fear seized my heart with cold, bony fingers. But my hands didn't shake when I nocked the arrow and lifted the bow.

Sunspots still flashed in front of my eyes. I blinked to chase them away and squinted, taking aim.

I'd killed a dragon once. I could do it again.

Only I couldn't kill this one, could I? If the king died, so would Elex...

Now, my hands trembled.

The dragon plunged toward me. I retreated all the way to the wall, pressing my back against the cool stone. He couldn't snatch me from here. The space between the inner and the outer walls in this part of the castle wasn't wide enough for his wingspan.

The shape of the dragon-king shrank and shifted. The man, not the dragon, landed on the cobblestones in front of me.

"You!" King Edkhar launched my way.

Fury rolled off him like a cloud of heat. He was angry, so angry that burning me from afar wouldn't be enough. He itched to end me with his own hands.

I jumped out of his reach. My bow dropped to the cobblestones. The arrow caught, dangling in my fingers.

"You'll pay for your sick little joke, human pest," the king gritted through his teeth.

He hadn't forgotten my leashing him. I didn't think he ever would.

With a giant leap, he caught me by the throat. I gasped for air, gripping his hand with mine. His hold was unyielding, like a tight iron collar around my neck.

Iron...

I had the arrow in my hand. My fingers tightened around it, gripping it just past the arrowhead.

Elex's voice echoed in my mind, the words he'd said as he'd held my hand with his dagger at his neck, *"Aim it here where the blood pulses, carrying the fire of life."*

Holding me by my neck, the king lifted me off the ground. "I'll enjoy squeezing every last drop of life out of you, wretched little rat."

My feet kicked uselessly against the wall behind me. My lungs burned, starved for air. My vision blurred as I tried to focus on that one spot on the side of his neck.

Where the blood pulses...

Lifting my hand, I struck.

The sharp arrowhead went into the flesh smoothly. Warm blood sprayed my hand. The king's emerald-green eyes widened. He was shocked I fought back.

Red sparks of Nerifir iron burst from the wound around the arrowhead. Releasing his grip, the king staggered back. I dropped to my knees, coughing and rubbing my neck.

I couldn't leave the arrow in his wound. I couldn't allow the iron to poison his blood.

I couldn't kill the king.

Unsteady on my feet, I lurched after him and grabbed the arrow, yanking it out of his neck. He pressed his hand to the wound, blood pulsing between his fingers.

Fae weren't easy to kill, were they? He couldn't die.

"Live, asshole," I spat out, breaking the bloodied arrow over my knee.

The king snarled. Spreading his arms, he grew in size, shifting back to his dragon form. Opening his wings as far as the walls allowed, he lifted off the ground.

A battle cry suddenly came from above, in a high, feminine voice. A dark figure leaped off the wall—muscular and graceful.

Isar!

She shifted into her salamander mid-jump and collided with the dragon in the air. Her curved claws pierced the scales of his underbelly.

"Isar, no!" I yelled.

But there was no stopping her. She growled and tore at the king-dragon. Golden-red scales rained down like shards of sunlight. Blood sprayed the black rocks of the walls. Her teeth glistened with poison when she sunk them into the king's flesh.

The dragon lurched to the side. His wings broke their rhythm. He crashed to the cobblestones between the walls, taking Isar with him. They rolled on the ground, locked in a deadly embrace.

I splayed myself against the wall, trying to get away. The dragon's tail lashed out, sweeping me off my feet. In a last desperate move, he threw Isar off him. And stilled.

"No, no..." I got up on all fours as the dragon's body turned into a man.

The naked king lay on the black cobblestones. His dragon horns morphed into the royal crown, and it rolled off his head, clinking on the stones. His torso had been ripped open. Shimmering steam of the venom was rising from the wounds.

Dead.

The king was dead.

"Elex." I pressed a fist to my chest. Inside it, the spark of him had lived, a part of him. Was it still there? I wasn't sure I could feel it. Was it buried deep in the rubble of the cold terror and ache?

Or was it gone?

As the dragon shrank, the black and gold salamander came into view just behind him. She shifted into a woman.

Was she dead too?

"Isar." I crawled past the dead king to her.

A long gash from the dragon-king's claws gaped on her side.

Red blood glistened like rubies against her dark skin. Her eyes were open, staring straight up into the bright spring sky. A smile played on her lips covered with blood and poison.

"Isar..." I cupped her cheek gently.

Sunshine filled her brown eyes with so much gold they looked amber. She turned them to me. Recognition warmed her expression. Her smile spread wider.

"I got my revenge, little human. For both Ertee and me..."

"For all of them, Isar," I whispered as tears welled in my eyes. "You avenged them all."

Her chest rose with a deep, labored breath. She winced, pressing her hand over the wound on her side.

"Now, I can finally rest." Her golden eyes closed.

Tears burned my eyes. "No, Isar, please don't go..."

I rocked on my knees at her side, my hands pressed to my chest.

The day grew darker as another shadow came between us and the sun with the rustling of wings.

"Amber!" came from the sky.

"Elex?" I leaped to my feet.

He landed and stepped over the body of the dead king on his way to me.

"Are you hurt?" He took my face between his hands, brushing my tears away with his thumbs. "What hurts? Where?"

"I'm fine. Are *you?*" I gripped his arms, then his shoulders, then placed my hands on his cheeks. "How are *you* feeling?"

I studied his beloved face for signs...of what? Fatigue? Decline? Death?

Would he just disappear into thin air now, slipping between my fingers like the most wonderful dream?

I dug my fingers into his shoulders, determined to hold on tight.

"The king is dead, Elex. God..." I exhaled a shuddering breath. "I'm scared." I held on to him so tightly, if he weren't a fae, it'd certainly hurt. "Please, stay with me."

"The king is dead..." he echoed mechanically.

He glanced at the dead body behind him, as if seeing it for the first time, then stared straight ahead of him. His eyes appeared unseeing, as if he were looking inside not out, searching his body for *the signs*, too.

"How are you feeling?" I asked again. My voice was so quiet, I barely heard myself.

He was alive. I didn't know how. Or for how long. But as long as Elex was here and breathing, I was afraid to move a single molecule in the Universe, afraid to change it all for the worse.

"I feel fine. Better than a little while ago, that's for sure." He blinked, glancing around. With a deep breath, focus and confidence returned to his expression. His gaze fell on Isar. "Who is the woman?"

I drew in some air, too, trying to gain a modicum of control over my fear. We couldn't just sit around waiting for the effects of the king's death to appear.

"It's Isar. The venomous one I told you about." Worry thudded in my chest as I kneeled next to her again. "She's hurt. Badly. She needs help."

If it's not too late.

Elex crouched by Isar and placed a hand on her neck, to the spot where "the fire of life pulsed."

Please, let it not be too late.

"She'll need a healer." He got up.

Holding on to the wall, I climbed to my feet, too. "All the *salamandras* of the Sanctuary are dead... Is there anyone else in the castle who can heal?"

"The royal hag—"

A blast of fire from the sky hit the wall above us. Rocks exploded. The pieces of wreckage crashed into the wall below, hitting the ground.

"Hide!" Elex jumped aside.

He spread his arms wide, looking up, as if inviting the fire to follow him, leading the danger away from Isar and me.

Several dragons circled over the passage between the two walls where we were. I recognize one of them as the High General by his charcoal-gray scales and his single eye.

What were they doing here? Searching for their king? Did they come to avenge his death? Or were they on the hunt for Elex?

Either way, it didn't look good for us. There were at least half a dozen of them that I could see. Maybe more. They were gliding and hovering over the castle walls like vultures.

Elex jogged farther away. He needed more space to shift.

The High General dove down from the group. His wings folded behind him, he propelled downwards at an astonishing speed, aiming for Isar and me.

I scrambled for my bow, then reached back for an arrow. But there was no time.

The dragon's mouth opened with a blast of fire shooting at me.

"Amber!" Elex bellowed.

I dropped my weapon and leaned over Isar, crossing my arms over my head in a pathetic effort to shield us both from the fire that burned people faster than candle wicks.

No.

This couldn't be it.

Everything inside me rebelled against dying like this. After everything I'd been through. After all that I'd survived. I didn't want to die. Not now. I spread my fingers wide, as if I could hold the wall of fire crashing down on us.

And suddenly, I could...

I held it.

The fire paused, as if hitting an invisible shield. Then it rolled over the outer wall of the castle and down the mountain, leaving us unharmed. My hands tingled in an odd way. But that was the only consequence of the blast. The fire was gone. The sky above us was clear once again.

I had no idea what had just happened, staring at my hands in shock.

With a deafening roar, Elex shifted into his dragon and took off into the sky. I *felt* his fury at my attacker. It burned through my chest. Elex was ruthless, crashing into the High General head on. He didn't even bother with fire, using his teeth and claws to rip the other dragon's throat out.

But Elex was largely outnumbered. The rest of the dragons homed in on him. Five against one.

Using the crumbling part of the inner wall, I climbed up to the very top to get as high to the sky and to Elex as I could.

The dragons met him with blasts of fire, turning the sky red. Black smoke churned, obscuring them from view.

Elex breathed fire, too. Stretching my arms up above my head, I reached for it, wishing to make it bigger, stronger, enough for him to fight against five dragons and more.

Miraculously, a lick of his flame separated from the blast. As the rest of it died out, dissipating into the cloud of black smoke, that one flame leaped my way, burning stronger than ever.

"Amber, hide!" Elex's voice boomed from the sky.

I felt his panic. His worry for me crushed my chest like a mountain. But this was *his* fire. No part of him could ever hurt me. I didn't know how I knew that, but I did.

The flame stretched from him to me like a bright, fiery serpent. I caught it with one hand and spun it into a circle over my head. It curled gracefully, like a ribbon, silently following my command.

The fight above halted as all the dragons watched me in awe. All six of them, including Elex.

I was in awe myself, spinning the ring of fire over my head like a giant hula hoop.

The king's dragons recovered quickly. One of them opened his mouth, ready to send a blast at Elex. I flicked my wrist, sending a small tendril of my flame his way. Slick and agile, the flame slinked down the dragon's throat. He choked as it burned him from the inside. His wings faltered, and he dropped from the sky, rolling down the mountain.

"Ha!" I kept spinning the fire over my head like a performer in some devious circus. "Who else wants some?"

The dragons regrouped. Two of them flew higher. Two tried to attack Elex from below. It looked like they wanted to lure him away from me. To separate us.

"Nice try." I moved along the wall to stay right below him.

Worlds had not separated Elex and me. The River of Mists hadn't pulled us apart. There was nothing that would keep us away from each other now.

Diving under his attackers, Elex flew to me.

"Climb up." He hovered next to the wall where I stood.

I jumped onto his shoulders, then straddled him, my legs on each side of his neck. As he took off again, I split my fire circle into two, one for each hand.

Elex turned his large head my way. For one tiny moment our eyes met. The awe in his expression was mixed with pride. His eyes twinkled.

"The one on the right is yours, my fire bender." He breathed fire at the dragon on his left.

The moment the one on the right opened his mouth, I flicked my hand. The ring of fire slipped from my wrist like a Frisbee. Smaller and less dramatic than a dragon's blast, it slid through the air, attracting little attention. It leaped into the dragon's throat, making him choke. He rolled in the air, his wings wrapping into a funnel.

Before his body even hit the rocks below, the remaining dragons stood back. Making a wide circle around us, they took off, away from the Bozyr Peak.

"That's right!" I yelled, bouncing on Elex's neck. "Get out of here." I tossed the remaining fire circle after them. "And don't ever come back!"

Twenty-Four

AMBER

A cloaked figure entered the royal chamber and approached the king's massive bed where Elex had brought Isar.

"Can you heal her, Grandmother?" he asked.

The woman fisted the folds of her worn cloak. The skin on her hands was crisscrossed by tiny fissures, like cracks in a stone. That was a sign of aging in gargoyles. Except that the hags didn't age, I heard. They *always* looked old. This woman could be my age, for all I knew. A hag's youth and beauty were the price she paid for the knowledge unattainable for any other fae.

Knowledge gave them power. Only this woman didn't look that powerful to me. Her back hunched over, she shuffled her bare feet, manacled together by a chain. She wasn't the respected and powerful royal hag in the castle. She was a prisoner in the Bozyr Peak, tricked by King Edkhar into serving him.

"What will I get if I help the *salamandra*?" the hag croaked from under her hood.

"Your freedom," Elex replied simply.

She paused, startled, then demanded, "Give me your promise."

"You have it," he assured her. "In fact, I'll free you right now if you tell me how. I'm sure a simple lock is not what keeps you in chains."

She glanced down at her feet. The metal cuffs around her ankles had chafed her skin into wounds that bled. "I'm bound to the king."

"King Edkhar is dead."

"Is he? And are you the new king?" she asked carefully. "Because if so, my vow of service to the king would pass to you with his crown."

Elex inclined his head, as if introducing himself to a new acquaintance. "Yes. I am the king now."

"Your Majesty." The hag bowed her head. "I'm in your service."

Elex wasn't wearing the king's crown yet. The ruby Crown of Dakath was in the Throne Room, waiting for the official ceremony to be placed on the new king's head. But he didn't need to wear the crown to act like the king he was born to be.

"Let me make this right." He kneeled at the feet of the woman and touched the chain that bound her ankles. "I, Elex, King of the Dakath Mountains, release you."

Magic swirled through the room, stirring the frayed hem of the hag's cloak. The chain clanked, dropping to the floor as the manacles clicked open.

"Ahhh." The hag stood straighter, her back no longer hunched over. She rolled her shoulders, stretching her neck, as if she'd just climbed out of a cage that was too small to stand upright.

"Now, please, share your gift and your skills with us," Elex requested. "If you help this woman, I'll reward you."

I watched him closely, afraid that if I moved my eyes away even for a second, he might disappear.

Who could tell me what would happen now? How long could

he exist when one of his ancestors died, breaking the chain that created him? How much time would it take? Would devastation have to work through centuries of generations to get to Elex? Would he disappear suddenly—I'd blink, and he'd be gone? Would he drop dead to the floor? Would he deteriorate gradually over time?

The more I thought about it, the more I felt like screaming.

"I need no reward," the hag said, "other than what you've already given to me, my king. But I need my things. Send one of your lads to fetch my basket from my cell in the dungeon."

Elex sent one of his men, who had gathered around us. The man was Gabrik. He'd questioned Elex back in the Desolate Peak but had proven smart and resourceful during the storming of the castle.

"How about the *biqirelle* crystals?" Elex gestured up at the shimmering cascade of crystals suspended under the ceiling. "Do you want to use them?"

"Would you waste their rare magic on a lowly *salamandra*?" The hag sounded shocked.

"That's their purpose, is it not? To heal people. Not to serve as trinkets for a vain king." He unfurled his wings, then flew up and started ripping the crystals from the ceiling by the armful.

The healer woman sat on the royal perch next to Isar. She took the crystals that Elex handed to her and started sorting them in her lap.

"It's been a very, very long time since I touched them last," she murmured, reverently stroking the iridescent facets of each piece.

Gabrik returned with her basket and set it down at her feet. She took out a cloth and a couple of jars to tend to Isar's wounds.

"My lady." Gabrik stepped closer to me. "Our men found a woman chained in a room below."

"Where? In the dungeon?" I imagined there would be more prisoners locked down there. We'd have to question and most likely release them all. King Edkhar's and Elex's definition of crime differed vastly.

"No. They say she's in a room next to the kitchen."

"The *salamandras*' bedroom?"

"I don't know." He shrugged apologetically. Gabrik wouldn't know about the *salamandras* of the Sanctuary and where they stayed.

I turned on my heel. "I have to see her."

"Amber? Where are you going?" Elex frowned, taking a step my way.

"I need to go down to the floor with the kitchen. They say there's a woman locked—"

"I'll come with you." He made a move to leave, but the hag stopped him.

"Sire, I'll need four more of these ones." She held up a milky white hexagon. "Then, maybe you could lend me some of the Dakath magic to help connect them better over this woman's wounds."

Maek, another one of Elex's men, marched in at that moment.

"My lord. We caught seven of King Edkhar's men on the outer wall. What do you want us to do with them?"

"Were they on their way in or out of the palace?" Elex asked.

"Two were sneaking out. Five were trying to get in."

Elex rubbed his eyes. The day was ending soon, and there was so much to do still.

I touched his hand. "I'll be fine, Elex. I'll go see the woman and be right back."

He caught my hand in his, squeezing it tightly. I needed the reassurance of his touch, too, as proof that he was still here, with me.

"Promise you'll be here when I return," I whispered only for him to hear.

Of course, he couldn't promise me that. Instead, he brought my hand to his lips and placed a tender kiss on my palm.

"Take Gabrik with you." He released my hand reluctantly. "And don't linger, my spark. Come back soon."

"I'll be back," I promised.

Gabrik escorted me down the stairs.

"Here." He stopped in front of the *salamandras'* old bedroom. "They found her in here."

The door to the room was wide open, like every door in the castle today. The early evening light flooded the gloomy space inside with a warm sepia glow, shrouding the perches into shadows.

My heart skipped a beat as I held my breath at the threshold. The *salamandras* of the Sanctuary were dead. I saw them die with my own eyes. Isar had avenged for far more lives than she knew when she murdered that bastard.

Could one of them have survived?

But how?

Afraid to hope, I stepped inside the room. The table with the breakfast food served days ago still stood by the open window. Most of the dishes were now stale or spoiled.

The rows of hard, narrow perches were empty, except for one. A woman lay on it. I recognized her dark, long braid even before she glared at me from under her arm.

"Zenada!" I rushed to her.

She sat up, drawing her knees to her chest. A clinking of metal exposed the manacle around her ankle.

"Why are you chained?" I lowered myself on the perch at her feet.

She swallowed and cleared her throat before replying, "Mother."

Her voice sounded rough. I noticed her chapped lips and sunken cheeks. If Mother was the one who'd locked her up, then Zenada had been here on this perch for two days now. The table full of food and drinks was just a few yards away, but it remained out of her reach since she was chained. Thirst and hunger wouldn't kill a fae for a very long time. But they would make them suffer.

"You're thirsty." I ran to the table and filled a goblet with water from a jug.

"Thanks," she croaked, grabbing the goblet from my hands and emptying it in a few greedy gulps.

I returned to the table to get more water and a bowl of plums, the only dish that still looked edible.

"Here." I placed the bowl into Zenada's lap and refilled her glass. "Now let me get this thing off you." I placed a hand on the metal cuff around her ankle, then searched for the hairpin in my braid with my other hand to pick the lock.

Gabrik cleared his throat, stepping closer.

"Allow me, my lady." He yanked the axe out of the holster on his back.

Zenada shrank back from him with a gasp.

I blinked at the sight of the massive axe in his hands. "Gabrik, we need the cuff removed, not to have her leg chopped off."

He smirked into his beard.

"Big doesn't mean clumsy. I can do some very fine things with this." He stroked his axe so gently, it almost looked like a caress.

I hesitated, but Zenada clearly wished to get out of the restraints as soon as possible. Scooting to the edge of the perch, she stretched her foot toward Gabrik.

He took her heel into his large hand, then slid the sharp toe hook of the axe into the ring that held the manacle around her ankle. Holding the manacle in place with his hand, he wrenched the long handle of the axe with the other. The metal cracked. The ring bent and the cuff fell open.

"Thank you." Zenada withdrew her foot from him, rubbing her ankle.

Gabrik grunted something under his breath, then stepped back to the door.

"Why did Mother chain you?" I asked Zenada.

She lifted her onyx eyes to mine. "Because I refused to go to the battlefield. I wouldn't fight for *him*."

I recalled her slumped shoulders as she'd left the Great Hall the last time I'd seen her. The king had chosen me over her for that last midday meal before the final battle. We'd had no chance to speak since that day. I never thought I'd get a chance at all. I thought she'd died along with the *salamandras*, burned on the side of the mountain.

"Zenada... I'm so happy you're alive. And I'm very sorry about what happened. You know I never wanted any of that. I never wanted King Edkhar—"

"I know." She interrupted, reaching for the bowl with plums. "That didn't make it any easier to accept, though."

She ate a plum in silence before speaking again. "I always knew I was just one in the long line of many. I knew that one day, someone else would catch his fancy, no matter how hard I tried to keep his attention on me." She stroked the strip of a scar below her neck. "Yet somehow, I allowed myself to have hope. He'd taken me flying. He'd never done that with any of the Sanctuary women before. And I thought..." She inhaled heavily. "I hoped that might mean something..." She chugged the water from the goblet as if it were wine. "I was stupid. And I've paid for that. But after that day, after he rejected me, I refused to fight for him. I could not *reject* him, but I was not going to help him win. I told Mother I wasn't coming to the battlefield, even under the threat of execution for desertion. That morning, I didn't get ready. I just sat on this very perch and told her that even if she carried me on her back down that mountain, I still would take no part in it. I thought she'd get the guards to kill me. But she just locked me up in here and said she'd deal with me later."

The "later" never came for Mother. Now, she was dead, her ashes strewn by the wind between the rocks and over the poppies.

"It was a good thing you didn't go, Zenada. They're all dead now."

She flinched as if I'd struck her. "All of them?"

I nodded. "Mother, too."

The weight of my own words pressed heavily on my chest.

Zenada blinked, turning to the window. "How? How did they die?"

"By dragon fire. They died instantly. And together."

She clenched her hands in her lap, staring out of the window. Her eyes brimmed with tears. For better or for worse, the Sanctuary had been Zenada's home for far longer than it had been for me. She'd lived with the *salamandras* side by side, surviving the hunger and the hatred of the villagers. Now, the women were dead. It must feel like losing a family. All at once.

I touched her knee. "Let me take you out of this room, please?"

She sniffled, brushing a tear off her cheek. "Where would I go?"

"To another room where..." Where the ghosts of the dead women wouldn't haunt us. Where the guilt of staying alive while everyone else was gone might be a little less excruciating. Where the sadness might be not as suffocating. "Where it's...nicer."

She nodded.

I held her under her arm, and she leaned heavily on me while getting off the perch.

Gabrik moved our way. "May I help, my lady?"

Zenada gave him a cautious look. "Who are you, anyway?"

He straightened his back with a grunt. "Gabrik. At your service."

"He's with Elex," I explained.

Zenada arched an eyebrow. "The king's favorite?"

I didn't correct her. She looked exhausted by everything as it was. The rest of the news could wait until she'd been made more comfortable.

"All right." She gave Gabrik her hand.

Instead of holding it, he wrapped her arm around his neck, then lifted her into his arms. She inhaled sharply but didn't protest, placing her other hand in her lap.

"Where to?" he asked me.

"This way." I led him up the stairs, then to Elex's old bedroom. This was the only decent room in the castle I knew and felt comfortable bringing Zenada into. I didn't want her to spend another night downstairs on that narrow perch of hers, next to the chain that had held her prisoner.

"This is beautiful," she said after Gabrik had placed her on a floor cushion by the window. "Who lives here?"

"You." As the new king, Elex would likely move to the royal chambers at some point. I didn't think he'd object if Zenada stayed in this room for now. "No one will bother you here. I'll just change the sheets on the perch for you."

I started stripping the sheets I'd slept in before, then took out a stack of clean bedding from one of the trunks.

"So much bedding for one person," Zenada commended.

I nodded. "You'll be comfortable here."

I sent Gabrik to get her some food and water. After he'd left, I helped Zenada move to the bed, then sat next to her.

She squeezed my hand. "Thank you, Amber. For everything. I'll never forget your kindness."

"You've done far more for me." I waved her off. Finding food for me in the Sanctuary while she was starving had been the biggest kindness anyone had shown me at that point.

She turned away, looking out of the window again. "We were disposable to him. All of us."

I realized she was talking about King Edkhar and the *salamandras*.

"Zenada." I sympathized with her feelings for the king, but I wasn't going to sugarcoat the truth to make him look better. "The women received no protection from the king. There was no one to defend them when they were attacked on that mountain. Not a single dragon came to their aid."

Even Elex had come too late, as he'd been looking for me farther down the mountain.

She exhaled a long breath, looking devastated but not very surprised.

"Where is the king now?"

I bit my tongue.

King Edkhar had met the end he absolutely deserved, in my

opinion. But how was I supposed to break the news to the woman who loved him?

Zenada swallowed hard before asking again, "Did he survive the battle?"

He did survive it, but that didn't change the fact that he was dead now.

I glanced away, unable to meet her questioning stare. "Zenada..."

With a soft whimper, she slapped a hand over her mouth. "He's dead?"

I nodded. "Elex is the new king now."

I debated whether to tell her about Isar but decided against it for now. Isar was fighting for her life. I didn't want to add the worry for her to everything Zenada was dealing with right now. She had a lot to process as it was.

She dropped her head with a quiet sob. A tear rolled down her cheek and dropped onto the blanket in her lap. They said a man had to be a true monster to have not a single woman cry upon his death. King Edkhar was a lucky son of a bitch to have a woman like Zenada shed a tear for him.

"I... I loved him," she confessed. "I knew I shouldn't have let that happen. I knew it would destroy me in the end. But for a while there, my love for him was the most beautiful thing in my life. And I couldn't stop... I *loved* loving him."

"You have a long life ahead of you. You'll love again. One day."

She dismissed my words with a wave of a hand. Finding love again was not on her mind right now. Something else seemed to bother her far more.

"Thank you again, Amber. But I won't burden you for long. As soon as I'm able, I'll leave here."

"What? Why would you do that? Now, when you can finally stay here in comfort? Elex is kind and just. You'll be taken care of, I promise."

She shook her head. "No. I can't stay."

220

"But where would you go?"

"Down to the valley, then up the river and into the Northern Mountains."

"Do you have a family there?" I didn't recall her talking about a family before. The fact that Zenada was in the Sanctuary in the first place meant that there was no one who cared about her.

She heaved a sigh, not meeting my eyes.

"A distant cousin and his wife." She didn't sound very enthusiastic about reuniting with them. And frankly, if they left her starving in the *Salamandra* Sanctuary for decades, they couldn't be that good of a family to begin with. Obviously, they didn't want her before. Why would they want her now?

"Will they let you live with them?" I asked.

She hesitated before replying, clutching her hands in her lap.

"I'll help them look after their child. I'll clean their house. Cook. Do whatever they'll need me to do." She drew in another long breath. "We'll make it." Her voice was firm with resolve. She sounded determined, though her hand still shook a little when she briefly placed it on her belly.

"*We?*" I stared at her hand.

She jerked it away from her belly. "I'll be fine."

Her dark eyes finally met mine. Pleading.

"Zenada, are you..."

She gripped my hand. "Please, Amber. You can't tell anyone. I'll leave. No one will have to know. Ever."

"You're pregnant," I breathed out. "With King Edkhar's baby?

The revelation shook me to the core. My mind was reeling. King Edkhar had left an heir, after all. Whether he knew about it or not before he died.

Zenada kept begging frantically, "Please... No one can know. I don't want my son to be a part of any of this." She waved her hand around the room.

"Your son? How do you know it's a boy?"

"Gargoyle women always know early. It is a boy. The dead

king's bastard child. If anyone finds out about him, he'll be in danger. Can't you see? With the new king on the throne, any descendants of King Edkhar will be considered a threat to the new bloodline. He'd be hunted and killed."

"No, he won't," I said. "You don't know Elex. He's the most decent, most honorable man I've ever met."

She tilted her head, giving me a faint smile. "Spoken as a woman in love."

I knew what she meant. I might trust Elex with my life, but for Zenada, he was a stranger. Why would she trust him with the future of her son?

"It doesn't have to be the new king who'd wish ill for my baby," she said. "There are plenty of people in the kingdom who will want to eradicate any trace of King Edkhar. Or some power-hungry High Lord may decide to use my Ahrit as a pawn in his political game. I can't let that happen."

"You'll name him Ahrit?" I smiled.

That was the name of the king who Elex said was his grandfather, the first time he and I met in King Edkhar's Great Hall.

If King Edkhar was Elex's great-great-grandfather, and King Ahrit was his grandfather, that meant Elex fit right between them in this succession line. In the line of his ancestors, he'd take the place of his own great-grandfather and his namesake, King Elex.

Voron was right. Future was but a black-and-white sketch, left for us to color in and give it substance. Elex's bloodline didn't end with the death of King Edkhar. It just took an unexpected detour.

"Ahrit was the name of my grandfather," Zenada explained. "He died when I was eight. And he was the only man in my life who ever loved me. Unconditionally."

I smiled and hugged her.

My heart soared, my head spinning. I felt like hugging the whole world.

There was a reason why Elex hadn't disappeared from existence, and now I believed he never would.

"You have no idea what this means, Zenada." I stared into her ink black eyes that looked so much like Elex's. At her braid that was so dark it appeared almost black if it wasn't for the copper highlights brought out by the setting sun. At her smooth, glowing skin, that was almost exactly the same beautiful shade of brown as that of the man I loved.

Elex carried little family resemblance with King Edkhar because he clearly took after another one of his ancestors, his great-great-grandmother Zenada. Who, by the crazy twist of fate also happened to be his great-grandmother.

For the first time since King Edkhar's death, I was able to draw a full breath, free of fear. "Oh, this makes me so, so happy, Zenada."

I hugged her again.

"What are you talking about?" She looked confused.

With a knock on the door, Gabrik entered, bringing Zenada her dinner.

The sun was hovering right over the horizon by now. There was no time for lengthy explanations. They would have to wait until tomorrow. But I had to tell her something.

"Have some food, sweetie." I placed the tray into her lap, then filled a glass with water for her. "You have to take care of yourself, eat well, and stay warm. And don't worry about a thing. Both you and Ahrit are safe. The future is ours. And we'll color it in the brightest, most beautiful colors from now on."

By the time I left Zenada's room, the sun had set. Gabrik remained on guard by her door in the corridor, making me feel like I was leaving her in good hands for the night.

I walked through the sleeping castle of the Bozyr Peak. The signs of the chaos of the day were everywhere. The sunset had caught people in all possible places and positions. There were servants cowering in the corners, unsure whether to run or stay.

Elex's people were everywhere in the corridors, turned to stone by the sunset while searching the endless halls and floors for King Edkhar's men.

Only Voron might be still awake somewhere, but I didn't find him. Maybe he was too tired to roam the castle at night and ended up catching some sleep in one of the many luxurious beds in here.

I found my gargoyle king in the Throne Room. And he truly looked like he belonged there.

He stood by the window, looking out. His arms were crossed over his chest. He had his wings out as gargoyles often did at night, ready to fly at the first ray of sun in the morning if needed.

"Hi." I climbed on the windowsill in front of him, bringing my face to his eye level.

His eyes were open. A deep crease between his eyebrows indicated the vast number of thoughts and worries he'd had roaming in his head as the sun had set. I was sure all of them were still there, keeping him awake. I wished to ease at least some of them.

I stroked the stone waves of his hair, then placed my hands on his cheeks.

"Guess who I found tonight, my love? Your great-great-grandmother. And she's not Lady Amree, thank God. To be honest, it makes perfect sense. Between King Edkhar's evil ways and Lady Amree's tendency to terrorize her servants, I wondered where all your good qualities came from. Now I know. From Zenada. She is the other surviving *salamandra* from the Sanctuary, the former lover of King Edkhar, remember? The fire dancer?"

I gave a moment for my words to settle in his stone head before continuing.

"She's also your great-grandmother, as she is the future mother of King Ahrit. He is in her belly already. Your grandpa. You see, you can't give birth to your own grandpa, of course. But you are filling in for your great-grandfather in the line of your ancestors, King Elex. Your namesake turns out to be you. It's mind boggling, at first. But when you really think about it, it all makes sense. A son of King Edkhar and Lady Amree had fewer chances to grow into the ruler that the next king would have to be. There are some exceptions, but generally apples don't fall far from the tree. You are the one who will bring the changes that this kingdom needs so badly. *You* will be the great king who will raise the next great monarch. So you, my love, are both the result and the beginning of the change for the better in the Mountains of Dakath. It looks like your life is a circle, Elex, not a straight line."

I gently rubbed the crease between his eyebrows, wishing I could smooth it out.

"One worry less for you tonight. Your bloodline is not in danger. You're not going anywhere soon. There is a life ahead of you. The life of a king. And..." I dropped my gaze to his chest. I couldn't look into his stone eyes if I wanted to say the next words out loud, but confessions like this were so much easier to make when he was in this form. "I'll be there for you if you'll have me. Every step of the way."

Holding on to his shoulders, I rose on my tiptoes and placed a kiss on his hard but warm lips.

"I love you, Elex. And by God, I'm so glad you're not going to disappear on me anytime soon." I smiled, kissing him one more time. "Have a good night, my darling. I'll see you in the morning."

Twenty-Five

AMBER

A ray of light caressed my face. I smiled at the slight tickle on my forehead and opened my eyes.

Elex crouched by the royal throne where I lay. Leaning over me, he brushed a strand of hair from my forehead.

The sun shone at him from the side, bringing out the burgundy highlights in the mahogany waves of his hair. His black eyes sparkled with fire from within.

I smiled wider and stretched my arms above my head.

Yesterday, Elex had the king's throne brought here, to the Throne Room where it belonged. Since this was the room where I'd found him by the window last night, I'd decided to spend the night close to him and curled up on the wide throne covered with furs. Last night, it had looked comfy enough to my tired eyes. But my back and shoulders felt rather stiff after spending the night in such a position.

"Did I oversleep?" I squinted in the sunlight, reaching for him.

"A little." He caught my hand and kissed it. "You look so beautiful this morning, my spark."

I made an effort not to snort a laugh at his words. My clothes were wrinkly. My braid looked like an angry porcupine with hairs sticking out all over. The damp spot on the shoulder of my tunic must be from me drooling in my sleep. And I was pretty sure I had the imprint of my sleeve on my cheek.

But beauty was in the eye of the beholder. And Elex's eyes told me he was telling the truth. To him, I was beautiful.

I leaned forward and kissed the tip of his nose.

"How long did I sleep?"

Bright sunlight flooded the room from its many tall windows. It was clearly way past sunrise.

"You slept as long as you needed. It was a busy day yesterday. I have guards by the door with the order not to disturb you. But I missed you." He looked guilty.

"So, you decided to wake me up?" I laughed.

"I just wanted to check on you. And..." he pointed at the tray of food on the low table nearby. "I brought you breakfast."

My empty stomach spasmed at the mention of food. All I'd had to eat last night were a few pieces of fruit I stole from Zenada's dinner. With everything that had happened, I wasn't feeling hungry back then. But I was starving now.

"Breakfast sounds wonderful. Thank you." I sat up on the throne. "How is Isar?"

"She's much better. Still resting but awake."

"Oh, thank goodness." I pressed a hand to my chest as a calming wave of relief washed over me.

"We'll go see her after breakfast. But you need to eat first."

"You don't have to ask me twice, darling. I'm so hungry, I could eat a—" I was covered by a blanket that I recognized as one from our old bedroom. "Did you go to see Zenada?"

He poured a glass of sweet berry juice with lemon and handed it to me with a nod.

"I did. I had to meet my great-great-grandmother." He smiled, pouring a glass for himself, too.

"Oh, you heard me then, last night?"

"Every word. Thank you for telling me. I wouldn't have slept at all otherwise. I..." He took a drink from his glass. His throat bobbed with a swallow. "I feared this would be the morning I might not wake up."

"Oh God, Elex..." I put the glass back on the table and hugged him around his neck. I'd feared the same thing before I'd spoken to Zenada, but I didn't wish to even recall that. "It's so, so good to have you here."

He wrapped his arms around me and kissed me before leaning back.

"Isn't it amazing how things work out sometimes?" The same deep line appeared between his long, dark eyebrows. Only this time, I smoothed it out with a kiss.

"As long as they get sorted out, darling. What did Zenada say?"

I let go of him, and he sat on the throne next to me, then pulled me into his lap, turning me to face him. The throne was wide enough for us to sit side by side, but I preferred it this way. And he clearly enjoyed me straddling his thighs.

I lifted my glass again and took a jam-filled pastry from the table, making myself comfortable in his lap.

"You two look so much alike, you and Zenada," I said between the bites of my breakfast. "I've no idea how I didn't realize there must be a family connection between you two. If you stood next to each other, anyone would see you're closely related, like brother and sister. Or...you know, a great-great-grandma and her great-great-grandson." I took a drink of my juice, shaking my head. "It sounds so crazy when I say it out loud."

He laughed. "I can't believe it myself. But you're right. There is every reason to believe Ahrit will be the next king and my grandfather."

"Did you explain that to Zenada?"

He pressed his lips together. "No. I decided not to tell anyone where I came from, unless it becomes unavoidable. There is no need for any added instability in the kingdom due to confusion about my origins. Right now, people believe I'm an illegitimate son of King Edkhar, and I'll leave it at that. As long as there is royal blood in me, my claim to the throne is valid. That's all that matters."

"All right." I finished my pastry and picked up a slice of pear from the breakfast tray. "So, people will accept Ahrit, too, because of his blood, right?"

"Ahrit will be raised as my legitimate son. That's what Zenada wants."

My hand with the pear slice paused on the way to my mouth. "What do you mean?"

"There is a point to Zenada's concerns about her son's future," he explained. "Since I pose as King Edkhar's son, it will make Ahrit my younger brother if we admit the king was his father, too. The moment I have a child of my own, Ahrit will no longer be in the direct succession line. To guarantee he gets the crown after me, he'll have to be presented to the world as *my* son, not King Edkhar's. That also fits into the future history of Dakath, remember? King Elex is the son of King Edkhar, with King Ahrit being the son of King Elex."

"Right." I twisted the pear in my fingers. "But how does it work, exactly? If you acknowledge Zenada's son as your *legitimate* child, doesn't it mean the two of you will have to get married?"

My stomach roiled. The pastry left a nasty taste in my mouth. It wasn't easy to accept that the man I loved might have his entire family pre-planned. And those plans did not include me. It was a hard pill to swallow, no matter how important this arrangement might be for the future of Dakath. Not to mention the icky feeling at the idea of Elex marrying his great-great-grandma.

My brain felt swollen from all of this. My head threatened to explode. I dropped the pear back onto the tray, suddenly losing my appetite.

"I need a coffee..." I mumbled.

"Amber." Elex slid a finger under my chin, making me meet

his eyes. "I wish to get married. With all of my heart. But not to Zenada."

"Okay, but then—"

He silenced me with a kiss. I couldn't push him away. It'd felt like forever since he'd kissed me like this—long, unhurriedly, and so sweet, my heart ached. I hooked my right arm around his neck, drawing him closer.

Elex got what he wanted. The Crown of Dakath was his. But *he* was mine. And I was not letting him go, no matter what.

He broke the kiss but didn't pull away from me.

"I've given you a ring, as is customary in your culture." He took my hand with the ruby lizard curled around my finger and kissed the inside of my wrist. "I've taken you flying, as is customary in Dakath. But I've never actually asked you the question." He took out a small box from his pocket. "Amber, my dearest spark of life and fire, will you marry me?"

Breath caught in my throat. Love and excitement pulsed inside me, begging for me to let them out. To laugh. To cry. To hug and kiss the living hell out of him. I struggled to hold it all in.

He popped the lid of the box open. A single scarlet spark glistened on the black velvet inside.

"What is it?" I asked, holding my breath.

He produced a tiny stud earring from the box. A speck of red in a golden setting.

"It's for here." He tapped the side of my nose where the hole of my favorite piercing remained empty ever since Mother had made me remove the small steel ring I'd had in there before.

"You got a stud for my nose?" I smiled widely.

He watched me carefully as he spoke. "It's a simple garnet set in gold. It doesn't cost much. It has no value other than what we put in it."

"Sentimental value," I said softly. "You remembered."

My heart felt like it was melting, filling my chest with sunshine and warmth.

"You haven't answered my question, my spark." There was some tension in his voice, filled with anticipation.

Did he worry, even for a second, that I might reject him? He was my life, my entire world. There was no future for me without him, no happiness.

"Of course it's a yes, Elex. I will marry you." I laughed as tears filled my eyes. "I'll marry the shit out of you, my love." I hugged him around his neck so tightly that he made a choking sound. I leaned back as concern reared its head again. "But what about Ahrit and Zenada?"

He beamed, looking so happy. Nothing marred his excitement at getting me as his bride.

"We'll take care of them. But there is no one else I want at my side as my wife but you."

He helped me put the stud into my nostril. I enjoyed the sensation of its slight weight. The gargoyle king proposed to me with a nose stud. And I wouldn't have it any other way.

"Nothing is more important to me than you, sweetheart. You're my one and only. My soulmate. My bonded one. You'll live as long as I do now. We have centuries together ahead of us. Do you feel me right here?" He pressed a hand to my chest, over my heart where happiness and love pulsed the strongest, where his very essence had lived rent free for days now. "Do you know who you are, Amber? You are the legendary Fire Queen, King Elex's wife. You proved it."

"Oh... Me?" I recalled what he told me about that particular ancestor of his. She was the fierce fire bending queen. "I'm her?"

He smoothed my hair, his eyes filled with admiration.

"She is you, my fearless queen. A human's love can transcend magic. It can also form a bond, which makes the couple stronger. As my bonded mate, you can use my magic. And judging by your performance on the wall yesterday, you've mastered it. You have the power over dragon fire. You can repel it without getting burned. And you can wield my fire, with dire consequences for our enemies."

Was I always meant to be the Fire Queen? Or did we "tweak" the future? I didn't really care. It all fit perfectly. Past and future had aligned like two pieces of a puzzle.

"Neat." I grinned.

It'd felt so good, fighting those dragons alongside Elex yesterday. For once, I was as powerful as him. And together, we were unstoppable.

He watched me with a tiny smile playing on his lips. Never in a million years would I have thought I'd find someone who'd make me feel this happy.

"I love you, Elex."

I kissed him again. He tasted like sweet berries and lemon, and from now on, that would forever be the taste of happiness for me.

Twenty-Six

AMBER

Elex was publicly declared the King of the Dakath Mountains that very afternoon. The next morning, the coronation took place. The golden ruby Crown of Dakath was placed on his head, the most deserving one to ever wear it, in my opinion.

I had no doubt Elex would become the great king he was destined to be. And I was delighted to become his queen just a few days later.

We planned a modest, by royal fae standards, wedding ceremony. Only a few thousand guests were expected to attend. The nine remaining High Lords had arrived at the castle along with their families and courtiers, as well as many gargoyles from the valley.

On the morning of our wedding day, I was getting dressed in the royal chamber. Three huge mirrors in carved walnut frames stood around me, allowing me to look at myself from nearly every angle.

I had several maids in attendance but had yet to formally choose any ladies-in-waiting. The castle burst with life and was filled with people, but most of them were complete strangers to me. I was extremely grateful for both Isar and Zenada when they agreed to help me with getting ready today.

Zenada took the task very seriously, closely supervising the maids as they brushed and styled my hair. Braided into a gazillion tiny braids and decorated with gold and gemstones, my hair had been arranged into gorgeous rosettes and flowers on top of my head, with more braids, waves, and strings of beads cascading down my back and shoulders.

"What do you think?" Zenada moved my head for me to better see the back of my hairdo in one of the mirrors. "Do you like it?"

"Oh, this is gorgeous." I couldn't offer a word of criticism even if I wished. I turned my head a little, making the golden clips gleam and the gemstones sparkle. "I look like a princess."

"Better than that, I hope." Zenada giggled. "You'll be *the queen* before nightfall."

That still felt like a dream. Before the next sunset, Elex and I will become husband and wife. I heaved a breath, trying to get my nerves under control. Marrying my gargoyle king didn't worry me in the slightest. I couldn't wait to be his wife. It was the ceremony that would be happening in front of thousands of people that made my insides jitter with nerves.

"Don't remind her," Isar chuckled. "The poor girl is pale like a cloud owl already."

Isar sat in the pillows by the window and used a giant hunting knife to adjust the clasps of a golden filigree corset that was a part of my outfit. She had fully recovered from her ordeal in the dungeon and the fight with King Edkhar. The magical crystals had healed her wounds practically overnight.

"You'll be fine." Zenada placed a quick kiss on my cheek. "We'll be there, too. You can hold my hand anytime you like during the ceremony."

"Thanks." I smiled as the maids placed a light-like-a-feather gauzy layer over the red jacquard of my dress.

The train of the see-through organza over my skirt stretched all the way across the room. The dress left my shoulders exposed. The wide, transparent sleeves started below my shoulders. They flared out wide like flower petals and were held together by wide, bejeweled cuffs at my wrists.

"Here. This should fit perfectly now." Isar gave the corset to the maids who placed it around my torso over my dress and closed the little beaded clasps with tiny chains.

Leaning back into the cushions, Isar smiled at me. "You look beautiful, Amber."

"You are the most gorgeous thing I've ever seen," Zenada gushed.

I laughed, hiding my blush. Compliments were so hard to take, even from the closest of friends.

"Thanks. It means a lot, coming from the most magnificent fae like yourselves." I was so grateful for both of them.

As the future queen's favorites, Isar and Zenada had been close to me during all the events that had taken place in the castle in the past several days. No one at court questioned their status as my favorites. Of all the women from the *Salamandra* Sanctuary, there were only the three of us left. People accepted that we shared a special bond after everything we'd been through together.

Zenada trusted me with her most precious secret. No one knew about her baby yet. We were going to announce the royal pregnancy shortly after the wedding, and I would have to present Zenada's son as mine, the legitimate first-born son of the royal couple. That was Zenada's wish, to ensure her son's future. Elex and I would be officially listed as Ahrit's parents in all records and documents. But Zenada was going to remain in her son's life every step of the way.

Her rooms were adjacent to the future nursery. There would be a bed placed for her next to the prince's crib. She'd be the one looking after him, nursing him, changing him, singing for him— raising him. And when Ahrit was old enough to keep the secret, he'd learn all about what his mother had done to ensure his safety and his rightful place in life.

The maids placed a wreath of red snow poppies on my head, the last of the season. Most of these flowers had already disappeared from the mountains. The black rocks of Dakath's peaks now were green with patches of new grass and leaves on the shrubs. The air had warmed enough for us to have the windows in the room open.

Not all the castle windows had glass yet. There was a lot to do still. But we had time to do it all.

Zenada spread down my back the golden ribbons tied to the wreath. "It's time to take you to your king. I'm sure the poor thing is dying to see you already. You've been apart since last night's dinner," she teased.

I couldn't hide a giddy smile, looking forward to seeing my king, too.

The maids joined Zenada, Isar, and me as we walked out of the royal chambers. Several guards escorted us down the main staircase to the Throne Room on the floor below.

The maids walked hand in hand with the castle guards. The villagers who had come from the valley joined us, along with Elex's men from the Desolate Peak. The new court was so new, neither the hierarchy nor the etiquette had been firmly established yet. And as far as I was concerned, I liked it that way.

As I walked into the Throne Room, I spotted Voron by the wall behind the main crowd. He gave me a smile and a wave.

Music was played by the royal musicians who hovered above the high ceiling. The soft rustling of their wings blended with the melody they played.

The royal throne was empty. King Elex stood in front of it, waiting for me. The moment our eyes locked, I saw no one else.

Dressed in the royal colors—black, gold, and red—Elex presented a truly majestic sight. A long cape edged with fur was draped over his wide shoulders. The thick waves of his hair were tamed under the heavy circle of the Crown of Dakath.

But his kind eyes, his warm smile, and the adoration on his beloved face as he looked at me hadn't changed at all.

I smiled so widely on my way to him, my face started to hurt by the time I reached him.

He took my hands, and I tilted my head back, keeping our eyes locked.

The music stopped. The High Priest, dressed in a golden robe, started reading the text of the ceremony. And everyone in the room went still.

Suddenly, it dawned on me that this ceremony didn't really matter either to Elex or to me. All of this—the music, the dress, and the priest with his long fancy scroll—was for the guests, for the people of Dakath, and for the official records.

As far as Elex and I were concerned, we already belonged to each other. I gave his hands a squeeze, wishing it was time for him to kiss me already.

He brought his head down, whispering for only me to hear, "You stole me, Amber. I've been yours ever since."

I stole him, and I could never give him up.

"You are my biggest treasure, Elex. And I'm keeping you until the day we die and beyond."

These were our vows. Just for us. And they were more precious to me than all the big words the High Priest made us repeat after him.

After the ceremony, we all moved to the Great Hall. Even in the short time that Elex had been the king, this space had changed. Gone were the perches of King Edkhar and his men. The precious crystals had been removed to be used for healing, as they were meant to be.

Several long tables stood around the room, set with the most appetizing dishes. Elex led me to the one draped in a red tablecloth and decorated with bouquets of spring flowers. Zenada and Isar shared the table with us, as did Voron and a few of Elex's men.

This didn't feel like a huge official celebration, but just a dinner with friends. I relaxed, enjoying the scrumptious meal. By the time dessert was served, the conversation flowed freely, more than one conversation, actually, as several of them seemed to be happening simultaneously.

"Have you decided what you'd like to do, Isar?" Elex asked my friend.

Due to the skills of the royal hag and the amazing qualities of the crystals, every trace of Isar's gruesome injuries was gone now. I'd seen her already practicing with her swords again.

"My offer stands," Elex continued. "Join my army, and you'll make it to the rank of a general in no time. You have the strength of character for that, and I reward courage and loyalty."

According to Elex, there were no more wars in Dakath for the foreseeable future. But peace had to be defended, too. Every king needed an army, and Elex had no intentions to dissolve his.

Isar inclined her head.

"I treasure your offer, my king. But there are a few things I wish to see and do in this world before making a commitment like that. I've decided to travel around Nerifir for a little while." She gave him a smile over the rim of her wine glass. "That'll give you some time to prove yourself as the king worth going into battle for. Show you can rule fairly and wisely, and I'll come back to join your army."

"Fair enough," he agreed. "Whenever you wish to return, we'll have a place for you in the Bozyr Peak."

I knew Isar had always wished to travel and see the world. I was glad her dream was about to come true, but my heart pinched with sadness at having to say goodbye to her so soon.

"How about you, Voron?" I asked the sky fae who sat at my left. "What position would you like to hold at the Bozyr Peak?"

Voron swirled the tart pomegranate wine in his glass, squinting at the garnet-red liquid.

"Actually, my queen, I think I'm ready to collect on my royal favor."

"Already? Have you decided what you want?"

He gave his glass another swirl. "I have."

"What is it?"

His blue-gray eyes focused on me, as if assessing how much one could trust a human to fulfill her promise. The intensity in his stare was a bit unnerving, making me squirm.

"Voron, what is it that you want to ask me for?"

He set his glass on the table. Hard.

"I wish to go back to the Sky Kingdom."

"You want to leave here?" My heart squeezed with a new pang of sadness—another goodbye. "You know with the royal couple as your friends you can have pretty much anything you want in Dakath Kingdom."

I smiled. He did too, but it didn't reach his eyes that remained cool, like a frosted pond in winter.

"You see, dear Amber, you've inspired me in a way."

"I have? How?"

He directed his gaze to the early afternoon sky in the open window.

"If a human woman could find her place among the stone-cold gargoyles and thrive, there must be a chance for me in the world I was born in, don't you think?" He glanced back at me. There was something new in his look. Hope? Vulnerability? Ambition? I believed I glimpsed all of that.

"I hope there is, Voron. And if so, I'm sure you'll find a way to thrive, too."

He smirked, taking a sip of his wine. "Would you ask your new husband to fly me up there, then?"

"Why can't you fly yourself?" I blurted out.

I'd heard that highborn sky fae like Voron could fly just as fast as gargoyles, if not faster.

He let go of his glass. His gaze traveled over the tables and the guests again, to the window and the sky beyond.

"Tell me, Amber, if a wingless dragon is a lizard, what is a wingless crow?"

I gaped at him as realization struck me. Voron couldn't fly. Like almost every gargoyle of the Desolate Peak, he had no wings.

He gave me a bitter smile. "Exactly. There is no word for something like that, is there? Other than *an abomination*."

Compassion tugged at my heart. If Voron looked at least a tiny bit more approachable, I'd squeeze him in a hug. The cool glint in his eyes, however, demanded I keep my distance.

"So?" he prompted. "Will your royal husband give me *a lift* back to where I came from?"

"Of course." I nodded, without even having to ask Elex. If he wouldn't do it for any reason, I was certain we'd find someone who would. If Voron wished to return home, I would find a way to make it happen.

"I'll miss you," I said to him.

"Don't." He leaned back in his chair. "Missing someone is a weakness, and a queen can't afford to have too many weaknesses." He took another swig of his wine. "I certainly am not going to miss you."

I didn't take it personally. There was some truth to his words. Missing someone left an open wound in one's heart, and there were just so many wounds a heart could bear.

"So, we'll never see you again, Voron?"

"No. But I wish you both well, you and your gargoyle king."

The afternoon sun moved closer to the mountains on the horizon as I stood in the window of the royal chamber.

The royal rooms had completely been re-done in the days

since our wedding. I'd made sure every trace of King Edkhar had been removed from our space.

Soft, handwoven rugs made by the weavers from the valley covered the stone floors. Colorful silk curtains hung in the tall windows that had panes of stained glass in them instead of wooden shutters. The windows were wide open, letting the fresh evening air in.

The fireplace wasn't lit, but it was warm without the fire. Spring had won full reign over the Dakath Mountains at last.

A gentle breeze played in the gauzy skirts of my pink-and-yellow dress as I stood by the open window. Shielding my eyes from the sunlight with my hand, I peered into the sky, searching for a winged shape among the white puffy clouds.

At last, it appeared. Like a tiny dot at first, it grew to the size of a sparrow. But I knew that the shape moving toward the Bozyr Peak was actually much bigger than any bird.

It was a dragon.

My dragon-king.

Letting go of the window frame, I stretched my arms toward him as he approached.

"Got you," he rumbled softly, snatching me from the royal chamber and taking me up into the sky.

I laughed, spreading my arms wide. Tilting my head back, I let the wind play with my hair and caress my face.

Strong arms replaced the hard claws around my waist. Elex had shifted from a dragon to a man.

"You're back." I threw my arms around his neck.

His hair was mussed by the wind. His cheeks looked flushed after the long flight.

"How is the Sky Kingdom?" I asked.

He chuckled. "Gods help them, now that Voron is back."

I hoped with all my heart that the sky fae would find what he was looking for in his old world.

"Did you miss me?" Elex murmured.

Keeping one hand under my butt, he used the other to slide

down the thin, golden chain that served as a shoulder strap of my dress.

I nuzzled his hair as he kissed my bare shoulder. "I always miss you. No matter how short your absence is."

It was true. A part of me seemed to hang in suspense when Elex wasn't around, waiting for him to come back. Everything fell into place only when he was near.

He tugged my dress down, exposing my breast.

"Gods, I missed you, too," he groaned, before sucking the nipple into his mouth.

Desire surged higher from his caress. I wrapped my legs around his middle, pressing myself to him. The light layers of my skirts fluttered in the breeze from his wings.

"How much time do we have before the sun goes down?" I raked my fingers through his hair. Need for my husband pulsed hot between my legs. I flexed my legs, rubbing myself against his hard abs.

He growled approvingly, sliding a hand under my skirts. "Long enough to make you scream my name once or twice."

I squirmed as he slid a finger inside me.

"Oh God..." I rocked my hips against his hand. "I think I'm about to start screaming soon..."

He tipped me backwards, with the castle being right below us now. My braid hung straight down as did my skirts. He shifted me, impaling me on his hard, hot erection.

"Yessss..." I let go of his neck, spreading my arms wide like wings.

For one brief moment, it felt like I was falling. But I knew he'd never let me fall.

Elex made me fly.

He gripped my hips, thrusting hard inside me. I flexed my legs tighter around him, taking in more of him. He leaned over me. Half-folding his wings, he dove into a free-fall with me.

A thrill rushed through me, fanning my desire. My breath caught in my throat, as my body burst into the flames of orgasm.

"Elex... I..." I screamed through moans, rocked by pleasure.

We spun in the air, our bodies intertwined.

Wind rushed by us, as we were falling, falling, falling...

Falling over the edge together.

The sharp black peaks of the mountains grew bigger below, coming closer.

With a sharp swish of air, Elex unfurled his wings. They caught the wind like sails, their delicate edges trembling in the strong currents rushing under them.

I heaved a breath, coming down from the height of pleasure.

"So...intense," I breathed out, wrapping my arms around his neck again.

"It couldn't be any other way with you, my spark." He grinned. "Every single time is pure magic."

We soared over the mountains, their ridges gilded by the glow of the evening sun. Patches of green grass and colorful flowers covered the slopes all the way to the brilliant valley below.

"This is such a beautiful world, my love." I pressed my temple to the side of his face.

"It is, Amber. And it's all ours. Yours and mine."

Epilogue

TWO YEARS LATER

ELEX

"Do you want to see Na-da dance, Ahrit?" Amber bounced the Crown Prince on her knee, making the baby giggle.

"Na-da." The little boy stretched his chubby hands to Zenada, who smiled and blew him a kiss from the middle of the Throne Room.

Dressed in a leather bustier and a pair of long pants, the queen's favorite lady-in-waiting pulled a ball on a chain from a large trunk.

"Of course you do," Amber cooed, kissing the boy's soft golden-red curls. "We all want to see Na-da dance, don't we?"

The musicians spread their wings, taking off into the air with their instruments. A moment later, energetic music filled the room.

Almost the entire court of the Bozyr Peak gathered here this morning after Zenada had announced she was performing today. Amber had told him Zenada had been practicing a new routine for months. Today, she was finally ready to share her gift with all of them.

"Na-da." The baby fussed, stretching his arms to his mother.

"Shhh." Amber bounced him on her knee again, but there wasn't much space left in her lap because of her eight-month pregnant belly.

"Give him to me." Elex smiled, taking the boy from her. "Come here, little guy. I have a better view. And a toy, look." He dangled the thick golden chain that hung around his neck, making the royal seal on it jump up and down.

The seal got Ahrit's attention. He grabbed the onyx disk and stuck it into his mouth, immediately calming down.

Amber gasped. "Is that thing clean enough for a baby?"

Elex laughed. "Of course it is. I make sure not to seal any dirty deals with it."

She rolled her eyes at him, hiding a smile, but said nothing as Zenada lit the ball on her chain on fire. She dangled it side to side slowly, as if testing its weight and trajectory.

As the music surged higher, Zenada jerked the chain, sending the ball up. The fire left a wide arc of light in its wake— star-bright in the dim lighting of the room.

It was a cloudy day outside. All the stained-glass windows were closed. Pale daylight filtered into the Throne Room in glowing patches of color that failed to fully illuminate the large space. There were no torches inside. The fireplace wasn't lit either. The brightest light came from the fireball at the end of Zenada's chain.

She spun faster, the ball spinning in a circle over her head. Flicking the other end of the chain, she made the other ball catch fire. Now, she wielded them both over and all around her.

The tension in her expression eased, giving way to a smile. The dance seemed effortless to her. She spun and twirled, making the two fireballs bounce and zip by her as if they were alive.

He remembered the dance Zenada had performed for King Edkhar. Back then, she looked nervous and scared. Rightfully so, as the king had hurt her.

It didn't surprise Elex that it took her this long to start

dancing again. But he was glad she finally did. The joy from doing what she loved shone through her expression without fear.

Zenada finished the first part of her dance, dipped the chain into a bucket of water to put the fire out, then went to the trunk to grab a different prop.

The room erupted into applause. She jerked, looking up.

"Beautiful!" people screamed.

"Amazing!" Amber clapped her hands.

A huge smile spread across Zenada's face. She rolled back her shoulders and sank into a gracious bow for the crowd.

"Magical!" a deep voice boomed to Elex's left. Gabrik clapped his big hands so hard, his wrists would surely be sore tomorrow.

"She's magnificent, isn't she?" Amber gushed from her seat on the right.

Elex moved his attention from Gabrik to his wife.

"She is," he agreed.

Amber glanced at Gabrik, who wouldn't tear his eyes from the dark-haired fire dancer.

Elex chuckled. "I wish Gabrik would do something more than just stare at her with forlorn eyes like that."

Amber gave him a sly grin. "I think he already has."

"What do you mean?"

She leaned over the armrest of her throne to him and lowered her voice. "Zenada let it slip recently that Gabrik is an amazing kisser. And I have every reason to believe she learned that from experience, not from some court gossip."

"Oooh." He straightened in his throne, giving Ahrit a bounce. "Good for her. For both of them. Gabrik is a good man."

Most of the former men of the Desolate Peak had proven to be good, loyal men. They all had found new homes. Some stayed at the castle, others moved down into the valley or elsewhere in Dakath. All have been building new, better lives for themselves.

The Bozyr Peak was more and more resembling the place where Elex grew up. There was hardly any trace left from the brutal rule of King Edkhar. The most lasting seemed to be the scars people still bore in their hearts and on their bodies.

Elex had offered to raze the *Salamandra* Sanctuary into the ground for Amber, but she'd asked him to spare the gloomy place. Instead, she'd been working on transforming it into something else. Something better. She said she wanted it to be a real sanctuary for everyone who had no other place to go.

Everyone who needed care but had no one to take care of them, all who found themselves adrift in the world with no purpose or no direction, were welcome to the new Sanctuary. They could stay for as long as they needed to get back on their feet, or forever if they so wished.

After just a couple of years, the results were astonishing. From an isolated, destitute place, the *Salamandra* Sanctuary had become a refuge and a place of hope for many, as well as a thriving part of the community.

Inspired by the results, Amber pledged to open Sanctuaries all over the kingdom. Every single one of them would be under the queen's personal protection. Elex could clearly see how the Order of *Salamandra* would eventually become the safe haven it was during the reign of his parents.

The future was not written in stone, but Amber and he had a good blueprint to follow. And the future looked brighter than ever.

Amber gasped softly, rubbing her cute, round belly.

"Is she moving?" He reached to touch his wife's belly and felt his daughter kick.

"Is she ever!" Amber laughed. "I think she's performing her own fire dance in there."

He rubbed her belly gently. "Can't wait to meet her."

His wife smiled. "Oh, I'm sure she can't wait to come out and finally stretch those strong little legs of hers, too."

The thrones of the seven Rebel Lords had remained empty. Their properties had become the crown's lands after the war. Their little princess would become the High Lady of one of them at birth. As far as Elex was concerned, he didn't mind filling the other six thrones in the same manner.

"Come here." He cupped her cheek. "I love you, my spark," he murmured against her smiling lips.

She pressed her mouth to his in a tender kiss. "I love you too, my precious gargoyle."

Burn for me

BONUS SCENE

<u>Note of caution</u>: The following scene does not fit into the main narrative of the Fire in Stone duet. It's slightly more erotic than the rest. It may be not for everyone. But I had to write it for one reason: curiosity.

If you married a man who could shift into a rock and a dragon, wouldn't you want to know what it's like to make love to him in his every shape and form? I figured Amber would be curious, too. She enjoys her husband's body when he is a man. She trusts Elex fully. It only makes sense she would want to try to *ride* her dragon-king, in whatever form he may be.

Warning: Non-shifted love scene ahead.

Subscribe to my newsletter to read *Burn for Me* for free:

https://dl.bookfunnel.com/6rxwrlyxi7

Next in the River of Mists

WINGLESS CROW

AMBER

Flapping of wings woke me up. The room was still dark. The sky outside our open bedroom windows was just beginning to light up with a new sunrise.

It was too early for the gargoyles to wake up. Yet I was certain I'd heard the sound of someone flying.

Or *something?*

A large, black bird landed on a windowsill. I'd recognized the crow. I just couldn't believe it would fly all the way from the Sky Kingdom.

With a tendril of worry curling around my heart, I climbed out of our bed where Elex had spread out in his warm stone form.

The crow held a tiny scroll in its beak. I held out my hand, and it dropped it onto my palm.

"Did you carry it all the way here? You are a smart bird, aren't you?"

The crow cawed once before taking off and quickly disappearing into the graying sky.

I opened the message, already knowing who it was from.

"I have a confession to make," it read. *"When I said I never wanted to see you again, I lied. How do you feel about having a glass of wine at the Sky Palace with me, dear Amber? Bring your royal spouse, too, of course."*

It was signed simply.

"Voron."

The note was short, but it made me smile.

I studied the puffy silver clouds in the sky, wondering which one of them might be hiding the mysterious Sky Kingdom high above us.

Please, read the preview of Call of Water, book 1 of Madame Tan's Freakshow, also set in the world of the River of Mists.

More in the River of Mists

CALL OF WATER

EXCERPT

With a bracing breath, I squeezed through the gap and into the fragrant semi-darkness of Madame Tan's menagerie.

Just one look, then I'd get out before Fleur was back. We would get some ice cream afterwards, and no one would ever need to know where I'd gone while she was using the bathroom.

Inside, I found myself in a dark, stuffy place behind yet another fabric partition. Just about three feet wide, it appeared to be a corridor, stretching along the outside wall in each direction. Following the music, I headed right, grateful for the rubber soles of my sandals that allowed me to pad along noiselessly.

The sound of music intensified, then the murmur of voices mingled in. One stood out above the rest—the melodious voice of Madame Tan who sounded as if she was telling an enchanting tale of old.

"Water Fae would probably be referred to as 'sirens' in your world. They are known for their enthralling voices and ethereal looks..."

Up ahead, I came flush with the thick velvet curtain blocking my way. Eerie, blue-green light cut through the darkness in the narrow gaps on each side of the curtain where it met the canvas walls of the corridor.

"Although their appearance closely resembles humans, Olathana Ocean Fae are not intelligent or even self-aware,"

Madame continued with her narration. "In fact, their IQ level is below that of a dog..."

Something must have happened behind the curtain because a series of loud gasps and murmurs reached me. The light in the gaps intensified.

Unable to stand the suspense of not knowing any longer, I leaned closer, tugging the curtain aside a little, just enough for me to peek through.

A large, tall water tank stood in the middle of the next room. Shimmering green and blue light shone from it, piercing through the waves of the fragrant smoke that curled over the heads of six people sitting at the bar in front of the tank.

They were having drinks and hors d'oeuvres while watching a figure floating in the water.

Judging by the shape of his body—wide shoulders of a swimmer, well-defined chest, and narrow hips—he was a male, despite the halo of long white hair streaming around his head in the water and the silver skirt with high slits on each side. The skirt was actually a long, loin cloth, I realized, upon a closer look. And it was the only clothing the male was wearing.

Madame stood next to the bar.

"Hear the siren's voice." She waved her arms in the air dramatically, and the sound of a somber but breathtakingly beautiful voice filled the space.

It was a wordless song—no lyrics—the emotions conveyed through the melody alone. Yet the suffering in it was so clear, my chest ached, and my eyes burned with tears.

The man in the tank remained upright, as if suspended in the glowing water. The glow appeared to be coming from him, his pale skin highlighted by the delicate blues, greens, and pinks, which shimmered through his long, silvery hair, too.

Suddenly, a few deep notes of the song sliced through me with recognition.

I knew this voice.

It was the same sound that had enchanted me back in the cabaret in Paris.

Some of the songs he sang back then might have been soulful and sad, but none had been this sorrowful.

Yet I had no doubts. This was the voice of the man with fascinating blue eyes and a warm smile that hid in the corners of his mouth, even when he was singing a song meant to make you cry.

Zeph.

I shot my gaze back to the tank, examining closely the face of the person inside it. He seemed paler than I remembered, his hair much longer. There was not a hint of a smile in his features this time. But it was certainly the same man, the one I'd spent a night with and hadn't been able to forget ever since.

My heart thundered so loud, I pressed both hands to my chest, afraid that the people at the bar would hear it.

"He's gorgeous!" A young woman exclaimed, raising a tall glass with luminous liquid to her lips.

A man sitting next to her gave her a side glance. "Looks rather human to me."

Madame leveled him with a stare. The next moment, however, her face lit up with another wide smile.

"But he is *not* human." She gestured somewhere behind her.

The same dark-haired girl with big, soulful eyes who sold us our tickets entered from the side, carrying a large crystal decanter filled with a shimmering cocktail. She refilled the man's glass with it.

"The differences between sirens and humans are not that apparent at a first glance," Madame continued the moment the girl had left.

I spotted Radax, the large, bearded man who had escorted me out of this tent earlier. Now he stood in the entrance where the girl with the decanter had departed. Another man, who looked nearly identical to Radax except that this one was clean-shaven, stood on the other side of the entrance. The arms of both were folded across their enormous chests.

"However, there *are* differences." Madame made another theatrical gesture toward the man in the tank...*Zeph*. "Aside from the ability to breathe underwater, as you can see, Water Fae swim better than any fish and infinitely better than a human. They can also regulate their body temperature and are not affected by cold."

"Still, looks human to me," the man at the bar retorted gruffly.

"No regular man could be this beautiful," a woman objected.

"So..." The man shrugged, dismissively. "A *pretty-boy* human, then."

With another gesture from Madame, a ripple ran through the water, carrying something that made Zeph's body arch. He threw his head back, his features crumbling into a grimace of pain, mouth open in a soundless scream.

This couldn't be right. Bounced around in my head.

Why would Zeph be here? How did he end up in that tank?

Zeph's jaw flexed as he bared his teeth. The singing never stopped, however, making me realize it must be a recording. He shot his hands to the side, his arms and legs rigid and straight.

Two pairs of magnificent fins opened, fanning out from his arms—elbow to wrist—and from the back of his legs—knee to ankle. The multi-colored glow in the water broke into iridescent swirls as Zeph slowly rotated inside the tank. When he turned with his back to the audience, they all broke into awed gasps.

A large, dorsal fin opened on his back like a shimmering sail of gossamer silk stretched between sharp spikes. It reflected the multicolored lights running through the water.

"But how is this attached?" A few people rose from their seats, leaning forward.

"It looks too real," someone said, their voice guarded.

"He doesn't seem to be very comfortable in there." An older woman reached over the counter.

Madame quickly slid in behind the bar, positioning herself in front of Zeph's tank.

"Please take your seats, ladies and gentlemen. Remember the rules. You cannot touch the glass," she reprimanded sternly.

With puzzled murmurs and gasps of awe and bewilderment, the audience settled down.

"Enjoy the refreshments," Madame prompted. Obediently, the six at the bar went back to drinking their cocktails and munching on the food.

Madame's smile returned. "I assure you, like all animals in my menagerie, the siren is kept in the utmost comfort. I make sure to maintain the optimal conditions for the wellbeing of my exhibits. Many would not have survived in the wild for as long as they do in my collection."

I stared at Zeph as he completed his rotation, facing the audience once again. His expression was now blank, the clear blue eyes gazing vacantly straight ahead. If I had not seen this face vividly animated when he was singing, talking, laughing a year ago, I would have been inclined to believe there was no thought, no self-awareness behind those eyes, just as Madame had claimed.

But I *did* know better. Because I did remember everything from that night. I knew that Zeph was a real man—smart, fun, and intelligent.

It did not matter right now how things had ended between us. Locking him in that tank was not right. Keeping him there could not be legal.

Fervently, I tried to decide on the best course of action. I should run back, find Fleur, and call the police.

As the light inside the tank dimmed. Radax and his beardless twin left. The people around the bar continued to eat and drink, with Madame telling them some out-of-this-world trivia about the food on their plates.

I had to get out of here before anyone spotted me. I was not looking forward to facing Madame if I were discovered trespassing on her property. Something about that woman made my skin crawl.

I was about to turn around, back to the gap in the wall I had used to enter, but the noise of footsteps and sounds of a conversation coming from that direction made me freeze in place.

Huddling into the shadows, I felt thankful for the darkness between the stuffy fabric walls. Whoever was approaching from the other end of the corridor wouldn't be able to see me right away. Yet the sounds traveled easily enough through the fabric, and I crouched down, afraid to breathe.

The footsteps were heavy, the conversation stilted. Not a real dialogue, but an abrupt exchange of cut-off sentences and short phrases. The strangled voices and some low grunts made me think that the men talking must be also carrying something heavy.

The loud thud of a load being set down on the ground confirmed that.

The footsteps then moved again.

In *my* direction!

Trying to keep the panic from rising, I checked both walls on each side of me. The inside partition was stretched over a frame. Taut fabric did not leave me enough space to crawl under. The bottom edge of the outside wall was weighed down by the sandbags outside. My attempt to raise it made a rattling sound of a tarp crinkling.

"What's that noise?" Radax's voice asked, close—way too close—to me.

"Sounds like someone is trying to sneak under the wall again," another deep male voice replied. The two would catch me before I managed to crawl half-way through any opening I could find or make.

"Cheap assholes," Radax grumbled. "No one wants to pay anymore. Everyone wants free entertainment."

Panic spiked hot in me, making it hard to think clearly. Glancing behind the velvet curtain again, I found the room there nearly empty now. The VIP clients had left. Madame was gone, too. The dark-haired girl carried out a pile of dirty dishes from the bar.

With not a second to lose, I slipped behind the curtain as the footsteps of Radax and his companion approached.

With the girl now gone, the VIP room was completely empty. Zeph's water tank was dark, too. It was hard to tell whether he remained inside. With the footsteps right behind me, I crouched low to the ground and scurried behind the bar. The curtain swished open, with the heavy stomping coming in a moment later.

"And?" Radax asked.

"Nope. No breach," the second voice answered. "Someone must be just poking around from the outside."

"Good. Let's help Amira spruce this place up. Madame already went to get the second group of VIP clients. They'll be here any minute."

The sound of chairs being re-arranged around the bar jolted me with another shot of alarm through my system. Next, someone would certainly come behind the bar to wipe the counter top off or to get some clean glasses, maybe.

Scrambling for a more secure hiding spot, I padded around the stand with the water tank. There was just about enough of a gap between the floor and the stand for me to fit under. Getting down on my belly, I wiggled from the rug behind the bar onto the packed dirt under the water tank. Trying my darndest not to sneeze in the dust, I fit my body between the tubes and hoses running from the bottom of the stand.

"Welcome to my special exhibit," Madame's pleasant voice greeted, followed by shuffling noises of people entering.

Another group of VIP clients.

How many did she have scheduled for today?

Listening to her speech about the Ocean Fae again, I wondered how *did* Zeph breathe underwater. It would be impossible for anyone to hold their breath for that long, and I didn't notice any tubes or masks inside the tank.

His fins appeared so incredibly realistic, as if they were a natural extension of Zeph's body. Were they some ingenious mechanical invention? A sophisticated costume? Or a crazy surgical modification?

The last possibility made my stomach churn.

Watching the reflection of the green-and-blue glow from the water tank on the floor in front of my hiding place, I wished I could see his face. The heart-breaking sound of his singing floated through the room once again. The wordless pain and longing of the song filled my chest with sorrow and compassion.

If it hadn't been for Radax and his buddy out there, I would have been on my way to get help for Zeph right this very moment. Instead, there I was, lying in dirt while he was being ogled and tortured up there.

Fleur must be losing her mind outside, looking for me.

The thought of her brought my cell phone to mind. With Zeph's magical voice filling the space, the risk of me being heard was less. Carefully, I slipped my hand to the phone in the back pocket of my shorts. Sliding it out, I quickly turned the ringer off, finding no messages from Fleur yet. Could she still be in the bathroom? Then I realized, I had absolutely no signal here.

Disheartened, I shoved the phone back in my pocket and remained still, listening to Madame's voice spinning her tales.

Apparently, Madame had two more groups of VIP clients scheduled for that evening. Unless she'd lied to me about the ten-thousand-dollar admission, which I didn't see any reason for, she'd made a lot of money today. And if she'd had but half that many visitors for each day of CNE, she'd make a fortune during this fair.

Did I rush to assume that Zeph was forced into that tank? Considering the amount of money involved, he could be a business partner of Madame or her employee, performing to earn enough money to buy that place by the ocean he'd dreamed about.

How well did I know him, anyway? Compassion made me initially view him as a victim, but now I questioned that. He could very well be performing willingly.

Showing up with the police would be stupid in that case. If anything, I risked being charged with trespassing.

Another question roamed my mind while I lay there. Why would people pay this much money just to see an actor float in the tank, no matter how handsome or talented he was?

"To see the things not found on Earth." Madame's words came to mind.

For the words to make sense, though, I'd have to believe that Zeph indeed was not of this world.

My legs started to fall asleep, and my back ached after lying in pretty much the same position for nearly two hours. The dust and the smoke that slithered under the tank made me incredibly thirsty, too.

Finally, the last group of VIPs had departed. The sounds of clinking dishes then the sweeping of the broom told me someone must be cleaning the place.

More people entered.

"It was a good day, but I'm tired now," Madame's voice announced. "Amira, bring my dinner to my trailer once you're done here. Then start packing up."

No audible reply followed, but I wondered if that was the name of the dark-haired ticket-booth girl. She seemed to do pretty much everything around here, from selling tickets, to waitressing, to cleaning up.

"Radax," Madame ordered to another one of her mostly silent helpers. "You have a few hours. We're leaving at sunrise."

A good few minutes passed in silence after Madame had exited. Then I heard the deep voice of Radax, "Go, get her dinner now, Amira, then take a nap for an hour. I'll manage without you for now."

As brief as the statement was, I caught a warm note in his voice I didn't expect from someone like him.

"Thank you," came in a barely audible whisper from the girl, Amira, then the soft padding of her shoes sounded as she left.

Radax stomped around the tank for a while as I lay still as a mouse, praying he wouldn't decide to check under it.

Once he finally left, I waited for a few more minutes, listening for any sound out there. This room must be deeper inside the group of the tents, with numerous walls and partitions effectively muffling the outside noise. All seemed quiet.

It was time to get out of here.

With a deep breath to calm my nerves, I crawled out onto the rug behind the bar. A faint glow from the streetlights filtered through the roof of the tent above, barely making a dent in the darkness.

Poking my head around the bar, I made sure no one was nearby then got to my feet and scurried to the velvet curtain, the way I had come in.

Before lifting it, though, I paused, staring back at the water tank. All the lights inside it were off, and the dark water made it impossible to see anything inside.

I hadn't heard any sound of Zeph getting out of it. Did they leave him inside for the night? That wouldn't be an appropriate way to treat a business partner or an employee.

Clutching the curtain in my hand, I recalled Zeph's listless expression and his wordless cry, more harrowing because it was soundless in the water. Was all of that an act?

Something didn't feel right about this place. Regardless of Zeph's position here, I decided to call the police the minute I got out of here if Fleur hadn't already.

A noise somewhere inside the tents snapped me back to the moment. Madame's people must have started to pack up as she'd ordered. Someone would come here, too, sooner or later.

Drawing back the curtain, I peeked into the corridor behind it to make sure no one was there. Then, I carefully started on my way back to the support pole and the gap in the wall I'd used to sneak in.

Right in the spot where it was, though, a massive wooden crate now stood, blocking my way. Frantically patting with my hands around the corner of the crate, I realized there simply was no space for me to squeeze behind it.

Unable to get out the way I'd came in, I searched for the bottom end of the canvas wall. If I yanked at it hard enough, I might be able to free it from the sandbags outside so I could crawl under it.

The canvas wall, edged with tarp, made the crinkling noise again when I tugged at it.

"Who's there?" A deep male voice suddenly boomed nearby, startling me into panic.

One of Madame's tattooed guards shuffled from around the crate.

Holding my breath, I pressed my back to the crate, frantically scrambling for an idea of what to do next as the guard moved my way.

Should I run back to the room with the tank and try to hide again? Or scream, in hope that someone outside would hear me?

Maybe I could just stay still, hidden by the crate?

A loud growl, accompanied by weird hissing noises, suddenly came from right behind me. I jumped forward, unable to hold back a strangled gasp of alarm, then realized too late that the sounds were coming from inside the crate.

The guard saw me.

"Hold there!"

The ray of light from the flashlight in his hand landed on my face, blinding me for a moment. Breathless from terror, I pivoted on my heel and ran as fast as I could back to the VIP room.

With his heavy steps gaining on me from behind, there was no time to stop and check if the space behind the curtain was still free of Madame's people. I rushed in at full speed and bumped into the hard-as-rock chest of Radax.

"What's going on?" he roared, catching me by the scruff of my t-shirt and lifting me up as if I were a cat.

"Found her snooping around the gorgonian's crate," the one chasing me replied, quickly catching his breath.

"Who are you?" Radax gave me a shake.

"Nobody," I panted, my heart lodged in my throat, choking me with panic. "Please, let me go."

"What the fuck were you doing by the crate?" the one with the flashlight demanded.

"Just, um..." I remembered Radax speaking about people sneaking in to see the show for free. "Wanted to see what you have here, without having to pay for the ticket." It wasn't even a lie. "I'll give you the twenty bucks right now." I patted the back pocket of my shorts. "Just let me go, please."

"What *did* you see?" Radax narrowed his eyes at me.

With my shirt in his firm grip, I could only stand on my tiptoes.

"Nothing," I lied, desperately hoping it came out convincingly enough. "Nothing at all."

"Weren't you the one I escorted out of here earlier?"

My heart dropped, he'd recognized me.

Denying felt stupid at this point, so I just kept quiet, scrambling for what to do next.

"You wanted to see the VIP exhibit, didn't you?" Radax asked next.

He was way too smart for his size.

"No. I have no idea what you're talking about..."

"Well, she's seen it, now." The other one scowled, tipping his head toward the tank.

A pale shape was clearly visible in the water. With both hands pressed against the glass, Zeph appeared to be watching us, although his eyes stared into the void unfocused, his expression remained impassive.

"She didn't eat *camyte*." The man with the flashlight scratched his bald head. "She can cause trouble if we let her go."

"I won't," I rushed to assure him. "I want no trouble. Promise. I just want to go home."

Getting the police involved felt absolutely necessary now, but I tried not to think about that, afraid it would reflect on my face somehow.

"Trez, go get Madame," Radax ordered to the other man.

"Oh God, no please," I whimpered, hating him for bringing her into this. "Not her. Just let me go, and she would never need to know about any of this. Please."

"This is her property." Radax dragged me to the exit of the room. "Her show and her business. She gets to decide what to do with you."

Yawning, her hair wrapped in a silk turban, Madame arrived in a smaller room somewhere inside the tents where Radax had brought me. Dressed in a pink kimono painted with golden birds, she tossed but one glance at me.

"Kill her."

AVAILABLE NOW

More in the River of Mists

Wingless Crow – coming soon

Fire in Stone Duet

Fire in Stone

Hearts of Fire

Serpent's Touch Duet

Serpent's Touch

Serpent's Claim

Madame Tan's Freakshow Trilogy

Call of Water

Madness of the Moon

Power of Rage

More by Marina Simcoe

PARANORMAL ROMANCE

Demons (Complete Series)

Demon Mine

The Forgotten

Grand Master

The Last Unforgiven - Cursed

The Last Unforgiven - Freed

Stand Alone Novels

The Real Thing

To Love A Monster

Midnight Coven Author Group

Wicked Warlock (Cursed Coven)

More by Marina Simcoe

SCIENCE-FICTION ROMANCE

My Holiday Tails

Married to Krampus

My Tiny Giant

My Birthday Getaway

New Year, New Planet

Mail Order Mom

My Pumpkin

Dark Anomaly Trilogy

Gravity

Power

Explosion

Stand Alone Novels

Experiment

Enduring (Valos Of Sonhadra)

About the Author

Marina Simcoe likes to write love stories with human heroines and non-human heroes who just can't live without them. She firmly believes that our contemporary world could always use a little bit of the extraordinary.

She has lots of fun exploring how her out-of-this-world characters with their own beliefs, values, and aspirations fit into our every-day life.

She lives in Canada with her very own extraordinary hero, their three little offspring, and a cat who is definitely out of this world.

facebook.com/MarinaSimcoeAuthor

twitter.com/MarinaSimcoe

instagram.com/marinasimcoeauthor

bookbub.com/profile/marina-simcoe

amazon.com/author/marinasimcoe

goodreads.com/MarinaSimcoe

tiktok.com/@marina.simcoe